THE SILK TRAIN MURDER

THE SILK TRAIN MURDER

A MYSTERY OF THE KLONDIKE

Sharon Rowse

CARROLL & GRAF PUBLISHERS
NEW YORK

THE SILK TRAIN MURDER
A Mystery of the Klondike

Carroll & Graf Publishers
An Imprint of Avalon Publishing Group Inc.
11 Cambridge Center
Cambridge, MA 02142

AVALON
publishing group incorporated

Copyright © 2007 by Sharon Rowse

First Carroll & Graf edition 2007

Cataloging-in-Publication Data is available from the Library of Congress.

ISBN-10: 0-7867-1946-X
ISBN-13: 978-0-7867-1946-4

9 8 7 6 5 4 3 2 1

Interior Design by Maria Fernandez

Printed in the United States of America

For all those who shared the journey – with thanks

ONE

Monday, December 4, 1899

"Shut the door! It's bleedin' cold out there."

John Lansdowne Granville glanced at the bartender through the smoky gloom and let the heavy cedar door slam behind him. Sauntering over to the bar, he hooked a stool with one foot, pulled it closer, and sat down.

"Whiskey, straight up," he said.

The shot was placed none too gently on the counter in front of him, but he needed that drink and didn't much care how it came. He lifted his glass in a silent toast to all those who'd prophesied he'd come to no good, grinning at the look his gesture earned him from the scrawny bartender.

The man had to be used to unpredictable guests. Not only was the Beaver Tavern the dreariest, most down-at-the-heels bar he'd seen since he left the Yukon, it was by far the most run-down he'd found on the bleak streets lining the Vancouver docks. Noisy, dim, and crowded, it was an establishment that fit his current mood perfectly, not to mention his pocketbook. With only enough money left for a meal or a drink or two, he'd chosen the latter, and planned to enjoy it.

Granville unbuttoned his heavy coat and brushed the snow from his face and beard, then tossed back the rest of the shot. The bartender was still watching, eyes narrowed and suspicious. He looked rather like a ferret, all sharp angles and twitches. Granville laughed inwardly, imagining what he was seeing. He was well aware he looked grimy, unkempt, and down at the heels, which he was. There was no sign of the gentleman he'd been two years before. But he'd made his choices and didn't regret them; he could live without the endless social parade, sleeping till noon every day and having a perfectly starched cravat, though being dead broke and having holes in his boots was starting to get tiresome.

Behind Granville, the door opened with a blast of cold, salty air and the clattering of wagons over cobblestones. A large man swept up to the bar, shaking snow in all directions. "Christ! It's freezing out. Barkeep!" he hollered, banging on the bar with a meaty fist.

Granville froze at the sound of that voice, then examined the broad face, bushy black beard, and deep-set brown eyes reflected in the tarnished mirror behind the bar. Sam Scott! He'd last seen his former partner more than three months earlier as they'd bade each other safe journey in Skagway. He'd been returning to England to make peace with his father, and Scott had been heading for Seattle. The big American hadn't changed a bit, except he looked better fed. But what was he doing here?

The reflexes he'd honed in fending off gold-hungry claim-jumpers obviously still worked. The big man sensed he was being watched. He met Granville's gaze in the mirror with a hard stare, followed by a dawning recognition. A grin split his thick beard and he turned, clapping Granville on the shoulder with a vigor that nearly knocked him off his stool.

"Granville, you scoundrel! Never thought I'd find you here! What happened? Jolly old England not quite so jolly?"

How to answer that one? With a shrug, Granville decided not to try and signaled for two whiskeys.

"What, you don't talk anymore? Never thought I'd see the day!"

Granville lifted one of the glasses that had been plunked down in front of him. Ignoring the bartender's obvious curiosity, he slid the other glass down the bar to Scott.

"You're thinking of yourself, old man," he said. "Cheers."

Scott laughed, shook his head, and downed his own drink. "I know who got called the Klondike storyteller and who didn't. What's the matter, your tongue still frozen?" Scott laughed, then turned so he was directly facing Granville and his expression sobered. "Christ, Granville! What in hell's wrong?"

Too much traveling with too little money and too little food, plus the news that his father was dead, Granville thought. But this wasn't the place to talk about it, and besides, he wasn't nearly drunk enough yet. He just shrugged, and signaled for another round. "You know how it goes."

Scott studied Granville's face, then canceled the order with an abrupt wave of his hand. Ignoring the bartender's continued interest, he threw a coin on the bar and said to his drinking companion, "I could use a steak, a thick, bloody one. How about you?"

"Sounds good," Granville said, with an expression that conveyed more than his words.

"So Turner ended up hiring me to guard the rail yards and the cars," Scott concluded, emphasizing the point by waving a chunk of steak impaled on his fork. He looked meaningfully at Granville's empty plate. "The pay is good and it's steady work—every night, in fact. I know it's no job for a gentleman, but I sure could use some help. Interested?"

Granville had to smile. They'd nearly frozen digging gold out of unforgiving rivers, and Scott was still worried about a job, any job, being beneath him? Still, he could see his friend was worried about him. And he knew he'd polished off the meal as if he hadn't eaten in days. Which was true, but that was his own business, and not something for Scott to be worrying about. He didn't want pity. He hadn't accepted charity from his brother and he wouldn't accept it now. "It doesn't sound like enough of a job for two men."

Scott shrugged, an innocent expression sitting oddly on his weather-beaten face. "The rail yard's a big place. And it's not easy to find a man I can trust." He grinned. "I already know I can't trust you, so I don't have to waste the time worrying about it."

"For the record, I don't trust you, either."

"Damn, but I've missed you, Granville." Scott grabbed his mug and downed a mouthful of coffee. "What do you say?"

"Hmmm. I need to think about it."

"Think fast. We've got to be on watch in a few more hours. Meanwhile, I have to keep my strength up. Want another steak?"

Without waiting for a reply, Scott yelled the order to the harried cook. If he wondered about the protruding cheekbones above the Englishman's ragged beard, he had the discretion not to ask.

Granville sat back, his stomach full. Only a small chunk of gristle remained of the second huge slab of meat Scott had ordered. At least tonight he wouldn't wake from dreaming of food to find his mouth watering and his stomach screaming.

Money had been short since he'd left the Yukon to set off on the long journey home. He winced with the memory of finally reaching

Toronto to find Henry's months-old letter waiting for him. Their father was dead and William now the sixth baron. "Come home," Henry had written. "All will be forgiven." Granville smiled bitterly. Not with William as head of the family, it wouldn't be.

Granville eyed his tablemate with affection, glad to see again the man he'd first teamed up with in the spring of '98. After a year and a half of backbreaking work on the creeks, with the money running out and no gold to show for it, they'd left Dawson City just before winter set in again. They'd both been scrawny and half-starved. But Scott now had the confident look of a man who knew where his next dollar was coming from and who'd been eating regularly.

Unlike himself. Granville's mouth twisted wryly. As he worked his way west, he'd clerked for a merchant in Toronto, helped round up cattle on a vast Alberta ranch, even swung a hammer as a navvy for the CPR. Gambling was the only way he knew to make real money, but he'd sworn on Edward's grave never to touch cards again.

Was Scott serious about the job? It seemed odd they'd need more than one man to guard an empty train, especially when that man was as big as Sam Scott. But what did it matter if the pay was good? He wasn't accepting charity, though. If it wasn't real work, he was gone. The word was they were looking for miners in the Kootenays, and he'd find a way to get there somehow.

Granville realized Scott was no longer eating and was looking at him quizzically.

"So are you in, partner?"

"Partner? I thought you needed someone to work for you."

"Nope. That was only if all I could get was a hireling. What I really want is a partner. And you're him."

Granville narrowed his eyes. "I'll work for you, but that's as far as I'll go."

"Partner or nothing."

"Then it's nothing. I won't accept charity, especially not from a friend."

"Can't you get it through your thick skull that I really *need* your help?"

Now there was a ring of truth in his voice that even Granville's pride couldn't ignore. He met Scott's gaze for a long moment, trying to gauge the truth of his words, then nodded slowly. "I'll work with you. But if it's not right, then you have no obligation to me."

Scott extended his hand. "Then shake on it."

Midnight found the two men standing in front of a string of boxcars in the Canadian Pacific Railway yards. The darkness was broken only by the wavering light of three hanging oil lamps. Just beyond the pool of light, the black waters of Burrard Inlet lapped softly against the wharves where the ships docked. Granville shivered and drew his torn coat more closely about him. He wished he'd brought a flask; a nip or two would keep the icy cold out of his bones. "You're sure your employers are willing to pay both of us to just stand in the yards?"

"Yup."

"It makes little sense to me."

"All that matters is that it makes sense to the boss."

"Still," Granville said. He was feeling argumentative, since it kept his mind off how cold his feet were. He'd have to use most of his first pay to buy new boots. An odd creaking from somewhere in the yard behind them took his mind off his feet. He touched Scott's shoulder and gestured in the direction of the sound.

The two of them moved carefully so each was covering the other. Granville had his knife ready, and he'd seen the size of the baseball bat Scott carried. They stood listening, barely breathing, and then the sound came again, followed by a metallic crack, hastily muffled.

Scott stepped forward, motioning for Granville to stay behind him. Hugging close to the shadows of the railcar, they circled toward the back. Scott stopped suddenly and Granville halted just behind him. He could taste the salt in the air. The smell of creosote was even stronger here, despite the rain.

The breeze shifted and he caught a whiff of cheap cigar smoke. Granville spun on his heel, ducking as he did so. The cudgel whistled by his ear, missing him by inches. Straightening, he caught his half-seen assailant's chin with a sharp left hook. It stopped the first man cold, but a second attacker close behind the first kept coming.

In the flickering shadows cast by the lamps it seemed they were moving in some exotic dance. Granville feinted, then tripped his opponent, striking the fellow with the haft of his knife on the way down. He looked warily about. Scott had dealt easily with a third man and it seemed there were only three of them.

The man he'd punched showed signs of stirring. Granville was about to employ the knife haft again when his partner stopped him.

"Just tie 'em up, will ya? I'll have a few questions for them when they all wake up," Scott said, tossing him a coil of oily rope.

Grabbing it, Granville did as he'd been asked. The men stirred, one muttering something.

"So why the interest in empty boxcars, boys?" Scott asked his groggy captive audience. He was answered by a thick silence. He asked again. Less patiently.

Granville crossed his arms and lounged back against the wall, his expression as fierce as he could make it. It had started to rain, a thin, drenching wetness.

"Who's behind this?"

"Nobody. It was our idea." This from the youngest of the three. His face gleamed too pale in the lamplight, and his voice cracked on the final word. He had only just begun to shave, Granville thought, wincing as he noted the bump rising behind the kid's ear. How had he become involved in a caper like this? Looking at his threadbare clothes, Granville knew the answer—money, of course. When was it ever anything else?

Whatever Scott was thinking, it didn't show on his face as he looked the kid up and down. Finally he drawled, "Your idea?" The scorn in his voice made the boy's ears go red.

"It was," he insisted. "It was *your* idea. Tell 'em, Da." He looked toward one of his fellow prisoners, who was sporting a deep scowl.

"Shut your face. You'll hang us all." The father's face was as gaunt as his son's.

"Very clever," Scott said, though his tone was still an insult. "So if this plan of yours succeeded and you ended up with the silk that's going into these boxcars, what were you planning to do with it?"

"Sell it."

"Hmmm. And where were you planning to sell two thousand bales of raw silk?"

The man's baffled silence spoke volumes. Twice he opened his mouth to say something, then closed it again under Scott's contemptuous gaze. Finally Granville entered the discussion. "You might as well come clean," he said. "It will go easier on all of you. Unless you really want to hang."

He put a hand on his knife as he strolled toward the boy. The father looked anxiously at Granville and his son. Sighing heavily, he licked his lips and coughed. At the sound, Granville paused. "Well?"

"I can't tell you who hired us."

"I think you can."

When no further information was forthcoming, Scott offered encouragement with a nudge in the ribs. "We're getting tired of waiting here."

The man on the ground swallowed hard, cleared his throat. "Jackson. It was Jackson," he whispered as his expression turned fearful.

Granville recognized the name: Clive Jackson was Benton's man. The soft hiss of Scott's indrawn breath confirmed everything Granville had been hearing about Robert Benton ever since he'd arrived in town a week ago. The word was he practically owned Vancouver's underworld, with ties to the highly profitable businesses of gambling, prostitution, and smuggling. Benton was even said to be linked to the Chinese-run opium dens.

"Are you willing to swear that before a judge?" Scott asked.

"Instead of jail time? The answer's yes. We're to be gone from here after tonight anyway. The only trick'll be to stay alive long enough to leave, if'n I swear against Jackson."

"You can think about it until tomorrow. Till then there's a nice, safe jail for folks like you. Just as soon as our watch is over."

"You mean you're going to leave us tied up in the rain till dawn?"

"So you know how long we're here." Scott observed. "Good work. Wonder who else knows. You got partners, waiting till we drag you off?"

"Maybe we should just shoot them," Granville offered. "Then they wouldn't have to worry about getting wet."

"True." He considered their prisoners. "Of course, if they agree to sign a statement now, then leave town for good, we could probably let them go . . ."

"We'll sign," said the first man. "Anything."

TWO

The café was warm and bright despite the early hour, and drops of condensation ran slowly down the windows. "So how long have you been standing around in the rain guarding boxcars?" Granville asked Scott over plates heaped with sizzling sausages.

His partner took a bite before replying. "Three months or so. It's a lot better than hunkering down in a blizzard scrabbling for nonexistent gold. And it sure beats starving."

Granville nodded. "I can see that. But tell me, why is anyone paying good money for you to guard empty boxcars?"

"Those aren't empty boxcars, those are the silks."

"The what?"

Scott seemed to be enjoying Granville's confusion. "The silk trains. Those particular boxcars are lined with steel, to keep from damaging the silk."

"Keep going."

"Once a month steamliners from the Orient bring in cargoes of raw silk, which are loaded into those specific boxcars, then shipped across the continent. We only guard the silks right before the liners dock. The rest of the time we just keep an eye out."

"They're still empty boxcars."

"Do you know what the silks are worth?"

"I'll let you tell me."

"Six of those cars full of silk fetch nearly three-quarters of a million dollars," Sam Scott said, grinning at his partner's expression. "How's that for motive? Turner was afraid somebody might get the bright idea of sabotaging the cars beforehand, make stopping the train a little easier."

Three-quarters of a million dollars. Granville whistled softly. It was an amount his brother William, with his estates sprawled across a corner of Buckinghamshire, would be quite comfortable with. For himself, it had become an unimaginable sum. He now lived in a world where he'd earned two dollars for a cold and dangerous night's work and judged himself lucky to be paid so well. "So how long do the cars sit in the yard?"

"Usually just a day or so. They have to be ready and waiting when the *Empresses* get in, then the silk is loaded as fast as they can do it, and the train's gone. The *India* is due in later today."

"The *Empresses*?"

"They've got three ships carry the silk, all in the *Empress* line; the *India*, the *Japan*, and the *China*."

"And there are no passengers?"

"Sure, the *Empresses* carry nearly a thousand passengers as well as the freight, but the silk trains only carry silk. They run faster that way. And when they're carrying silk, every lost hour is lost dollars."

Granville raised an eyebrow.

Scott laughed. "Insurance," he said. "With so many train robbers out there waiting for the silks, rates are sky-high. And silk in transit is insured by the day. So you get CP racing the Canadian National and Northern Pacific lines to get the silk from China and Japan to New York the fastest."

Granville whistled. "By the day?"

"Uh huh."

"So it would be worth a fair bit to CP to get these attacks stopped?"

"Anything that valuable, there's always people determined to steal it. Stopping them is easier said than done."

"And last night's attack? You think it was about sabotage? Ordered by Benton?"

Scott drained his coffee and set the mug back on the table with a thunk. "Maybe, maybe not. He's got his fingers into nearly everything in this town, and Jackson is still his top lieutenant. But I've heard rumors that Jackson's cutting his own deals on the side."

"Well, he can't be too bright. Crossing Benton can't be a very healthy thing to do."

"Not if he finds out, it isn't."

That afternoon, Granville strolled along Seymour Street. He'd eaten and slept better than he had in months. All he needed now was a whiskey, with perhaps a bath and a shave first, he thought, fingering his thick beard, which itched. He glanced across the street, spotting a barbershop. His luck must be changing. Whistling "There Is a Tavern in the Town," he stepped off the board sidewalk, then leaped out of the way as a wagon rolled by, heavily laden with logs.

"Damn fool," Granville muttered, stepping out of the pothole he'd landed in, shaking the water from one foot. Not that it did any good;

his socks were soaked through. New boots definitely came before whiskey, and with the money Scott had advanced him, he could afford a decent pair.

"Granville! Granville! Is that you?"

Granville spun to face the man calling him, his hand going to the revolver on his hip. Seeing only Walter Blayney's fair hair and foolish face, Granville relaxed. "Yes, it's me."

"I thought so. Well, I'll be. I almost didn't recognize you with all that facial hair," the other said excitedly in his unmistakably English voice. "Never thought I'd run into you here, wasn't sure you were even alive! When'd you leave the Klondike?"

"September."

Blayney's pale blue eyes swept from Granville's decrepit boots to his ragged coat. "So you never did hit the mother lode?"

Granville grinned. Blayney had always had a keen appreciation of the obvious. Which, unfortunately for his long-suffering family, who had hoped for more from their second son, was not a talent likely ever to support him. "No, I never did."

"Still, I'd have thought you'd recoup your loses. Cards not running your way?"

Dangerous images flashed in Granville's mind: the smoky buzz of a gambling hall, cards spread on the green baize, the thrill in his blood when he held a winning hand . . . Edward lying facedown in a pool of his own blood. "No," he said, his voice harsh in his own ears. "I don't gamble anymore."

"The luckiest man in London has given up cards? I don't believe it, by Jove, I don't."

Granville ignored the dig. He needed to change the subject. "And you? What about yourself?"

Blayney ducked his head, scuffing one toe along the ground.

Despite being the second son of a viscount, he was still the least socially comfortable man Granville had ever met.

But personal experience had taught Granville what failure felt like, what it tasted like, and what it looked like, and Blayney did not fit the mode. Rather, his boots were polished and his coat, of good quality wool, tailored to fit. So what was he hiding? "Hear anything from home?" Granville asked, instantly regretting the words. England was no longer home.

"I'm afraid I'm out of favor at the moment."

And likely to remain so, Granville thought, which meant no remittance from Papa. Still, Blayney seemed not to be suffering. "You're working, then?"

At this, Blayney looked up, his face beaming. "I'm a sort of general manager for a fellow named Gipson."

"Gipson? George Gipson?"

"You know him?"

Granville nodded. Oh, yes, he knew George Gipson. Too well. The last time he'd met anyone working for that old weasel, Gipson had hired a couple of toughs to ambush Granville and stake him on the frozen edge of a Yukon lake for the night. If Scott had been even ten minutes longer in finding him, he'd have died there.

"Gipson struck it rich, you know," Blayney was saying. "He struck gold on the edge of a claim he'd worked forever, and finally his patience paid off."

"Gipson struck gold?" If Gipson had found gold, it hadn't been on his own claim, Granville thought. Of all the miners Granville had met in his eighteen months in and around the creeks of the Yukon, Gipson was the least skilled and the most corrupt—and patience was not a quality he had ever been known for.

"More gold than even you or I dreamed of."

"So what does a man who's already made his fortune need a general manager for?" And why would he hire Blayney, of all people?

Certainly Blayney had an English public-school education, the same one as Granville's own. Heavy on the classics, light on everything else—a training as useless out here on the edge of a new world as anything he could think of. So why had Gipson hired Blayney? It was a puzzle, and Granville had never been able to resist puzzles. It was what had drawn him to games of chance.

Blayney brushed a speck of mud off his coat. "This and that. So, may I buy you a drink?"

Granville abandoned the idea of new boots without a qualm. "Indeed you may."

Blayney turned and led the way into the Dancing Dog across the street. "Two whiskeys," he called out.

The smell of smoke, beer, wet wool, and unwashed bodies hit Granville the moment he walked in. Every bar he'd been in from San Francisco to Dawson City smelled the same. It was about as far from a Pall Mall club as you could get, but the whiskey was as good, and, to his mind, the company was better.

"So, Granville. What have you been up to?"

Granville shrugged. "This and that," he said.

"What are you doing now you're here?" his companion persisted.

Granville took a slug of his whiskey. "I hooked up with my partner from the goldfields, and he's found me a job guarding empty boxcars."

Blayney spluttered. Granville regarded him with mild concern. The man still couldn't drink.

"I'm fine. I'm fine," Blayney said when he'd caught his breath. "But empty boxcars? Sounds odd, old chap."

"Odd it may be, but the CPR pays well, and jobs are hard to come by in this town. Especially for traveling British gentlemen, it seems."

"The CPR?" Blayney said. "You're working for Canadian Pacific?"

Granville nodded. "I am now guarding the silk trains. You may have heard of them?"

Blayney pulled out a gold pocket watch. "Look, I'm most awfully sorry, but I just remembered a most important appointment, worth my life if I'm late. I must dash, but have another drink on me." He threw some coins on the table.

Granville shook his head as he watched him leave. Now, what was that all about? Blayney had practically had heart failure on the spot, but why?

Was it the mention of the boxcars they were guarding? Perhaps Scott's tales of the silk robberies weren't quite so far-fetched, after all. And what was Gipson up to with his newfound wealth? Whatever it was, Granville doubted it was legal, though personally, he intended to stay as far away from Gipson as possible.

Meanwhile, he needed to see about that bath, shave, and haircut, then he'd do something about these boots and perhaps the coat, too. He hadn't missed the pity in Blayney's eyes, and whatever his brother might think, he hadn't sunk so far as that yet.

Stepping onto the planked walkway several hours later, Granville rubbed a hand against the newly revealed squareness of his chin. Following the new fashion, he'd even dispensed with a mustache, and he felt shorn, literally as well as figuratively, as though in cutting off the beard and leaving only neatly clipped dark hair the barber had left him too exposed to the world. He snorted with sudden laughter at his own thoughts. He could just imagine his partner's reaction if he knew what Granville was thinking. He'd never hear the end of it.

He drew the double-breasted greatcoat more closely about him, reveling in the warmth and the fit of it, both of which were a welcome change from what he'd worn for nearly two years. Granville recalled with amusement the tailor's face when he'd walked in. Sheer horror at his attire had been rapidly replaced with the gleeful recognition of a solution to an expensive problem. Mr. Tittle, it seemed, was in possession of "a beautiful overcoat, sir, commissioned special for a gent just your size, who failed to collect it."

And it was rather nice, thought Granville, especially for the price he'd paid, once he'd convinced the little tailor to admit the down payment already made on the coat, and to factor that into the final price. Between the coat, the hat, and his new boots, also compliments of the unknown gent, he pretty much resembled the upper-class Englishman he'd been raised to be. Granville smiled cynically and headed for the docks.

"Well, now, don't you clean up pretty," Scott drawled from behind him.

Granville spun around and threw a quick punch at him, which the big man dodged without effort.

"Who you calling pretty, you big lummox?"

Scott looked him up and down, then wrinkled his nose and inhaled lustily. "You even smell pretty."

"Well, that's better than smelling like you," Granville retorted. "Now, tell me, what do you hear about Gipson?"

Scott scowled. "That scum? Why?"

"I ran into an old acquaintance, name of Blayney, quite down at the heels last time I saw him. Now cleaned up and all, it seems, due to Gipson."

Scott looked Granville up and down, from his neatly barbered hair to his gleaming boots, but didn't say a word. Luckily for him, Granville thought darkly.

"Anyway, it seems Blayney is working for Gipson. Poor fellow. But something's up, he lost all his color when he heard I was working with you at the yard."

"Working for Gipson, is it? Doing what?"

"It's hard to tell. What's Gipson's business these days?"

"He's set himself up as an honest businessman, but rumor says it's a front."

"I'd say that rumor is correct."

"I see you haven't lost your love of the man."

"It's a weakness, I know, but I can't help hating people who try to kill me."

"He thought you were after his claim."

"So he said."

"You're still here, aren't you?"

"Thanks to you."

"Well, if you're lucky, Benton will handle Gipson for you. Rumor also has it Gipson's poaching on his territory."

"Gipson's moving onto Benton's territory? I thought that Jackson was doing the poaching, or are they working together?"

Scott looked thoughtful. "Not that I've heard."

"So what makes that dried-up old weasel think he can challenge Benton?"

"That weasel's got money now. And if Benton presses him, well, ain't nothin' nastier than a cornered weasel. Now, come on, partner. We've got a boxcar to guard."

"I thought the *India* was due in today."

"She got caught in a storm at sea and delayed. She made it to Victoria today, should be here tomorrow."

THREE

Wednesday, December 6, 1899

It was a quiet night, if long and even colder than the previous one. It warmed enough to start snowing sometime after nine, thick flakes floating down, obscuring sight and muffling sound. Toward dawn it turned to rain, steadily growing to a downpour. By the time sunrise streaked the heavy clouds with pink, Granville was cold, wet, and miserable despite his new coat. He was also heartily bored; they hadn't seen or heard anyone all night; it had been just Scott and himself and the boxcars.

He scowled at his partner, who looked untroubled by the long hours, the cold, and the lack of sleep. Scott had refused to discuss Gipson or his doings any further, changing the subject each time Granville mentioned the name. He was even less forthcoming on the subject of Benton and Jackson. Was something going on, something Scott wasn't telling him? Granville wondered for the sixteenth time that night. His mind worried at the question, turning over the few facts he had, looking for patterns in what felt like the beginnings of an elaborate puzzle.

When the daytime guard relieved them at six, Scott and Granville headed off. Feet squishing wetly, they walked north and west, heading for Cambie Street. On their left was a row of boxcars, paralleling the docks. On their right was Water Street, lined with brick warehouses. They walked in silence for several minutes, too cold and wet for idle conversation.

Granville noticed a light burning over the doorway of the four-story Hudson's Bay warehouse, and was thinking how advanced the city of Vancouver was in some ways—even the warehouses were wired for electricity—when, beside him, Scott stopped abruptly. Granville froze, every sense alert. His hand fell to his revolver. "What is it?"

Scott moved toward a dark mound lying half-hidden under one of the boxcars. A bleak certainty of what they'd find filled Granville; he had seen death in too many guises not to recognize it here.

Scott bent to the corpse, rolling it over. He bent a little closer. "He's dead. Shot, looks like." He fingered a singed hole in the man's coat, above the heart, then picked up an arm, let it drop.

There was nothing they could do for him now. Granville scanned the area around them, but nothing moved, nothing claimed his attention. He looked from the body to the empty boxcar. Had the man been killed here, or shot elsewhere and dumped? And why here? "Neither of us heard anything. The snow would have muffled sounds."

The dead man was a dark shape against the pale gravel. "Do you know who he is?"

Scott nodded, his face expressionless in the half-light. "Oh, yeah. It's Jackson, Benton's right-hand man."

"You're certain?"

Scott nodded. "And there'll be the devil to pay."

Granville stared hard at what had once been a man. Undoubtedly Jackson was a scoundrel, but no one deserved to die like this. "He's the best-dressed dead corpse I've seen in quite some time," he said lightly. "The evening coat is a particularly nice touch. But he looks surprised about something."

"Probably being shot," Scott said. "I've heard it takes people that way."

Granville laughed. "So will the city police handle this?"

"Someone has to tell them first."

"Very amusing. You spotted him and identified the body. I think that should be you."

"Walking will be warmer than standing here anyway. We'll be back soon."

As the sound of Scott's footsteps faded, Granville stood contemplating the body. After a quick look around, he bent down for a closer look at the icy hands. They showed no sign of bruising on the knuckles, and the fingernails were clean. They were also manicured, Granville noted. It didn't look like Jackson had been in a struggle before he was shot.

His curiosity unsatisfied, he ran a hand into the dead man's pockets. In one pocket he found a handbill, brightly colored and crudely lettered, and was unfolding it when the crunching of heavy feet on gravel startled him. He straightened, quickly placing the paper in his pocket.

When Scott and two policemen in the dark blue uniforms and peaked caps of the city force came into view, Granville was standing several feet from the corpse, looking respectful. In the barrage of questions that followed, he stayed in the background, listening hard. He wasn't really involved, hadn't found the body, didn't know the dead man, but the questions interested him. It wasn't the fact that

Jackson was dead—that seemed almost expected—it was where he'd died and when that appeared to concern them most.

As the questions hurled at Scott seemed to become more pointed, however, Granville stepped forward. "We kept watch together last night and were leaving the yard together this morning," he said.

One of the policemen, a short, burly man, turned toward him. His expression was not friendly. "All night? From what time? And how do you know this fellow didn't just walk off and return without your noticing?"

His insolent tone irritated Granville. "Yes, all night, from eight o'clock last evening, and we were within sight of each other all night."

"And what time did you say you left the yard?"

He hadn't said. "Six, wasn't it, Scott?"

His partner nodded.

"How long has this person been dead?" Granville asked.

The other officer was checking the dead man's pockets. In the back one, which Granville hadn't had time to check, he'd discovered a dark, flat wallet, which he now examined.

"I'd say since long before ten, but we need the coroner to be sure. You sent for him yet?" the shorter one said.

The other man nodded. "Station'll have done that." He looked at Granville. "You're sure you both left at six?"

"Yes."

"And you saw nothing out of the ordinary?"

"Nothing."

"Hrmphhh."

The short officer clearly wasn't satisfied and probably didn't believe him. Several days of headlines in the *World* had informed Granville of the difference between these city police and the upright Mounties he'd dealt with in the Klondike. Vancouver's latest scandal had involved bribes and other favors some members of the local constabulary were accused of accepting to turn a blind eye to the gambling and the "ladies" on Dupont Street. Wearing a uniform was no guarantee of honesty, though it did mean you held the upper hand.

"You're sure you saw nothing?" the second policeman was now repeating.

"No, nothing," Granville said.

The arrival of the coroner ended the questioning. He poked and prodded at the corpse, muttering to himself, then gestured to the two officers to cover the body again. "One shot, missed the heart, looks like he bled to death. Probably sometime yesterday, perhaps last night. Can't tell more yet."

"Can you give us a closer time of death?"

"Too cold out. I'll need to do an autopsy. Get the body to the morgue," the coroner said, and bustled off.

After the coroner was out of earshot, the taller policeman looked at the other and grimaced. "He's right, it is cold. Are we done here?"

The shorter man gave his partner a sharp look, then turned to Scott and Granville. "As for you two, don't leave town, you hear me?"

Shortie's attitude was beginning to annoy Granville. He opened his mouth to say something scathing, but Scott spoke first. "We'll be here. Can we go?"

"For now."

When they were out of earshot, Granville turned so he could see Scott's expression in the lamplight. "What was that about?"

"His name's Craddock. I knew him back in Chicago and he hates my guts. If he can find a way to pin this on me, he will."

"I see."

"He didn't seem to like you much, either."

"The feeling was mutual."

"I could tell."

Later, Scott and Granville stood on the pier and watched the *Empress of India* steam into the harbor. She was a beauty, Granville thought, an elegant white steam liner with a clipper bow. As she drew closer, he could see evidence of the storm she'd been through: part of the molding along one side had been stripped away, and one of the metallic lifeboats was staved in. The two men watched the passengers disembark, laughing and chattering, then the unloading of the baggage. Finally, the process of transferring the cargo began. A crane lifted wooden crates from the hold and began to fill the boxcars he and Scott had spent the last two nights guarding. Over the scene the clouds hung low and ominous, and the dockworkers hurried to finish the job before the rain began again.

Funny, Granville thought, silk was something to which he'd never given a moment's attention. Herrick's line, how did it go?

When as in silk my Julia goes,
Then, then, methinks, how sweetly flows
That liquefaction of her clothes.

Which brought to mind another Julia, who was part of the reason he was here in the first place. "Damn," he muttered.

For several more minutes they watched the activity, until the last of the boxcars was full. Suddenly he realized how tired he felt, and that the cold had started to seep back into his bones. A whiskey or two would warm him, and then he could sleep.

FOUR

Friday, December 8, 1899

A gray light was seeping through every crack in the wooden shutters when a loud banging woke Granville from a sound sleep.

"What . . . ?"

"Police. Open up."

Blinking, Granville stumbled out of bed. Throwing open the door, he glared at the two men standing in the dingy corridor, rain dripping from the brims of their hats. It was the two policemen from the other morning.

"What?"

"The chief has a few questions he'd like to ask you. You'll have to come with us."

Too little sleep and too much whiskey left Granville at a disadvantage. "What questions?"

"Just come with us. Now."

He stared at them, half hoping they would vanish once his brain began to function. They didn't. "What time is it?"

"Half past eleven. And you have five minutes until we drag you out." Craddock looked as if this was the option he'd prefer.

Let them try, Granville told himself, then realized he would gain nothing by putting up a fight. Far better to find out what they wanted first.

In six minutes, the room was empty.

Glaring at Chief McKenzie, Granville slammed a fist on the desk that separated them. "What do you mean you've arrested my partner for murder?"

McKenzie, a big, heavyset man with deep pouches beneath his eyes, pulled at the end of his thick mustache. "Calm yourself, Granville. Thumping the furniture won't help anything. If Sam Scott didn't kill Jackson, he has nothing to fear. If he did, then he's right where he should be."

"Surely there should have been a coroner's inquest?"

"Dr. Barwill held an inquiry yesterday. Warrant was sworn out for your friend right after."

"A warrant? On what evidence?"

"You'll find that out in court. Until then, Scott will remain our guest."

Granville pictured what time in a cell would do to Scott, who hated confinement of any kind. His anger rose. "You cannot simply hold him here. What about bail?"

"Well, now, that would be up to the judge to decide. The hearing should be in a day or two."

Granville wasn't liking the sound of this. "And if there is a trial? When would that be?"

"The next criminal court date is December nineteenth."

Which meant Scott could be facing eleven days in jail. "And which judge would that be?"

"He'd be brought in front of Judge Thomas."

Even though Granville was a newcomer, he knew the man's reputation. "The one they call the Hanging Judge?"

"Judge Thomas is a fair man. If your friend is innocent, he has nothing to fear."

"And who is to prove him innocent?"

"Well, I'm thinking you'd best be looking for a good solicitor."

If there was such a thing as a good lawyer in this upstart town on the edge of nowhere, Granville thought. "Can I see him?"

Vancouver's chief of police looked Granville up and down, while Granville thanked God he'd bought new clothes the previous day. At least he looked the gentleman he'd once been. British Columbia, for all its wilderness, was part of Her Majesty's empire, with an instinctive respect for the well born.

"Aye, I don't see why not. Leave that revolver with us until you visit, and don't cause a disturbance. And I'll thank you to remember in the future that this is a law-abiding town. We don't allow our citizens to carry guns, except in pursuit of their duties."

"What?"

The chief nodded. "Next time, you'll be arrested on the spot."

Granville couldn't believe what he was hearing.

"Unless your life is in danger, of course," the chief continued. "But you'd have to prove that to our satisfaction."

A quick glance around Scott's cell told him that it was dry and mostly draft free, but that was all that could be said for it. Scott sat on the end of one of two narrow bunks, and Granville chose the straight-backed wooden chair for himself. His partner looked miserable, Granville thought. He seemed to have shrunk somehow, as though his big frame was trying to fold in on itself.

"Why did they arrest you?"

Scott shrugged. He was not meeting Granville's worried gaze.

"They have to have told you something!"

"Said they figured I had the most likely motive for killing Jackson. And I was there."

"Motive? What motive?"

"Maybe I owed him money," he said, his voice so low Granville had to strain to hear him. "Maybe Jackson was harassing me about it."

"How much did you owe him? And why did you mention nothing of this?"

Scott was silent.

"Damnit, Sam, I want to help you. If a hearing doesn't clear you, they'll be bringing you in front of the Hanging Judge."

Scott still said nothing.

"Look, Scott. I don't know the rules here. How likely is it that the hearing will get you out of here?"

"Not very likely."

It was what he'd been picking up from McKenzie. "Sam, I don't want to stand by and see you die. If I'm going to get you out of here, I need to know what's going on. You have to talk to me."

"I owed him—Jackson—six hundred dollars," Scott said, each word like a pebble dropping into the silence. "And he was hounding me for it."

Granville shook his head in disbelief.

"Yeah." Scott's voice was still low. "I didn't trust him, but I had no choice. I needed that money bad. Nobody else was going to give it to me."

"Why did you need it?"

The only reply was further silence, and a stubborn look.

Scott wasn't just holding out on him, he was lying about something,

Granville was sure of it. Dishonesty was completely out of character for his blunt friend. Granville had never seen Scott back away from a fight, and he'd never seen him lie for his own gain. So why was he lying now? Looking thoughtfully at his jailed partner, Granville could think of only one reason: to protect someone else. But whom?

"What was Jackson like?" Granville asked, changing his tactic.

"A bully. Benton counted on him to do his dirty work, but Jackson made sure he had sidelines of his own."

"Sidelines. What sort of sidelines?"

"He had money in a couple of the houses over on Dupont."

"Prostitution?"

Scott nodded.

"What else?"

"You name it. But that's the one I know about for sure."

"So he must have made some enemies."

It wasn't a question, but Scott answered anyway. "He did."

"Then why are they pinning his murder on you?"

"Craddock hates me?" Scott said, making an attempt at humor.

"You did mention that. But whatever did you do to the poor man? Beat him at arm wrestling?"

"Not exactly." There was an odd expression on his face.

"Well, we both know there has to be a reason the police focused on you so quickly."

"The money. Plus I was nearby when Jackson died. They don't believe you when you say we were together."

"Yes, I had rather gathered that," Granville said. But he was thinking about the strange expression he'd seen cross his partner's face. Something was very wrong here, and he didn't know what. Or what he was going to do about it. He just knew he had to do something.

None of Granville's thoughts showed on his face. "You have

nothing to worry about," he told Scott with a confidence he didn't feel. "You're innocent, and I intend to prove it if I have to find Jackson's murderer myself to do it."

"But can you prove it in eleven days?"

Granville shrugged. "You know I love a challenge."

FIVE

Four hours later, soggy and frustrated, Granville sat nursing a whiskey in a grimy saloon by the docks, already wishing he'd never taken up the challenge of freeing Scott. He had eleven days to save him, ten and a half now. It had seemed longer this morning, before he'd found out exactly how hard it was going to be to pry information loose in this town.

No one was willing to talk about Jackson; even dead, he seemed to beget fear. When Granville asked questions, people treated him as if he were contagious. And Jackson seemed to have been invisible; no one remembered him, no one had seen him anywhere near the docks, no one knew where he had been or was going. It was absolute horseshit, but Granville could not shake their stories.

Without money to grease their memories and overcome their fear, he wasn't going to get anywhere. And because he didn't have money, his friend was at risk of losing his life. For the first time, Granville regretted his stubborn refusal to accept the remittance from home that most emigrant gentlemen of his class depended on. He'd always been too proud, too determined to prove he could succeed on his own, and now it was too late to change his mind. If he asked for help now, always supposing his pompous ass of an eldest brother would honor their father's wishes and send the money, it would come too late—Scott would be dead.

It also didn't help that Granville was new to Vancouver. Up in Dawson City, he would have known exactly whom to talk to and how to get them talking. There he knew most of the invisible connections that tied people together, while here he only knew Scott and Blayney, one of whom was in jail and refusing to tell him what he needed to know, while the other for the moment had vanished.

Someone had killed Clive Jackson, and probably for good reason, but Granville was damned if he knew what that reason was. He had spent hours on the docks without getting a single answer he could use.

Even the paper he'd found in the dead man's pocket hadn't given him a lead. It was a cheaply printed handbill for a burlesque performance at a place called the Carlton, on Columbia. "Don't miss Franny from Frisco," it screamed. "Two shows nightly, ten and midnight." He'd gone to look at the place right after talking to Scott. It had been deserted, though, meaning he'd have to return this evening. Until then he had time on his hands and no idea where to look next.

Granville swore and called for another whiskey. Watching the bartender pour the drink, he was struck by how often he'd watched that same action. In how many bars, in how many cities? And for all the griminess of this one, with the wind blowing through the cracks, how different was it from all the others?

The door over there probably led to a back room, with the

inevitable poker game. But it was too early. Just thinking about it, though, made the tips of his fingers tingle. It had been too long since he'd handled the cards, felt the crisp snap of the pasteboard.

He picked up his glass, stared at it, slammed it back on the counter. It might make him feel better, but it wouldn't save Scott. He thought some more. Considered. There might be another way to proceed. But only if he was prepared to forgo the oath he'd sworn on Edward's grave.

A second death would hardly make the first any more bearable, or his conscience any easier. He signaled the bartender, his decision made. Granville knew what he needed to do. And he knew, finally, how he'd make the money to clear Scott.

When the bartender looked from the half-drunk whiskey to him, Granville put two quarters on the bar and leaned forward. "I'm partial to a good game of poker," he said in a low voice. "Can you tell me where I'd find one?"

The bartender looked hard at him, then half nodded. "Sure can. Low or high?"

"High."

"Try the bar at the Terminus Hotel or the Balmoral Club."

"And where would they be?"

"Terminus is straight up Westminster on Hastings, Balmoral Club's in behind the Savoy."

"And do the games run all day?"

"High ones start around seven or so. Just watch out for the law."

"Thanks, I'll be sure to do that."

The bartender was right. Granville found the action in a small back room off the Terminus bar. It was loud, smoky, and frantic, the cries of the winners and groans of the losers echoing off the battered, pine-clad walls.

He circulated slowly through the crowd. Most of the gamblers were gathered at round tables, either placing bets or watching the action. He found the game he was looking for on the far side of the room, partially screened by thin painted partitions.

Granville ordered a drink and lit a cigar, watching the faces. He'd seen them all before—the predators, the reckless ones, the ones hooked on the hope of easy money—but none of the faces were familiar. He hadn't really expected them to be, though he still hoped to find Blayney.

Watching the play, he suddenly felt the old sensations. Now, here, he could give in to them. With a fervent apology to Edward's ghost, Granville sat down at a table where a new game was being dealt.

Five games, one whiskey, and two cigars later, Granville folded his cards, picked up his winnings, and pushed back his chair. He had the money he needed to pursue Jackson's real killer, and he felt a bone-deep satisfaction in knowing it. Granville made his way into the equally crowded and smoky bar, where sawdust crunched under his feet. He exited into the crisp night air with a feeling of relief.

Turning his collar up against the light rain, he walked south on Westminster and turned west on Dupont. In just one block the air went from damp but fresh to a thick dankness that proclaimed its origin in the mudflats the street was built on. It was likely most of the landlords on Dupont were Chinese, Granville thought cynically. It'd be the only place they were allowed to buy, on land nobody else wanted.

Walking briskly, Granville kept a careful eye on the shadows between buildings. Electricity hadn't reached this part of town, and the oil lantern streetlights were few and far between. He passed a butcher shop, a decaying rooming house, two white-painted bawdy houses with red lanterns glowing over their doors, an opium den with its row after row of beds clearly visible through the open door, a laundry, another white-painted house, several dilapidated shanty houses, and a produce store. Light seeping from doorways and partially curtained windows cast odd shadows on the men, both white and Chinese, who hurried by. The tinkling of pianos played in the parlors of the bawdy houses provided an odd background to the eerie scene.

The Savoy Hotel was the second to the last building on the block. There was a dark narrow passageway running beside it. Granville left the street and turned into that narrow lane, his senses alert for danger, his hand on the knife he always carried. The passageway was Stygian, with only an occasional light in a high window to break the gloom.

From this vantage point the Balmoral Club was hard to miss; light streamed from its windows and he could hear a babble of voices. It was a ramshackle wooden building, two stories high, that ran the full length of the Savoy and the hotel beside it. Someone had slapped on a coat of white paint, but it didn't look like they'd been serious about it. Here and there strips of raw wood showed dark in the lamplight.

Inside, the volume was so loud he had to stop for a minute to get his bearings. There had to be a hundred men in here, all of them clustered around blackjack or poker tables. No wonder the barkeep had told him to watch out for the police. Granville wondered how often this place was raided. He could just picture Craddock rampaging through here, swinging his club, eyes glittering.

Granville scanned the crowd. He believed he would find Blayney in here, but such a throng meant it would take some time. He eased through the crowd, headed for the bar, when a hand on his arm froze him where he stood. Granville spun around, knife half-drawn, and found himself facing the scared eyes of the kid who'd tried to sabotage the silk cars.

"Sorry, mister," the boy stammered. "Please. I just wanted to talk to you."

Granville released his breath harshly. "So talk."

The kid looked over one shoulder, then the other. "Not here. It's not safe."

It took all of Granville's self-control not to laugh out loud. Then he remembered his own approach to the world at the same age, the exaggeration and melodrama, the longing for adventure. But he was on the hunt for Jackson's killer, and the boy's connections to Jackson meant he might know something. "I thought you agreed to leave town if we let you go."

The kid nodded. "Pa left. I stayed."

"Why?"

"I found a job."

"Another train to rob?"

His companion bristled. "A real job. It's legit this time."

"Oh?"

"It's not like that. I'm working for Mr. Turner."

Turner? The one who'd hired Scott? "So why were you looking for me?"

"Well, I was really trying to find the other man, the one you were with."

"Scott?" Granville took a hard look at the boy. "Why are you after him?"

At his tone the boy seemed to shrink, then he looked quickly behind him. "Not here."

Impatient now, Granville nodded. "All right. What's out back?"

"Not much, just an alley."

"We'll talk there. Lead the way."

They passed through a half-hidden side door, down a long narrow hallway that smelled of mold and stale soup, exiting through a door at the rear of the building. No one seemed to notice them go.

The back lane was malodorous and dark, with the sole illumination from two small windows set high in the wall behind them. With any luck they wouldn't be observed or overheard. He turned to the boy.

"Now tell me. Why did you want to talk to Scott?"

The kid hesitated.

Granville watched him impatiently for all of thirty seconds, then reminded him, "I have better things to do with my time than stand about in alleys waiting to be shot at. Either you start talking or . . ."

He stopped short. At his words, his listener had ducked. He was terrified, and much younger than Granville had first thought.

"No one is gunning for us," Granville said calmly. "Believe me, I wouldn't be standing here if they were. Now, it's time to answer my question."

The boy straightened slowly but remained mute. Then with no warning, he started to talk. "We were broke. And we'd been hungry awhile. That's what started it. Pa . . . Pa, he said there was a way to get money . . . that he knew a man."

Granville could hear him swallow hard.

"He . . . Pa . . . met with Mr. Jackson. I didn't know anything at first, but then he asked about me, said I'd be useful."

"How well did you know Jackson?"

The boy hesitated again.

Granville sighed. "Look, kid . . . what's your name, anyhow?"

The kid bit his lip, looking as if he'd said too much already.

"It's all right, you can trust me," Granville reassured him, but his impatience was growing.

No response.

"You have to trust someone, right?"

The answer came all in a rush, as if the words had been held back far too long. "My name is Davis, Trenton Davis. But call me Trent, sir. Everyone does."

"Fine, Trent. And I'm Granville."

"Thank you, Mr. Granville, sir."

"Just Granville. And don't call me 'sir.'"

"No, sir. I mean, no, Mr. . . . I mean, Granville."

This was far harder work than guarding empty boxcars. "So, Trent, tell me about what you and your pa were doing for Jackson."

Trent nodded. "He hired us to run errands. That's what he said. Sometimes for him, sometimes for Mr. Blayney."

"Blayney?"

Trent hunched his shoulders. "Yes, sir."

"Go on." Suddenly Granville was even more interested in what Trent had to say. "What kind of errands?"

"Fetching and carrying. That's all, really."

"Fetching and carrying what?"

"Envelopes. Bundles. Whatever they gave us."

"What was in these packages?"

"Don't know. They were sealed tight."

"Where did you deliver them?"

"All over town."

"And how did Blayney fit into this employment?"

"I'm not sure," Trent admitted. "He doesn't really work for Jackson but for some other fellow."

"Gipson."

"Yeah, that's the one. But how did you know?"

"Never mind. What more do you know about Jackson?"

"Nothing. And I wouldn't want to, either," Trent said.

Delivering packages was only part of the story. "How did you end up trying to sabotage the train?"

The boy didn't reply, just stood there shivering.

Granville wished he had a drink. "Trent?"

Trent's voice was miserable. "Mr. Jackson told us what we had to do. He made it clear we had to get it right."

No one so young should sound like that. Granville fought to keep the pity out of his voice, knowing from his own experience that it would be anything but welcome. "There were three of you. Who was the third?"

"Charlie Jones. He was supposed to be in charge, but he's no real thief, either. After all, we got caught, right?"

"Right," said Granville dryly. "So why are you still in town?"

"Because I found work. It seemed worth it to take the chance."

"And why did you want to talk to Scott?"

"I need help."

"He can't help you now, kid."

"I'd rather ask him myself." The words were courteously spoken, but the underlying will was fierce.

"Scott's in jail," Granville snapped, suddenly angry with himself for wasting time. "Why don't you just tell me what you want from him?"

"In jail? He can't be!"

At the despair in Trent's voice, Granville nearly promised to help him if he could. He stopped himself, knowing he didn't have time for another lost cause. "Well, he is. And you didn't answer my question."

"What? Oh. I needed to talk to him about Mr. Jackson."

"Why? Jackson's dead," Granville said.

Trent looked at him in shock, staggered, and would have fallen if Granville hadn't moved quickly, putting a steadying hand on his shoulder.

"Who killed him?" There was stark terror in the boy's voice.

He hadn't known Jackson was dead? What was going on here? Granville wondered. "They've arrested Scott for the murder," he said, making an effort to keep his tone matter-of-fact.

"Are they crazy?"

The amazement in Trent's voice drew surprised laughter from Granville. Here was someone who believed in Scott's innocence as much as he did, even if he was only an unfledged kid.

The growling of his stomach suddenly reminded him that he hadn't actually eaten anything that day. He made an impulsive decision, based as much on Trent's drawn face and scrawny frame as his need to find out any more from him about Jackson. "Look, there's no point in continuing our conversation here. I know a place where they make one hell of a steak. You hungry?"

He led the boy to Garrity's Steakhouse, where Scott had taken him the previous day. The rough-and-ready ambiance hadn't impressed him, but the steaks had. As Granville chewed on a thick bite, he watched the top of Trent's dark head, where a cowlick stood up in spikes. The kid was eating with happy concentration. Catching the waiter's eye, Granville ordered two more steaks.

When Trent finally looked up, Granville offered a grin. "And now it's time for you to sing for your supper."

Trent looked confused. "Sing? Here?"

"Talk," he said softly. "It's time for you to talk now. What did you want to ask Scott about Jackson? And why Scott?"

"Oh." Trent paused, his fingers turning a fork over and over again, then in a hurried motion he put it down and folded his hands on the table. His eyes met Granville's.

"I didn't trust what Mr. Jackson might be saying, and I wanted Mr. Benton to know I've gone legit," he said with great dignity. "That I won't be running errands no more. Anymore," he corrected himself.

"So all you actually wanted was to talk to Benton?"

Trent nodded.

"Wouldn't he have been a little annoyed with you about the botched job at the yard and the fact you told us about Jackson's involvement?"

Trent's face flushed, and he seemed to be studying the splinters in the tabletop. "He doesn't know I was involved. It was just supposed to be Pa and Charlie. They weren't paying for me."

Granville sighed. "But you were there anyway."

Trent nodded eagerly, then he seemed to remember the outcome and his expression dimmed.

"Then why do you need Scott's help?"

"Mr. Benton isn't easy to get to talk to. I wanted Mr. Scott to set up a meeting for me. I didn't want there to be any misunderstanding between Mr. Benton and me," he said with a gravity that was at odds with his youth.

"But why Scott?"

Now the boy looked worried. "I thought you two were partners."

"We are."

"Then how come you don't know that he knows Mr. Benton?" Trent crossed his arms over his chest and sat back, watching Granville with a wary expression.

Granville would have been amused to see his own mannerisms copied if he hadn't been so shaken. If Trent was right, why *hadn't* Scott told him? It had him wondering—again—what else Scott wasn't telling him, and how well he really knew his friend.

In the Yukon, all that mattered was how a man acted, not who he had been. Granville had to ask himself what he really knew about Sam Scott, about his background. He knew he was an orphan, had grown up in Chicago and then gradually wandered west, like so many men eventually following the lure of gold north. Not much information, when you came to think about it. But back then all he'd needed to know was that Scott was courageous, loyal, quick with his fists, and an accurate shot. Now it wasn't enough.

How well did he really know anyone? What things he did know about Scott were the things that mattered; he had saved his life and his sanity. Hell, Scott was probably the closest thing to family Granville had here.

He turned to the kid. "I've only got your word for it. Exactly what have you heard about Scott and Benton?"

Trent looked like he was debating whether to answer or to run, but finally said, "Rumors, mostly. That's all."

Granville's mind was racing. How had Scott gotten involved with Benton? Or was Trent lying? What he needed, still, was to locate Blayney and see if he had any information to offer.

He looked at Trent speculatively, decided it was worth a try. "Any idea where I'd find Blayney?"

Trent nodded. "On Friday nights he's always at Gipson's warehouse. It's payday."

Granville stood up, dropping some coins on the table. "Where is this warehouse?"

"On Water Street, past the Union Steamship wharf."

Granville nodded, he knew the area. "I'll find it. Thanks, Trent."

"I'm coming with you," Trent said, putting his cutlery down with a clatter.

"No, you are *not*."

"Then I'll follow you." Trent stood up.

Granville stopped dead. He didn't have time for such nonsense, he thought, putting one hand to his hip, where his revolver would have been if he'd been carrying it. "You are not coming."

"I know some more stuff about Jackson."

"What?" Granville asked, only half sure he believed him.

"I'll tell you later. After we find Blayney."

"You do realize I could put a bullet in you as you stand there," he said mildly.

"But then I'd be dead, and you'd never get your answers."

"Not if I placed the bullet strategically. Through an arm, say. Or a leg."

"Do that, and you're no better than Jackson was," Trent said, and waited.

Granville knew when he was defeated. "All right. But stay in the background."

Trent followed him out of the restaurant, looking pleased with himself.

SIX

The first blow caught Trent solidly on the chin. Granville winced in sympathy even as he tripped his own assailant. A pair of arms gripped his from behind, and he jerked an elbow back into a beefy midriff. A loud groan followed, and he was released. He spun toward Trent's assailant and got in one blow, then a sound from behind had him half ducking, but not fast enough to avoid the blow.

When consciousness returned, Granville found himself trussed up like a chicken ready for spitting. A quick assessment revealed a ringing head and a few new bruises, but nothing that felt permanent. From the corner of his eye he could see Trent, similarly bound. The kid didn't appear to have fared too well. One eye was puffy and closing fast. His lip was cut and bleeding. Granville winced. He should have refused to bring him along, no matter how the boy had insisted. It was no business of his, after all.

A pair of shiny shoes stopped in front of him. "What are you doing here, Granville?"

Blayney sounded as ineffectual as ever, despite the fact that he was the one holding a gun.

"I was looking for you," Granville said.

Blayney ignored this. He studied Granville closely, taking in his new coat and boots. "Well, well. You're cleaned up since the last time I saw you."

Granville had never considered Blayney dangerous, but something in the other man's expression made him rethink that assumption. Perhaps it had something to do with being trussed up, or perhaps it was the four thugs positioned like bookends on either side of them.

Blayney looked down at the revolver he was holding, then without changing expression or tone of voice, he cocked it and aimed at Granville.

"Now, if it's all the same to you, I need to know why you were looking for me and how you knew to come here."

And just what are you hiding? wondered Granville. But before he could speak, Trent did.

"It was my fault."

We're in for it now, Granville thought, bracing himself for what the kid would say, but Trent surprised him.

"I told him about the warehouse, that you'd be here, I mean," he explained. There was an open, honest expression on his face. "And when Granville was so worried and wanting to talk to you about his friend, well, I remembered delivering stuff here, so I brought him. I didn't mean to cause a problem, really I didn't."

Somehow Trent had figured out what to say, and he had managed to look and sound entirely guileless. Amazingly, it seemed to have turned the trick, because for now Blayney was lowering his gun.

"What friend?" The question was thrown at Granville.

"Scott's in jail. He's been arrested for Jackson's murder."

Blayney looked stunned for a moment. Then he began to laugh. "The man thought he had connections and that would protect him," he said, a bright thread of malice running through every word. "You can't fight the law, though, can you?"

Now what did Blayney mean by that? "That's why I want your help."

"My help? Never thought I'd see the day. What d'you want my help with, old chap?"

Blayney wasn't making any attempt to untie them, Granville noted as he carefully chose his next words. "You've been here longer than I have, Blayney. I've set myself the job of learning just why Scott's been targeted for this killing. I'm bound and determined to get him off."

"Get him off? Get Scott off on a charge of murder? My dear Granville, I don't think so. The man will undoubtedly hang within the month."

Why had he never realized what a detestable creature Blayney was? With an effort, Granville kept his voice level. "Can you tell me anything about his enemies, then?"

Blayney appeared to find the question amusing. "Well, the chief one is probably Clive Jackson. The late Clive Jackson, I might add."

"And who else?"

"It's a rather large list, I should say."

Granville couldn't keep the contempt he felt from showing.

Blayney reacted with a pettishness that quickly switched to aggression. "Perhaps I should shoot you," he said. "It would probably save a lot of inconvenience if I just shot you both."

Probably? Granville thought. The man was an idiot who would never have the nerve to shoot them in cold blood. He might not have a problem telling someone else to do it, though. There was no point in taking chances. "My disappearance would raise questions that you might find rather, shall we say, awkward to answer. My brother wouldn't take kindly to his kin being murdered."

"That would be your elder brother William now, wouldn't it?" Blayney said in thoughtful tones. "From what I hear, the baron might be rather pleased if someone murdered you."

That was a hit, but Granville was damned if he'd acknowledge it. "Oh, I think you heard wrong," he drawled. "William would be quite happy to kill me himself. However, he would be most unhappy if anyone else did it for him." He paused. "Most unhappy," he repeated, watching Blayney's face.

Granville let the silence stretch out. From behind him came a muted buzz of voices and activity. The flickering of the oil lamps cast grotesque shadows on the warped boards. Electric lighting was probably too costly for this end of town, but he'd have thought Blayney would be more concerned about the possibility of fire. The place was piled with boxes and crates, and the building was made of wood, roughly constructed, and old. What were they storing here, anyhow?

Blayney's nervous laughter snapped Granville's attention back to him.

"You're slipping," he said with an attempt at heartiness that rang hollow in Granville's ears. "I've never been able to fool you before. As if I'd really shoot such an old chum."

"Untie them," Blayney said to the thugs. Then to Granville, "Now, what can I tell you about Scott?"

Unsure what had caused Blayney to release them, Granville shrugged, which relieved the ache that had been building up in his shoulders. He let his now-unbound hands fall to his sides.

"Anything you know about Scott's business or acquaintances in town," he said, ignoring the fierce pain as the blood slowly began returning to his hands and feet.

"You know Scott was in with Jackson, of course." A pause.

"Of course," Granville said, then added offhandedly, "What I don't know is why."

Blayney shrugged. "Money, probably. You'd have to ask him."

"Go on."

"When Scott first arrived, he picked up work here and there, then got himself hired by Turner at the CPR."

"All common knowledge, Blayney. I thought if anyone knew the real story, it would be you."

The flattery worked. Blayney preened. He moved several steps closer, lowering his voice until Granville had to strain to hear. "Scott was seeing a woman, some cheap fan dancer from what I hear. She works out of a club on Columbia."

"Do you have a name?"

"Franny, Fanny, something like that."

Suddenly that handbill he'd filched from the dead man's pocket took on new meaning. Could Scott be protecting a woman? It would explain much.

"And what about any enemies Scott might have made?"

For a fleeting instant malice was stamped on Blayney's face, then he smirked. "From what I hear, the recently deceased Jackson was none too pleased with your partner."

"But why?"

"Scott was Benton's man."

There it was again, but did that mean it was true? "So? So was Jackson."

"Well, let's just say Jackson had been Benton's man."

"Had been?"

"Rumor has it that Jackson was going to set up on his own."

"Then why is Scott in jail and not Benton?" Granville demanded.

Blayney gave him a pitying look.

He'd had enough of this nonsense. Granville stood up, keeping his expression casual but watching Blayney's reaction closely. "Thanks for the information. Come on, Trent."

Turning, Granville strode toward the door, the boy following. Blayney stood irresolute, watching them go. As they reached the relative safety of the street, Granville drew a relieved breath. He paused for a moment, then turned right and strode briskly down Water Street.

"That was great, Granville," Trent burst out. "I didn't think we were going to get out of that one, but you played him like an old trout."

Granville rolled his eyes skyward.

"His information's out of date, though, don't you think?" Trent continued.

"Out of date? What do you mean?"

"Benton and Jackson were tight again."

"What?"

"Yup. Way I heard it, Benton hired Jackson as manager for his lumber mill. Gave him part ownership and everything."

Now that was interesting. What motive could lie behind that? "Why didn't you tell me this earlier?"

"I figured you'd already know."

Granville gave him a sharp look. Perhaps you did, and perhaps not, he thought. "Then why didn't Blayney know?"

"I don't think Jackson much liked him. And Mr. Blayney isn't any too bright, is he?"

"But then . . . ," Granville began, when a movement in a thick patch of shadow ahead of them alerted him. He stopped and yanked Trent behind him with one hand, the other going to his knife. The boy stayed quiet, seemingly listening as intently as Granville was. For a long, long moment, there was no sound beyond the steady patter of the rain that had begun again while they were in the warehouse.

Then there was a sudden outburst of motion in the darkness, a loud yowling, and a small cat streaked across their path, followed immediately by a larger one.

This whole business had him jumping at shadows. Behind him, Trent had started breathing again.

"If Jackson didn't like Blayney, why did he have you run errands for him?" Granville could think of a number of reasons, but he wanted to know what the kid knew.

Trent shook his head. "Dunno," he said. "Where we goin' now?"

"I'm going to see a show and you're going home."

"Can't I come?"

"No."

"How are you going to stop me? I'm here now, aren't I?"

At that age, Granville had thought himself invincible, too. "Come on, then," he said, still unsure why this boy was so determined to tag along. Curiosity? The chance for adventure? Or was it something else?

SEVEN

The main room at the Carlton was loud and smoky. At the far end, a voluptuous blonde was shimmying on a small stage, wearing nothing but sheer scarves and a few strategically placed feathers. Granville glanced at Trent, standing beside him. He was oblivious, all his attention focused on the dancer.

"Ever see a burlesque dancer before, Trent?"

Trent didn't take his eyes off the stage. "No, sir."

Granville let his gaze rove around the packed bar. Most of the patrons wore expressions almost identical to Trent's. So where was this Franny from Frisco? Grabbing Trent's elbow, Granville maneuvered them both over to the bar, with Trent nearly tripping twice because he never took his eyes off the stage.

"One whiskey, one soda."

The bartender set up the glasses.

"I've been seeing posters for Franny."

The huge bartender grinned, showing two missing front teeth. Judging by the muscles rippling in his arms and upper torso, Granville was willing to bet the man had won more fights than he'd lost.

"You and half the town," the bartender said as he handed over the whiskey. "She's our biggest draw."

"So when is she on?"

"Right after Annette over there," he said, gesturing at the blonde, who was slowly molting feathers.

"Thanks." Granville handed the soda to Trent and began to work his way to the edge of the stage. Trent followed.

With a final thrust of her hip, the last feather fluttered to the stage. Amid wolf whistles and applause that seemed to shake the flimsy walls, Annette gave a wink and a wave and disappeared backstage.

The whistling and applause died away and there was a long silence. Granville looked around him in surprise. Usually in a place like this the noise would continue until the next dancer appeared, growing louder if she took too long. Instead, the silence seemed to deepen, until finally it was broken by a drumroll. Another silence, another drumroll. Now a long, shapely pair of legs encased in black net stockings glided into the spotlight, topped by a huge feather fan.

Granville joined in the thunder of applause that broke out. It seemed that Franny—if this was indeed she—had a real sense of showmanship. She wasn't afraid of her audience either, he thought, as legs and fan came to a complete stop. Slowly the noise died away, then came the sinuous wail of a lone clarinet, followed first by a trumpet, then by the drums. The fan began to sway backward and forward, still revealing nothing except those spellbinding legs.

Now the chant began, swelling until it filled the building.

"Fran-*ny!* Fran-*ny!*" The stomping of booted feet shook the floor so violently that Granville found himself hoping the building was sound. Then, at last, Franny began to dance. Still only those legs and the fan were visible, but the legs were kicking, higher and higher with every hollered "Fran-*ny!*" It was enthralling. It was also highly arousing. Granville ran a hand under his collar and reminded himself forcefully that he was here to help his partner.

He glanced over at Trent, whose eyes were huge in a pale face. Granville sighed. He'd known it was a mistake to bring him, but everyone had to grow up sometime. At least this was nothing like the brothel William had dragged him to when he turned fourteen, Granville thought, shuddering at the memory of painted faces, groping hands, and jeering laughter. "Fourteen, is he? Ooh, he's a cute one, he is. C'mon, lad, let's see what you're made of." The voices cawed in his head, and he thrust them away; it was an occasion he preferred not to remember.

An increase in the noise level focused his attention back on the stage. The fan had begun to dip lower, revealing dark brown hair with glints of red where the light caught it. The spotlight dimmed and the other lights began to come up very, very slowly. The din around him intensified as the woman herself began to appear, inch by inch. "Fran-*ny!* Fran-*ny!*"

A pair of strongly marked brows appeared, set in a broad white forehead, then eyes that flashed in the dim light. Strong cheekbones and a nose with a hint of a tilt were next, then full, sensuous lips, pouting slightly, and a chin that was perhaps a shade too sharp, all set on a long, graceful neck. In any setting, it was a face you would not soon forget. In this place, Franny from Frisco had the kind of beauty that seemed to dare and challenge every man there.

And they were responding. The cheers, whistles, and foot-stomping increased. And all she was showing was her face and her legs, thought Granville in amazement. What was next?

Her face disappeared behind her fan again, and the spectators went abruptly silent. The ensuing quiet seemed to echo off the thin walls. Then a clarinet wailed out, the lighting on the stage brightened, the drum began to throb, and a trumpet to moan. The fan swayed in rhythm, from side to side, allowing a glimpse of arm here, a flash of bosom there. Behind her fan, Franny seemed to be clad in something that glistened and shimmered where it caught the light.

Suddenly the trumpet blared. The fan snapped shut. Franny from Frisco, revealed at last in a short golden costume that covered her from neck to thigh, began to gyrate, and her audience roared approval.

Granville tore his gaze from those shapely hips and studied her face. She looked lost in the music as she danced, but there was a hint of a smile curving the corners of her red, red mouth, and a definite gleam in the down-swept eyes. She was playing with them, and loving every minute of it. He studied the enthralled men around him; they knew it, and loved her for it.

She sat in a deep armchair in her small dressing room, the air sweet with powder and scent. "Call me Frances," she said in a clear voice, accompanied by an enigmatic smile.

"I'm Trent."

His voice was as eager as his expression as he rushed forward to shake her hand. Granville hid a smile as he stretched his own hand out to take hers. Scott's name had gotten them access backstage without even a question. Which was apparently not usual;

Franny from Frisco saw no one after her show. It made him even more curious to see how she would react to his own name.

"John Lansdowne Granville. Scott calls me Granville," he said, watching her.

Frances's grip was firm, her hand, lingering in his, long and shapely. The glint of laughter in her eyes was a challenge.

"Sam's told me about you," was all she said.

"You know where he is?"

She nodded.

He eyed her up and down, wondering where she fit into the picture. She was even more attractive seen up close than she'd been onstage. Clad now in a floor-length dressing gown of red brocade, with her wavy hair loose about her shoulders, she radiated sensual appeal, yet her face gave nothing away.

As he looked her over, Frances's expression froze and her eyes lost their laugh. Fleetingly she reminded him of his paternal grandmother, a woman capable of delivering a very sharp put-down. "I assume you're here for a reason?"

Granville almost laughed at his own sudden discomfort. He knew he had been rude, and he felt like a small boy who has been reprimanded. "I want to get Scott out of jail."

"And just how do you plan to accomplish that?"

"With your help." It was worth a try, though, judging by her present expression, she wouldn't help Granville to a glass of water if he were dying of thirst. He should have been less obvious in his studied appraisal of her.

"How?"

The single word was a cold as a February morning on the Klondike River. Either she was mortally offended, or she was a hell of an actress. He was betting on the latter, though he wondered why she'd bother. She was a burlesque dancer; she must be used to the frank stares she got from men.

"I need to know more about the relationship between Scott and Jackson, and why everyone here seems so quick to jump to the conclusion that Scott murdered Jackson."

"Why?"

"Because they are going to hang him." Granville bit out the words, glaring at her. It was one in the morning and he was exhausted and no closer to helping Scott than he'd been when he set out. He needed answers and he was sick of playing games.

The minute the words were out of his mouth he was wishing he could call them back. He knew better. This was the wrong place and she was the wrong woman to be losing his temper with.

"But why did you come to me?" Her expression remained chilly.

"I was told you and Scott knew each other."

"I know many people."

"Listen to me. Scott has ten days left before he faces trial. Now, do you want to help Scott or don't you?"

Frances put her head to one side, as if considering him and his question. After a long moment she said, "Jackson was threatening me. Sam didn't like it."

"Threatening you with what?"

"Threatening to blacken my name with Benton. He owns this place."

Somehow he didn't think that was the whole story, but he'd let it pass, for now. "And what exactly is Scott to you?" he asked, anticipating the answer. She surprised him.

"Sam's my brother."

For a moment Granville was too stunned to ask another question. No wonder she'd taken offense at his behavior. That was not how he would have treated Scott's sister—if he'd ever known he had one. That idiot, keeping secrets like this from him. How was he ever going to keep the noose from around Scott's neck if he didn't have the most basic facts at his disposal?

"I'm his younger sister," she explained, her voice softening somewhat. "From Denver, by way of San Francisco."

"So why did you come to Vancouver?" Trent broke in.

It was a good question. Granville waited to see if she'd answer.

She gave a tiny shrug. "It was time to move on."

Interesting, Granville thought.

"So you came here because your brother was here?" Trent persisted.

Frances paused before replying. "No, Sam was in the Yukon when I got here. I liked the sound of Vancouver, and someone I knew offered me a job here."

"Anyone I know?" Granville asked.

She acted as if she hadn't heard him. "So here I am," she finished.

"Who met Jackson first, you or Scott?"

Frances gave him a cool look. "I did, when I got a job dancing here. Benton used to have Jackson oversee the place."

"Used to?"

A tiny smile lifted her lips, then was gone. "They had a difference of opinion about how it should be run."

Granville couldn't help wondering exactly what her role had been in that disagreement. "Can you tell me what was between Scott and Jackson?" he shot at her.

An odd expression crossed her face, but disappeared too quickly for Granville to interpret. "You'll have to ask Sam that."

"I tried. He just told me that he owed Jackson money."

"If Sam won't tell you, then I can't."

"Do you want to see your brother hang?" Granville asked, hoping to shock her. She surprised him again. Was that pity in her eyes as she looked at him?

"Sam's choices are his alone. I can't make them for him, and I can't save him from them."

Granville shook his head. He couldn't believe what he was hearing. Didn't she care if her brother hanged? Or was Scott's family as crazy as his own? "Who is he protecting?"

"That's for Sam to tell you. Or not."

At least Frances hadn't denied that Scott was protecting someone. But from the sound of it, it wasn't her.

EIGHT

Saturday, December 9, 1899

Granville woke the next morning with the dry taste of failure in his mouth. He wasn't happy to realize that the lump of discarded clothing against the cheap wardrobe was actually Trent, bedded down under a couple of thin blankets. The cheap hotel room he rented by the week had barely enough space for one person.

"Oh, good, you're awake."

Granville scowled at his unexpected sleeping companion. "Why are you here?" He sat up and swung his legs off the bed in one motion, glaring at the kid as he did so.

"You said I should stay," Trent reminded him. "That it wasn't safe to head home on my own." He paused, rubbed the end of his nose.

It was coming back to him, all of it. Granville pulled his trousers on and strode to the window, narrowing his eyes to slits as he pulled back the shutter. By the look of things, it was late, and his pocket watch confirmed that it was nearly ten. But then, it had been nearly four when they got home, after he'd hit practically every bar between the warehouse and the docks, hoping to turn up any useful snippet of information.

The sun was pouring in through the big windows in Mary's Café, and by the time he'd finished six flapjacks, three eggs, two rashers of bacon, and his third cup of coffee, Granville felt revived. Until a hand fell on his shoulder.

"We'll be asking you to come down to the station now."

Granville had known someone was behind him from the fear in Trent's widening eyes, so he didn't jump. He didn't even turn around, didn't need to. He recognized the voice. "Morning, Craddock. What can I do for you?"

"There's been another murder, and you're wanted for questioning."

"I see. Well, I'd suggest that you remove your hand from my shoulder before we discuss the matter. Unless you want to lose it, of course."

Granville could see the admiration in Trent's eyes and sighed to himself. "Thank you. Now, what was it you wanted to discuss with me?"

"We have some questions about a man whose throat was slit last night."

Granville sighed again. He didn't have time for this; perhaps he could cut short the dance he was sure Craddock was dying to start. "Practically the only person I know in this town is Walter Blayney. Unless he's your victim, I suggest you look for someone else to question, someone who might have a motive."

It was a brilliant strategy, with one small flaw.

"Tell me again where you went after Blayney let you go," Chief McKenzie said, both face and voice expressionless.

"I've told you. Three times. Nothing is going to change if I tell you again."

McKenzie merely repeated the question.

Granville groaned. "I watched the show at the Carlton, went to a few bars. I don't remember the names."

"Why?"

"As I said earlier, I was asking questions. I'm trying to help my partner, whom you're holding here. You already know that. I would have been happy to run across Blayney and in a few places even inquired after him."

"Why, when you'd already seen him?"

"I'd thought of a few more questions for him."

"And what did you do when you found him?"

"I *didn't* find him."

"Why did you kill Blayney?"

This was getting tiresome. "I did *not* kill him."

McKenzie leaned forward. "You're not cooperating here, Granville. Guess we'll have to let you think for a bit." He nodded at Craddock, who was standing stiffly by the door. "Put him in with his pal."

"Hey! You can't arrest me."

"I'm not arresting you. You just need a little time to cool off."

"I haven't done anything." Granville looked from McKenzie to Craddock and back. "I want my solicitor."

McKenzie squinted at him. "Solicitor, huh? I hope he's good. What's his name?"

Granville said nothing. It had been a bluff. He hadn't even begun making inquiries about hiring a solicitor for Scott. Obviously it was past time he did so.

Chief McKenzie let the silence drag on for a moment. "That's what I figured." He motioned to Craddock. "Lock him up."

Scott opened one eye at the noise of the doors being unlocked, then sat bolt upright as Craddock shoved Granville into the cell across from his.

"Look at you," Scott said ironically. "One day you're trying to get me out of here, and the next you're locked up, too."

"Oh, shut up." Turning around, Granville pounded on the iron bars. "Hey. Any chance of some coffee in here?"

"You'll be sorry."

"I'll take my chances. But more important than coffee, why the hell didn't you ever say that you had a sister?"

"It never came up," was the answer. "I take it you've met Frances."

Granville sat down on the other narrow bunk, which creaked alarmingly under his weight. "So how does she figure into the mess you're in?"

"The mess I'm in? Looks to me like you're in the same mess."

"Answer my question."

Scott went back to contemplating the rough weave of the gray blanket he sat on.

"I had a rough night, and I'm not a patient man at the best of times. I need answers, Scott."

The big man wasn't intimidated.

Granville tried another tack. "Frances says she grew up in Denver. I thought you were from Chicago."

"I grew up in Chicago. Pa moved the family to Denver when she was eleven or so."

"You're how much older?"

"'Bout seven years."

"So you were eighteen when you left Chicago?"

"Nope. They moved, I stayed. Didn't head west till I was twenty-two."

Nine years ago, Granville thought. "Where did you go from Chicago? Denver?"

"San Francisco. I'd heard good things about the city."

"Did you go to join your sister?"

Scott shook his head. "She was still in Denver."

"I thought Frances was from Frisco."

"Yeah," Scott said, standing and pacing the cell. "She came to San Francisco a couple of years after I did. Looked me up." He paused and shot a grin over his shoulder at Granville. "You should've seen her there. She was a huge success in San Francisco. They loved her."

"I'll bet." Granville was turning over these facts. "What about your parents?"

"They stayed in Denver. Died a few years later. Influenza."

"I'm sorry."

"Yeah." Scott's face was blank.

Time to move to something less personal. "So you knew Craddock in Chicago?"

"Yup. We bumped into each other now and again. Then I had a little run-in with the law. Figured it was time to get out of town."

"Craddock was the law there, too?"

Scott let out a crack of laughter. "Craddock? Not likely. He was part of a gang tried to wipe out me and my pals."

"Let me guess. He lost."

"He's hated my guts ever since," Scott confirmed.

"I don't suppose Craddock went to San Francisco, too?"

"Nope. I heard later he'd gone to Denver."

That seemed to dispose of Craddock. "Did you know Jackson before you moved here?" Granville asked.

"No." Scott shifted on the bunk, his gaze fixed on a spot behind Granville's head.

"Your sister says she introduced the two of you."

"What else did she say?"

"That if I wanted to know anything else, I should ask you myself."

"That's my girl."

He was getting nowhere, Granville thought in frustration. "How did she meet Jackson?" Before Scott could say anything, Granville held up one hand. "And don't tell me that I need to talk to her about it."

"You do need to talk to her about it."

"Do you want to die? Is that what this is about? You fought like a madman so we wouldn't freeze to death last winter. Now you want to be hanged by the neck until you're dead?"

Scott shook his head. "Just let it be, Granville. There's stuff you don't know, stuff I can't tell you. If they end up hangin' me, then that's how it is."

"I can't let it be. Don't you understand? I can't just stand by and watch you die because you refuse to explain your actions to anyone. I cannot do it. I will not do it. You're my friend. I owe you my life, and I am getting you out of here whether you like it or not."

Scott grinned. "Maybe you should worry about getting yourself out first."

"Oh, hell." Granville stood up, strode to the barred door, and began banging on the bars. "Jailer! Hey, jailer! I need to talk to the chief. Now!"

Granville looked from the imposing stone facade to the turret that sprung from the building's side, then checked the address. In this section of town, all of the houses looked alike, right down to the monkey puzzle trees imported for the express purpose of keeping up with the neighbors. This was the right house. He strode up the stone steps and across a wide veranda, then pulled the door chimes. After what seemed a long wait, a maid in cap and apron opened the door.

"Yes?"

"Is Mr. Turner in? I have business with him. My card." Granville said, handing over the all-important calling card he'd just had printed. The address, though fake, was in the right area of town.

She looked him over, taking in the closely cropped dark hair, the new suit. Her eyes slid to the small pasteboard rectangle she held, and she opened the door wider. "Please come into the parlor, sir, and I'll see if Mr. Turner is at home."

Granville followed her into a room on the left, pausing at the doorway. He could be in England. From the heavily carved furniture to the elaborate wallpaper, everything was familiar, especially the bric-a-brac that thronged every surface. Unsettled, Granville strode to the fireplace and stood looking into the small fire on the grate. Mentally he began to run through the questions he needed to ask.

Since Scott wouldn't tell him what he needed to know, he had to find out everything he could of his friend's actions since his arrival in Vancouver. Starting with his employer. He'd have preferred to meet with Turner at his office downtown, but on learning Turner wouldn't be in that afternoon, he'd decided he couldn't afford to wait.

"Mr. Granville?"

The voice from behind him made Granville turn. Standing in the doorway was a plump man of medium height. He had dark hair, a full beard cropped close to his chin, and a considering expression.

"Mr. Turner?"

Now Turner was frowning slightly, his bushy brows almost meeting. "Do I know you?"

Granville moved forward, hand outstretched. "John Granville. You employ me." He savored the man's confused look for a moment, before adding, "Sam Scott is my partner."

Angus Turner's frown deepened.

"Scott and I guard the silk cars."

Turner nodded. "Yes, I know. This is not a place of business. Why are you here?"

Turner made no move to ask him to sit down, Granville noted, wondering whether it would have made a difference if his card had carried his honorific as well as his name.

Even as a fourth son, he was the Honorable John Granville. Glancing at the pretentious room, he decided it would have made all the difference, but everything in him balked at trading so blatantly on his family name. "I am sorry to disturb you at home. The matter is of some urgency."

"Urgent enough to disturb me here?"

"Indeed. Scott has been arrested."

Turner nodded again. "Yes, so I've heard. Under suspicion of murder, I gather?" His nostrils pinched slightly together as he spoke, as if he'd smelled something nasty.

The man did not seem at all concerned about Scott's probable fate, or even whether he was guilty. Granville fought to keep his voice level. "That's correct. I'm investigating the death, working to clear Scott's name."

"Admirable. And?" *And why are you bothering me?* lay unspoken between them.

Granville gritted his teeth. "Since you're Scott's employer, I'd like to ask you a few questions. If I may."

Turner pulled out a heavily engraved gold pocket watch from his vest pocket and glanced at it. "I suppose I have a few moments. What did you want to ask?"

"When did Scott join your employ?"

"Three months ago."

"How did you come to hire him?"

"I advertised the position. He answered the ad."

"Did he give references?"

One corner of Turner's mouth twitched. "He gave Jackson's name. And a Mr. Gipson, as I recall."

Gipson. That was a name Granville hadn't expected to hear. He filed away the questions it raised for future consideration. "And did you check those references?"

"Naturally."

"And?"

"I don't see that is any of your business."

"It is if I don't want Scott to hang."

Turner looked disconcerted, but only for a moment. "Mmph. Very well. Both references were good."

"What did Jackson say?"

"That Scott was reliable. The rest I could see for myself."

He was referring to Scott's size and muscle, of course. Well, Granville had no quarrel with that. "And Gipson?"

"Said much the same."

No help there. "In the three months Scott worked for you was there ever trouble? Apart from the little matter the other night, that is."

"What little matter?"

"A failed attempt to tamper with one of the silk cars while it stood empty in the station. We intervened and ran them out of town. Surely you heard about it?"

"No, I did not hear about it," Turner said, his voice sharp. "Why were the police not called in?"

"They weren't very efficient thieves. In the Yukon, idiots like that were given a blue card and run out of town. It seemed to be an effective solution."

"As I have told your partner on several occasions, this is not the Yukon. Vancouver has a police force and a justice system. I expect him, and you, to make use of it. Do I make myself clear?"

"Yes, very clear."

"Now, if that will be all . . ."

"I just have one or two more questions about Scott's references."

"Oh, very well."

"Had you dealt with Jackson before?"

"No."

Some subtle change in the man's expression prompted Granville to probe further. "Not even in some minor way?"

"I said no." He ostentatiously consulted the watch he still held. "I'm afraid I haven't the time for any further questions."

Granville watched this performance with great interest. "What about Gipson? Had you ever dealt with him?"

Turner walked to the door and opened it. "Good day, Granville."

Deciding it would be a waste of time to ask further questions, he inclined his head slightly as he strolled out the door. "Good day, Mr. Turner. Thank you for your time."

Three pairs of eyes watched him go. Angus Turner stared after Granville's departing back. Sally, the maid, peeped at him from the passageway to the kitchen. "He was ever so nice-looking," she would later tell the cook. And Emily Turner, the youngest daughter of the house, watched him from a nook beside the parlor. She'd sought refuge there when she'd realized her father was about to open the door against which her ear had been pressed.

When the door had closed behind Granville, Emily allowed a few moments to pass, then bestirred herself. "What was that about, Papa?" she asked, strolling into the room.

Her father gave a start, turning from the fireplace into which he'd been gazing to give his too-inquisitive daughter a sharp look. "What was what about?" he echoed her.

"The man who just left."

"Merely a business acquaintance."

"Oh, does he work for the CPR, too?"

Past experience had taught Turner to be wary of where Emily's questions might lead. This one seemed innocent enough, however, so he answered her. "In a way. He was hired by a man I hired."

"Oh? Who?"

"No one you know." But Emily's determined expression told him it would be simplest just to tell her what she wanted to know. Unlike her two sisters, she was not easily discouraged. "A man named Sam Scott."

"Sam Scott. Is he not the man who was recently arrested for murdering a Mr. Jackson?"

Turner's face darkened. She'd been reading his paper again. He'd thought he'd put an end to that the last time. "You should not even know about such matters. And I will not encourage your unladylike interest by answering any further questions. Now go and find your mother."

"But, Papa . . ."

"Never mind, young lady. Just do as you are told. For once!"

There was no arguing with him when he had that look on his face. But the questions the visitor had been asking had made her want to know more. Not for the first time, she wished Father wasn't so incredibly old-fashioned.

It was nearly a new century. How could Papa expect her to remain in ignorance of the things that were happening in the world? It was her world, too! And a far more interesting one than that of the afternoon teas and society dances she was expected to confine herself to.

Walking slowly up the stairs, Emily relived the shiver that had gone through her when she'd read about the murder. It hadn't been excitement so much as a kind of awe that life could be so dangerous outside the safe little circle she occupied. Now the partner of the arrested man, this John Granville, had come to ask questions of her father. Something about Mr. Granville intrigued her, and it wasn't just his arresting features.

Emily entered the sewing room on the second floor, where her mother and sisters sat working on their embroidery and chatting. Picking up her embroidery hoop, she let out a small sigh.

"What is it now, Emily?" her mother asked. "And where did you go?"

"Nothing. I just had a question to ask Papa."

Margaret Turner, a small blonde lady as plump as her husband but with rather more brain, gave her daughter a hard look, then resumed her stitching without comment. Emily stabbed her own needle through the fine linen and tried to pay attention to what she was doing.

Striding away from the Turner residence, Granville was unaware of the extent of the interest he'd stirred up. Oh, he'd seen the glance the maid had given him, but he had no inclination to follow up on it. He needed to talk to Gipson, and soon, except he had no idea where to begin looking for him.

Blayney had been his only point of contact, and Blayney was dead. Waiting for the electric streetcar to take him back downtown, Granville considered the question. The solution, when it came to him, was glaringly obvious. Gipson would be listed in the new telephone directory that everyone was so proud of.

And listed he was: George W. Gipson, Private Banker and Broker, with an address on lower Granville Street, in the heart of the business district. A larger ad proclaimed that he specialized in making advances on mining stocks and insurance policies, as well as selling stocks and mortgages. Granville particularly liked the "advances" on mining stock. It was the perfect setup for a con man. It would be enlightening to know exactly which mines Gipson had an interest in, and whether they even existed. Whatever Gipson was up to, Granville didn't believe the man had the moral fiber to have turned respectable, not unless it was part of an elaborate confidence game he was perpetrating.

NINE

Twenty minutes later, Granville was seated on one side of a vast expanse of mahogany, staring at this latest incarnation of his former antagonist. Who would have thought the old weasel would clean up so well? Dressed in a nicely cut suit, with his hair and beard clean and neatly trimmed, Gipson certainly looked businesslike, even distinguished. His fourth-floor office was opulent, with thick rugs, carved furniture, somber landscape paintings, and a corner window looking out to the harbor.

It was an impressive facade, and as far removed from the mud and sweat of the goldfields as it was possible to get. The only incongruous note was a large lump of quartz shot through with glitter sitting on Gipson's desk. Granville's experienced eye recognized it immediately as iron pyrite. Fool's gold. The corner of his mouth twitched. How apt.

"And what can I do for you today, sir?"

Even his voice was mellow, the vowels round and full. For the first time, Granville wondered about Gipson's background, the years before he'd washed up in the Yukon broke and bitter. Whatever he seemed to be now, under all those fine clothes was a twisted soul. Gipson obviously hadn't recognized him; he'd be calling him something much less polite than "sir" if he had. Wordlessly, Granville handed over his card, watching closely as he read it and looked up, his eyes narrowed. "Granville, is it? And why are you here to see me?"

Now Granville recognized the Gipson he'd known in Dawson City, the man who'd tried to steal another man's claim, then poisoned and nearly killed him when that failed. Gipson had loudly proclaimed the poisoning to be accidental, and the Mounties had been unable to prove otherwise. But no one had believed him innocent.

"Sam Scott, my partner, has been arrested for the murder of Clive Jackson. I intend to prove him innocent. I hoped you would be willing to answer a few questions."

Gipson's expression didn't change. "Why come to me?" He was keeping up the pretense of no shared history.

This was the hard part. Granville had considered what approach to take and decided on honesty. No matter what he said, the man sitting in front of him would expect him to have a hidden motive, and by sticking to the facts he'd at the very least keep his story straight. "Scott gave your name as a reference when he applied to the CPR."

Gipson gave him a smile that would have looked good on an adder. "What are your questions?"

"Why did he give your name as a reference?"

"Because he didn't know anyone else in town. And because he'd done some work for me."

Scott, working for Gipson? Granville couldn't picture his partner, the man he'd thought he knew so well, working for this fraud. "When was that?"

"Nearly four months ago. When he first hit town."

Granville had known Scott was broke when he left Dawson City—they both were—but he hadn't known his partner was desperate. In fact, he would have sworn he wasn't. So what had changed when he got to Vancouver? Would it have had something to do with his sister? "How long did he work for you?"

Gipson chuckled. "Well, now, I didn't say Scott worked for me. I said he'd done some work for me."

"What sort?"

"Loading shipments, shifting the supplies in my warehouse, that kind of thing. I hired him when I needed heavy loads shifted."

Gipson had never been subtle, Granville reflected. This new version of Gipson had just made clear his low opinion of Scott, and his expression said that opinion extended to Scott's partner. Granville decided to see if he could shake that smooth facade. "Yes, I've seen your warehouse."

"So I gathered."

Now that was interesting. How had Gipson known Blayney had discovered him at the warehouse, unless Blayney had told him? And Blayney had been murdered later that same night.

"Anything that happens in this town that concerns me, I know about," Gipson was quick to add.

"Like Blayney's murder?"

"Yes, poor fellow."

"When did you last see him?"

"Blayney? Day before yesterday."

Then how did you know I was in your warehouse? Granville thought. "Do you know how he died?"

"I know someone slit his throat, but not why, if that is what you're asking. I also know that the perpetrator will be caught, and hanged."

He paused. "And I know that the police were very interested in talking to you," he added, eyes watchful. "Yet here you sit, free."

Granville nearly grinned. Chief McKenzie had been unimpressed to learn that Granville had an alibi in the form of Trent, but he'd had to let him go. Not without warning him not to leave town, however. Granville hadn't wanted to involve the kid, but when Scott still wouldn't tell him what was going on, he couldn't afford to waste any more time cooling his heels in jail. "They wanted to ask me a few questions," he said.

"Hmmm."

Time was running short, and Gipson still hadn't told him anything useful. He needed answers. "How long did Scott work for you?"

Gipson gave a half shrug. "Two weeks? Three? I can't recall exactly."

Which would put it around late September, and Scott hadn't been hired by Turner until October. "Why did he stop working for you?"

"He was no longer interested in the wages I was prepared to pay."

Or he couldn't stand being on your payroll any longer, Granville thought. "Did you know Jackson?"

"I knew who he was, of course."

"And who do you think killed him?"

"Well, I know Scott hated Jackson, and I gather they had words last week, though I don't know what the problem might have been."

And you wouldn't tell me even if you did know, Granville thought, raising one eyebrow. "Well, I expect that explains why Scott was arrested."

"I'm afraid so. And the only one who knows the full story is your partner. You did say you were still partners?"

Now the old weasel was pretending to look compassionate, and there was no way Granville was going to stand for that. "That's right.

We'd just formed our partnership, but it's a new one. We're opening our own detective agency." He had no idea where the words came from, but he needed something that would wipe that phony look off Gipson's face.

It worked, too.

"A detective agency? Well, now, that is interesting."

"We think so."

"A little difficult to start a business, though, wouldn't you say, with your partner slated to hang for murder?"

"That's the beauty of it. When I trap the killer and clear Scott's name, it will be a perfect advertisement for our new business, particularly when I expose Blayney's killer at the same time."

Let's see what he makes of that, Granville thought. But for once Gipson was speechless, which gave Granville a deep sense of satisfaction, the first he'd felt since Scott's arrest.

Granville stepped outside the brick-and-plaster block that held Gipson's office and looked around him. Christmas lights blinked red and green in the display windows of the Hudson's Bay store across the street. With worrying about Scott, he had forgotten it was nearly Christmas. He considered the oblivious faces hurrying by, none of whom seemed to be in a festive mood any more than he was, then shrugged. Unless he could get Scott free, he wouldn't be doing much celebrating.

The temperature had risen several degrees, but it was misting slightly. Granville turned up his collar against the damp and settled his hat a little lower on his forehead. Now what? Why would his partner have accepted a position with Gipson? Scott said he'd needed money badly enough to have borrowed from Jackson. Granville wasn't sure he believed that story, but there were too many facts he didn't have yet, such as why Scott had needed the money, and why he'd hated Jackson so much. He wasn't going to get any answers from Scott, nor from Frances, so where did that leave him?

Paying a call on Benton, that was where. It wasn't enough to uncover the problem between Scott and Jackson; Granville had to find Jackson's killer, and after a day and a half of asking questions, he still knew virtually nothing about Jackson. He knew little more about Scott's relationship with the dead man. Perhaps the spider at the center of the web could be persuaded to tell him more.

He had no trouble getting in to see Benton, but the ease of it only increased his conviction he was doing the right thing. Benton's office could not have been more different from Gipson's. Located in one of the busy lumber warehouses on Alexander, it was on the second floor, up a flight of wide wooden steps. On the main floor, the air smelled of freshly cut pine and cedar and echoed with the shouts of the men unloading lumber, but the office itself was oddly quiet, thick walls shutting out most of the noise from below.

The man himself was a surprise. Robert Benton was short, barely reaching Granville's shoulder, and sturdily built, with solid muscle evident in his shoulders and the thickness of his neck. Clad in a dapper black suit with a black bow tie, he had a strong handshake and an engaging smile. Granville found himself smiling back without intending to do so.

"What can I do for you?"

"I'm here about the death of Clive Jackson."

"Oh? I know most of the local police constables. You aren't one of them."

Granville could tell Benton was toying with him and prepared to enjoy it. He decided to play the game. "You're correct."

"Then . . . ?"

"My partner and I have been retained to look into the matter. We're private detectives." The fictional business he'd concocted for Gipson might just prove useful, Granville thought.

"Ah, I see. But I'm not familiar with your name, Mr. Granville."

"We're new in town."

Benton gave him a sharp look, then nodded. "What d'you want to know?"

"When did you last see Jackson?"

"Mmmm. Let's see." Benton reached across his desk and pulled out a leather-bound book. Flipping through it, he paused on one page, then turned several more. "Ah, yes. That would be on the Tuesday the fifth."

Granville strained to read what was on the page, but Benton was holding it so that he couldn't. "What time?"

Again the sharp look. "Jackson was killed the next morning, wasn't he?"

"Or later that night."

"Whatever. He was here that afternoon, at four."

"And did Jackson have any enemies?"

Benton's eyes gleamed. "Did Jackson have enemies? Ah, now there's a question."

Granville crossed one booted leg over the other. He waited.

Benton watched him for a moment. "Putting it bluntly, he was a bully. I found that useful in an employee, for reasons I'm sure you can imagine, but he made enemies. In fact, Clive Jackson had more natural ability to make enemies than any man I've ever met."

"Any of them want him dead?"

"Oh, yes. Most of them, in fact."

"Then perhaps the question should be, why did he live so long?"

Benton smiled. "Fear of repercussions. Jackson was my man, you see."

Granville revised his initial view of the man: it took someone very sure of his own power to be so honest. Benton was more dangerous than he'd first thought, a puma to Gipson's weasel. "And now your man is dead. What are you doing about it?"

"It'll be handled, never fear."

Watching the way Benton's eyes narrowed as he spoke, Granville was sure of it. "And what of the man who has been arrested?"

"Scott? He's not my business."

Granville pounced on the information Benton had just given him, intentionally or not. "Then you know Scott is innocent of killing Jackson."

The corners of Benton's mouth quirked upward. "I didn't say that. That's a matter for the police."

"But whoever killed Jackson is your business."

"Oh, yes. I can't allow someone to go around killing my people. It'd send the wrong message."

Granville felt a surge of relief, and in that moment, he realized he hadn't been entirely sure Scott hadn't killed Jackson. "Proving Scott innocent is my business."

Benton raised an eyebrow.

"Perhaps you can tell me about the relationship between Jackson and Scott."

"As far as I know, they didn't have one."

"I heard they had a public quarrel not long before Jackson was murdered."

"That I didn't know."

Granville didn't believe him. The man had too much information not to know about the quarrel. "And Scott's sister?"

Benton's expression didn't change. "The lovely Frances? She isn't involved in this."

"Her brother is charged with murder and she isn't involved? Come now, you can't expect me to believe that."

"She isn't involved."

Benton's face had hardened and his tone was flat. He was showing more emotion than he had since the conversation began, and it was over Scott's sister. Time to push a little. "But she did know Jackson, didn't she?"

"Only as my employee."

"Funny. She said she introduced Scott to Jackson."

Benton's eyes turned flinty. "Maybe she did, but I wish to keep her out of this. You understand, I'm sure."

It was not a question, but Granville couldn't leave it alone, not now, when Benton finally had lost his detached air. "She's involved as long as her brother is in jail. Perhaps if you told me who killed Jackson, I could get Scott out of jail. Then she'd be involved no longer."

"It's not that simple."

"I don't see why not."

"I wouldn't expect you to. You'll have to take my word for it."

"And if I cannot do that?"

"Then you'll be buying yourself a lot of trouble. That would be stupid, and I don't think you're a stupid man."

"Stupid or not, I do have a job to do."

"Find some other way to get Scott out of jail. With a one-armed jailer guarding him, how hard could that be?"

"I prefer to work within the law." Unless I have no other choice, Granville added to himself.

"Noble of you. Foolish, but noble."

"If Jackson's killer is a dead man anyway, why not just tell me who he is?"

"I think this meeting has reached its end," Benton said, standing. He extended his hand. "It's been very interesting meeting you, Mr.

Granville. I have a feeling you're going to contribute to our little town, and I'll watch you do so with some interest. A word of caution, though—it's easy to get ahead of yourself here. See that you don't."

It was raining lightly when he left Benton's warehouse. The streets were nearly empty, with only the occasional wagon lurching past. Granville barely noticed. The interminable Yukon winter had increased his tolerance for short days and long evenings, and his mind was focused on the puzzle Benton had presented. The strange thing was, he had actually liked the man, threats and all. There was no question Benton was dangerous, or that he would have him killed without a second thought, but Benton was also intelligent and he'd been honest. Both were qualities that Granville valued but found all too rarely in his fellow man.

Why had Benton refused to name the killer? He'd been open enough that he intended to deal with him, so what would Benton have to lose in disclosing his name? Assuming he actually knew it, that is. Could it have been an elaborate bluff, designed to dead-end Granville's investigation?

That question occupied Granville's thoughts so thoroughly he nearly missed the whistling sound. Only reflexes developed through endless hours in London's boxing saloons enabled him to duck in time, the blow narrowly missed his head. He spun to face his two assailants just as the second slashed at him with a knife. Granville moved, but not fast enough. The blow caught him in the upper arm, and he felt it burn, then a gush of warm blood. Ignoring the blossom of pain, he kicked the knife wielder in the crotch, then ducked another blow from the cudgel.

From the cold numbness of his arm, Granville knew he was losing blood; he needed to end this fight. The slighter of the two assailants was still doubled over, but the bigger man was winding up for another blow and Granville's own knife would be useless against that cudgel. He scanned the area. They stood at the entrance to an alley, piled high with old crates and empty barrels. If the first assailant was as slow as he seemed, it might be enough. Granville grabbed for a crate, yanked it free, and flung it in the direction of the cudgel. Then he leaped clear, while with a groan and a rattle, half a dozen barrels tumbled free, each one hitting its mark. With one hand clutching his bleeding arm and a satisfied expression on his face, Granville set a fast pace toward a better-lit section of town. Experience told him the cut wasn't too serious, but thugs too often have buddies.

As he walked, he reviewed the faces of his assailants. He'd never seen the one with the knife before, but the other was one of the bookends from the warehouse the previous night, which meant Gipson had sent them. Granville smiled a grim little smile. If Gipson had thought Granville was a threat before, he was in for a shock. "I'll see him hang this time," Granville vowed to the empty street.

Under the dim streetlights on Cordova, the three- and four-story brick buildings lining the street looked shadowy and menacing. His hotel loomed ahead. Most of the rooms were dark and shuttered, though the bar on the far corner was still open, judging by the lights spilling out. Granville was relieved to be nearly back to his rooms. His right arm felt leaden and useless. They'd stitched and bound it for him at the hospital, but the five blocks he'd walked from there had seemed interminable. The day had been too long, the answers too few. Now all he wanted was a whiskey and a good night's sleep.

"Mr. Granville? Sir?" The boy stepped out of the shadows.

"Trent. Where have you come from?"

"I was worried about you. 'Specially after the cops came looking for me."

"The police were looking for you? Why?"

"Dunno. I ran before they asked me anything."

"So what're you doing standing there?"

There was a sudden gleam of teeth in the darkness. "Hiding. Waiting for you."

Granville sighed. He was tired, his arm hurt, and time was running short. "Don't you have somewhere else to go?"

"Not anymore."

The reality of Trent's situation silenced Granville. Thanks to him, the boy's father had been driven out of town, and whatever job Trent had found was obviously not enough to pay for both food and shelter. With a sigh, he started up the hotel steps, beckoning Trent to follow.

"So who killed Mr. Blayney?" Trent asked as he followed.

Granville kept silent until he'd closed the rickety wooden door behind them with a snap that nearly splintered one of the door panels. He turned to face his eager companion. "I don't know who killed him. I only know it wasn't me."

"But it must've been just after he let us go, right?"

"Undoubtedly."

"So the killer might even have been there."

Granville wished the idea filled him with one-tenth the enthusiasm Trent obviously felt. Instead, he just felt old and tired and very aware of how much his arm hurt. "Not likely."

"But if he had been, who do you think might have killed him?"

"We'll talk about it in the morning. Go wash up."

Trent scowled, but took a threadbare towel and headed for the small, grimy bathroom at the end of the hall.

TEN

Sunday, December 10, 1899

Late the following morning Granville reluctantly opened his eyes. His whole body ached. Turning his head slightly, he could see the lump of bedclothes in the corner. He hadn't dreamed Trent's return. He levered himself upright. Only the thought of a pot of hot coffee and a huge plate of bacon, eggs, and fried potatoes kept him from falling back and pulling the covers over his head. Swinging his legs over the side of the bed, Granville reached for his trousers, wincing as the movement pulled on his stitches. As he put on his shirt, he heard a gasp from behind him. Turning, he saw that Trent was awake and gaping at him.

"What happened to you?"

"What do you mean, what happened?" Granville said, buttoning the shirt.

"Where did the bandage come from?"

He almost sounds as if he's accusing me of something, Granville thought. But he could sense the worry behind the boy's words. "The local hospital. I had a little argument in an alley."

"A little argument? There's blood on that bandage!"

"That's what bandages are for."

"It isn't funny. You're hurt."

"And you are not my keeper. Now, get dressed and we'll go find some breakfast. I'm in dire need of sustenance." That seemed to silence Trent, Granville thought in amusement as the boy scrambled into his clothes.

"So what're we doing today?" Trent's eager voice demanded.

"*We* aren't doing anything. I thought you had a job. Don't they expect you to show up?"

"The Turners don't need an errand boy this week."

Granville eyed him with suspicion. "Very convenient of them. And exactly why don't they need you this week, might I ask?"

Trent flushed. "They only have enough errands for Bertie this week."

"I see. And who would Bertie be?"

"It is me."

The soft voice at his elbow nearly made Granville drop his coffee cup. He spun in his chair to see a short, slender young man, wearing baggy gray pantaloons and a long pigtail.

"Bertie?"

He bowed his head.

"Is that your real name?"

"It is Wong Xi Yan, but Mr. Turner find that too hard. It is Miss Emily who choose my new name."

"Miss Emily?"

"She's Mr. Turner's youngest daughter." This was Trent.

"But why Bertie?"

"She say the name is a favorite of hers. He was husband to the queen."

The notion amused Granville, though he allowed nothing of it to show on his face. "I'm pleased to know you, then, Bertie. Why are you here, though? Do the Turners need Trent today, after all?"

"No. I look for you. Miss Emily send me to find you."

"Why would a daughter of Turner's send you to look for me?" Granville asked Bertie, then turned to glare at Trent. "And what's your role in this?"

"Me? None! Well, maybe I did tell Miss Emily about meeting you, and how you were tracking Mr. Jackson's real killer . . ."

Granville groaned.

The tips of Trent's ears turned red, and he wouldn't meet Granville's eyes.

"If I might," Bertie's soft voice sounded louder in the sudden silence. "Miss Emily is kind to help me. My uncle's last son, Wong Yu Fung, is lost, and she think maybe you can help."

"She did, did she? And how does she think I could help?"

"Bertie's cousin was on that steamer that arrived, the one from China."

"The *Empress of India*?"

Trent nodded.

"You mean the one you and your father tried to steal the silk from?"

Trent looked stricken, but he persevered. "That's the one. It was delayed by a big storm. When she docked, Bertie's cousin was gone. They figure he got washed overboard, but Bertie here says that can't be."

Granville looked at Bertie, who was shaking his head slowly.

A sudden suspicion struck Granville. "Does Miss Emily know I work for her father?"

Trent nodded.

"Did she overhear our conversation?"

Trent shrugged but his ears turned red again.

Granville nodded. It was beginning to make a kind of sense; he'd told Turner he was investigating Jackson's death, deliberately making it sound official. "She thinks I'm a detective." He turned to Bertie. "Why don't you think your cousin was washed overboard in the storm?"

"He get most seasick. He stay below-decks."

"But he might have gone up on deck for fresh air." Granville watched Bertie decisively shaking his head. "Is there something else?"

"He bring opium for my uncle's factory. His bag is found, but no opium."

"How much opium?"

"Fifty pound."

Granville whistled. "That's a lot. Why come to me?"

"We think a white man steal the opium."

"Why? I thought all the factories were run by Chinese."

Bertie nodded. "In Victoria, yes. In Vancouver, too, for licensed ones. But we hear of illegal factory, and smugglers to United States. Can you help us?"

"No, I'm sorry. Miss Emily was wrong. I can't help you."

"Why?"

"Yeah, why?"

Granville let out an exasperated sigh. "Because I am not a detective. And because I must find Jackson's killer." Hearing the contradiction in his words, Granville wished he'd phrased it differently; he had a feeling Bertie would not be easy to discourage. He was right. Bertie looked at him in silence for a long moment, as if weighing him against some invisible measure, and it wasn't a comfortable feeling.

"If you help me, I help you," Bertie finally said.

"You know something about Jackson's death?"

Bertie's face showed nothing of his thoughts. "If you help me, I help you."

"OK, I'll help you. But first I need to clear my partner."

Bertie inclined his head. "You come with me."

Granville followed Bertie down one of the alleys that ran north of Dupont Street, where narrow buildings loomed over them, four and five stories high. The recessed balconies and wrought-iron railings that decorated the building facades were nowhere in evidence here, only steep walls of sooty red brick. Granville was glad it was still daylight.

Ahead of him, Bertie's pigtail bounced between his shoulder blades with every quick step, while Trent paced at his side. Granville's eyes darted from one rubbish heap to another, from dark doorway to dark doorway, alert for any motion, any sound, but the alley seemed deserted. He looked behind him. Nothing moved, yet he could feel the heat of unseen eyes burning into his back, and he was relieved when Bertie reached the end of the alley. Granville expected him to turn back to the street, but Bertie stopped in front of a plain green door.

He knocked, and after a moment a peephole set in the door opened. An eye considered them, then the peephole closed and the door silently opened inward. They were ushered through a short covered passage into a courtyard, surrounded by buildings on all four sides. Granville looked around him in astonishment; it was like a city within a city. Chinese shoppers clad in tunics and pantaloons and carrying baskets hurried by. Granville's and Trent's were the only white faces in sight, and this was earning them uneasy glances. Bertie, however, didn't hesitate, cutting straight through the crowd toward the buildings on the far side of the square, Trent in his wake.

With a last glance around him, Granville lengthened his stride and followed. The farther he got from the door where they'd come in, the more the back of his neck prickled.

After they'd negotiated several twisting passageways, Bertie ushered them into a long, narrow room. There were no windows, but in the warm glow of the oil lamps Granville saw that scrolls and paintings covered the walls. Waist-high dragon statues grinned on either side of the fireplace, their bronze flanks catching the flickering light. Granville regarded the man who sat at the far end of the room.

"This is my uncle, Wong Ah Sun," said Bertie in formal tones as a lean, white-haired gentleman wearing an elaborate robe stood up behind the wide rosewood desk. "Honorable uncle, here is detective I tell you about, Mr. Granville."

Wong Ah Sun bowed. "It is a pleasure to meet you, sir." His English had a British accent laid over a rising and falling intonation, which Granville found fascinating.

Granville bowed in return; it seemed the thing to do. "Your English is very good."

"Thank you," Wong Ah Sun said. "I studied in British schools in Hong Kong."

"And this is Trent," Bertie said.

Wong Ah Sun bowed to the boy, and Granville saw Trent redden then awkwardly return the bow.

I'm sure that's not a courtesy he learned from his father, he thought, pleased that the boy was turning out to be such a quick study.

"Mr. Granville, has my nephew told you of our loss?" Wong Ah Sun asked.

Granville nodded. "He has. I am sorry."

"I thank you. And also I thank you for agreeing to help us. Not many would have done so. There are things that you as a white man are able to do that we cannot."

Wait a minute, Granville thought, I haven't agreed to anything yet. "You must understand," he said, choosing each word with care. He was intensely aware that this was foreign territory, tantamount to a different country from that on the other side of the green door. "I am not free to help you until I have freed my partner."

The older man inclined his head. "So my nephew has informed me. You seek the killer of Clive Jackson."

"Yes, I do."

"I can offer my assistance with that problem if you in return will assist me with my own."

Granville nodded. "That would seem fair. But you understand that I must find Jackson's murderer first."

Wong Ah Sun bowed. "I understand. Then we are agreed."

Granville bowed in return. "We are," he said, then waited.

A brief smile flickered across Wong Ah Sun's face, then his formality returned. "You have learned patience, I see. It is not a common thing among your countrymen."

It is among those of us who have sluiced endless pans full of gravel to find a few flecks of gold, Granville thought. He said nothing.

Wong Ah Sun chuckled, the sound like dry twigs snapping. "Very well. I will give you what information I can. Your partner did not kill Mr. Jackson. He was shot by a woman."

"A woman!" The words were startled out of him. "But who?"

"That I do not know. Only that she was tall, with dark hair. And that she was white."

For a moment Granville was too stunned to think what to ask

next. Trent solved the problem for him. "Was it Miss Frances, Franny from Frisco she's billed as?" he blurted. "It wasn't, was it?"

"I am sorry, I do not know."

"Have you any idea why?" Granville asked. "Why a woman, I mean?"

"Mr. Jackson was involved in very many things. Some say he owned an establishment where he treated the women badly. If you were to ask questions there, it might be that you would find your answers."

"Where is this establishment?"

Something passed across Wong Ah Sun's face, but it was gone before Granville could read it. "It is said that it can be found at the end of Dupont Street. Number Twenty-one."

Nearly to Westminster. "Anything else I should know?"

"There is nothing more I am able to tell you at this moment."

Clearly the audience was over. Granville bowed. "Thank you for your assistance. You have been most helpful. I look forward to returning the favor."

Wong Ah Sun bowed in return. "The pleasure was mine. We will talk again when your partner is released from the jail."

"Until then." Granville turned to Bertie, who led them back along the alleys and through the green door.

"So now what?" Trent asked Granville as they watched Bertie hurry away.

"Now we start looking for the killer, whether it's a man or a woman."

"You don't think it was Miss Frances, do you?" Trent asked, glancing up at Granville, then quickly away. "I mean, I know she's tall and has dark hair and all, but she couldn't be a killer. Could she?"

It might explain why Scott was being so closemouthed, thought

Granville. Looking into Trent's anxious eyes, he said, "She was probably working that night."

"Oh, right. Of course, she'd be working. I forgot."

Granville didn't remind him that she wouldn't have been onstage the entire evening. "Now the question is, do we talk to Miss Frances first? Or do we go talk to the ladies at Number Twenty-one?"

ELEVEN

Emily Turner sat with her mother and sisters in the stuffy sewing room, demurely stitching a sampler; her expression was calm, yet her mind darted from thought to thought. She had vowed to herself that she would blend in with her sisters today, especially as there were several subjects that she preferred not to discuss. Like what errand she'd sent Bertie on, and why she'd persuaded Cook to give their new errand boy several days off. Mama knew she was up to something, though; Emily could tell, because she kept giving her sharp little looks.

I'm being too docile, she decided, it isn't like me to stitch without protest. Besides, I can't bear to sit still any longer! Putting aside her embroidery hoop with relief, Emily looked at the three heads bent so intently over their work, then glanced around the small overdecorated room. She drew in a deep breath and stood up, shaking out her long gray skirt and arranging it to fall just so. "I think I will go for a walk, Mama," she said. "I need some fresh air."

"Very well, if you must. Take Sally with you, then, unless one of your sisters would go?"

Miriam and Jane both shook their heads. They far preferred stitching to walking, especially in December.

"Yes, Mama."

"Be sure to wear your heavy jacket."

"Yes, Mama."

"And do not go dashing about. It is unbecoming."

"Yes, Mama." But she wasn't going to invite a companion along on her escape. The maid had more important things to do than be her chaperone, anyway.

Finally free, Emily strode along Georgia, the sharp wind whipping at her long skirts. She took an appreciative sniff of the crisp air and sighed happily. The smell of snow was on the wind, which meant they were sure to have a white Christmas. Maybe the Fraser River would freeze again as it had last year, and they could all go skating.

Even Papa approved of skating, which was odd, because he strongly disapproved of her bicycling. To her mind, the sense of freedom was the best part of both sports. It was when she felt most alive. For a moment, Emily regretted the cold weather and the slippery streets, which made bicycling impractical now. She quickened her stride. Even walking could be invigorating; not for her the drooping posture, the ladylike gait.

Perhaps if she walked far enough, she might meet Bertie coming back. She desperately wanted to know how his meeting with Mr. Granville had gone.

"Why, it's Miss Emily Turner."

The voice of one of her mother's friends broke into her reverie. To be caught walking without a maid, and by such a gossip, meant Mama would soon know she'd disobeyed her. Ignoring Mrs.

Smithers's disapproving look, Emily exchanged pleasantries with her and her daughters, then the three of them took their leave. Emily sighed. She really should have brought Sally along, but the girl dawdled so. Ah, well, it was too late now.

It was beginning to grow dark, though, she noted. Mama would be annoyed enough that she'd gone out alone; she'd be furious if she knew she'd been out alone after dark. Turning to retrace her steps, she heard the clatter of the streetcar and paused, hoping to see Bertie hanging off the back. Spotting him, in fact, she was pleased to note he carried a brimming basket of produce, as that had been her excuse to send him out. At least I won't have to walk home alone, she thought, waiting for him, then realized her mother might prefer that to her being seen in the company of the houseboy. She shrugged. Hearing about Bertie's meeting with Mr. Granville was more important than society's silly strictures about young women walking alone.

Granville lounged with one shoulder against the open door of Frances Scott's dressing room. The air was heavy with the scent of tea rose toilet water. Frances, eyebrow pencil in hand, glanced up from the looking glass she'd been peering into and frowned. Her gaze went from Granville to Trent. "Why are you here?"

"I need information."

"Yes, and I told you to ask Sam for it."

"This is not information that Sam would have."

"What sort of information do you need?"

"The sort that tells me what you were doing the night Jackson was killed."

"The night Jackson was killed? I was here, of course."

"And is your show always at the same time?"

"Same times," she corrected him. "And of course it is. I'm the headliner. I do two shows a night."

"And about what time would you have been onstage?"

"I go on at ten and then again at midnight."

"How long are your shows?"

"Just under half an hour. It's all timed to the music, you know."

"And how long does it take you to get ready?"

There was a flush of color high on her cheekbones now; she'd seen where his questions were leading. "Another half an hour." She met his gaze, her eyes level and clear. "What time did Jackson die?"

Granville shook his head. "I'll have to confirm that. Can anyone say when you arrived and when you left that night?"

Trent was looking worried, his eyes darting back and forth between them.

She pursed her lips softly. "I don't know. Some of the girls, probably. I'll ask them and let you know."

I prefer to ask them myself, Granville thought. "That would be helpful," he said. Frances gave him a sharp look, as if she'd read his thoughts, but she said nothing further.

"Say goodnight, Trent," Granville said. "Miss Frances needs to finish getting ready."

"Goodnight," Trent echoed. Watching her touch a powder puff to her nose, he blushed. Then he practically tripped over himself trying to get out the door before his face got any redder.

Frances laughed softly. "Come again." Granville couldn't read the look she threw him.

As they made their way back through the rowdy crowd toward the front door, Granville steered Trent toward the bar. "I have a few more questions for the bartender," he shouted in Trent's ear.

Their quarry was a large fellow, with a nose that looked like it had been broken repeatedly. He seemed to be in constant motion, his movements unexpectedly graceful as he poured a shot of whiskey here and sent a pint of beer shooting down the bar there. Granville watched him for a few minutes, then turned away.

"We'll come back when he has time to answer questions," he said to Trent, then realized the boy was no longer there. "Trent?" Spotting him standing closer to the stage, he reached out and grabbed him by the elbow.

"Miss Frances is about to come on. We have to stay."

"Another time," Granville said, dragging his reluctant charge along behind him. "We've got work to do."

Number 21 Dupont Street was a run-down building in one of the city's worst neighborhoods. The walls were warped and flaking from the rain. The windows were cracked, the door stuck, and the entrance smelled of wet wool and boiled beef. No one was there to greet them. Trent wrinkled his nose and looked over at Granville.

There was a burst of raucous laughter from the end of the hall. Motioning to Trent, Granville followed the sound, which led him to a large, over-furnished, overheated parlor. Several men clustered around two blondes wearing skimpily cut scarlet gowns. A thin brunette wearing a purple dress cut so low her breasts looked in danger of spilling out was clutching the arm of a dapper little man and laughing shrilly. The room reeked of bad whiskey. In the corner a buxom redhead wearing bright yellow satin caught sight of them.

"Hello, handsome," she said, strolling up to Granville. "What can we do for you?"

The smell of whiskey was so strong Granville nearly choked. "I'd like to speak to whomever is in charge here," he said.

The redhead laughed, then looked up at Granville through heavily darkened eyelashes. "But he's not available anymore," she said, stumbling slightly on the words. "You'll have to talk to me." She gave him a broad smile, showing a gaping hole where an incisor should have been.

Granville felt Trent move closer to his side. "That would have been Clive Jackson?" he asked.

The smile vanished, and her eyes narrowed as she looked him up and down. "So why's it your business?"

"He owed me money."

She laughed, short and hard. "Jackson owed everyone money. He was so tight, he'd rather starve than buy a meal."

"So where is he?"

"You hadn't heard? He's dead. Someone shot the son of a bitch, and it couldn't have happened to anyone who deserved it more."

"Who did it?"

She paused, but only for an instant. "Dunno. I hear they've got someone in custody, but with the cops we've got in this town, who knows if it's the right guy. If it is, he deserves a medal."

"Not a high opinion of the late Mr. Jackson?"

She grimaced.

A hint of the girl she'd once been showed in her eyes for a moment, and Granville felt a sudden pang of compassion for all that she'd lost. "Why didn't you run?"

She gave him a weary look. "'Cause he had the connections, didn't he? He'd just haul us back again."

"What connections?"

She shrugged. "Don't know, do I? One time our Gracie tried to run off, the cops brung her back."

"The police brought her back?"

She grinned at him. "Don't know much about this town, do you?

As long as the fines're paid, and a bit extra, they leave us alone." She winked. "Mostly."

"So Jackson bought off the police?"

"A few."

"Do you know which ones?"

Her expression changed. "No. No names," she said flatly.

Granville wondered if Craddock was one of the men Jackson had bought off. He thought about asking, decided against it. Considering her for a moment, he asked, "Did you hate Jackson enough to kill him?"

"Oh, yeah. I never did, though. Wish I had." She swayed slightly on her feet, then looked thoughtful. "Don't know if the others did, though. Hey, Darla. Colette."

The two blondes looked up.

"Either of you girls shoot our Clive?"

"Nah, didn't think of it, Flo," said the taller of the two. "Would have been a good idea."

"Me, neither," said the other with a giggle. "What about you, Gracie?"

The brunette, her bright red lips now pressed tightly together, shook her head. She said nothing, but there was a lost look in her eyes.

Somehow this wasn't how Granville had envisioned the questioning going. "Know anyone else who might have wanted Jackson dead?"

"Oh, yeah. Hundreds of 'em," quipped the redhead. "They were standing in line."

"Who?"

"Now why would I be telling you?"

She seemed drunk, but her instinct for self-preservation worked just fine, Granville thought. "Jackson's dead now. What difference can it make?"

A chuckle shook her. "So he is. Guess he can't do anything about it, neither. Right, then, let's see. Aside from the four of us, plus any other girl who ever worked for him, there's about a hundred guys he fleeced at cards, and old Gipson, and some of his boys. Some say Benton had it in for him, too. His fancy piece, that dancer, she sure didn't like him any, though."

"Benton's fancy piece?"

"Yeah, you know, with the fan. What's her name? Hey, Gracie, what's Benton's girl call herself?"

"She calls herself Franny from Frisco," Gracie said.

"That's right. Knew it was some hifalutin name. And her no better than any of us."

Granville felt a momentary regret. So that was the connection between Frances and Benton—she belonged to him. No wonder he was protective of her. Behind him, he could sense Trent bristling. He put a hand on the boy's shoulder to keep him from doing anything rash. "Why didn't she like Jackson?"

"Don't know as I ever heard."

"I know for a fact he tried to queer her with Benton," offered Gracie, who'd joined the conversation, the sad look still haunting her face.

"Yeah?" Flo said.

"Uh huh."

"No wonder she had it in for poor ole Clive."

"Didn't work, though."

"Jackson tried to come between Frances and Benton?" Granville asked. "Why would he do that?"

Flo shook her head at him. "Jackson liked power. Maybe Frances was getting too close to Benton." Her tone was condescending.

"I gather Jackson failed?"

"Sure did."

"How did Benton feel about Jackson's interference?"

Flo offered another pitying look. "Doubt he ever knew. Jackson was good. He'd have pitched it as concern for Mr. B.'s safety, or some such."

"And Frances's reaction?"

"Way I heard it, she swore she'd get even. Someday." Gracie gave him a sly glance. "I'd not want to get on the wrong side of that one."

Granville couldn't help wondering about Scott's sister, and the secrets she and her brother seemed to share. "What about Gipson? You said he and his boys didn't like Jackson, either."

"The usual disputes," said Gracie.

"Usual?"

"Sure," she replied. Seen close-up, Gracie was both too thin and too pale for health. "Benton owns half the town, and Jackson ran the smuggling and the whorehouses for him. Gipson wanted in on the action."

"I thought Gipson was supposed to be a banker," Granville said, just to see how they'd react.

The two women burst out laughing, swaying against one another. "That's a good one, that is!" gasped Flo when she could speak again. "He's into the banking so's he can clean up all that cash he's got coming in from smuggling and girls. 'Course, he's not above fleecing an idiot or two wants to invest in a mine somewhere."

Granville didn't doubt for a moment that Gipson was a crook, but could he trust what they were saying? They were giving him more information while breathing fumes at him and propping each other up than he'd gotten since Scott was jailed. "How do you know all this?"

Flo and Gracie looked at him, then at each other. It was Gracie who answered. Flo was still laughing too hard to speak. "Haven't you ever heard of pillow talk? We hear everything that happens on this side of town, and more than you'd guess about the other side."

"Everything?"

She nodded. "Sure."

"So who killed Jackson?"

Gracie gave him a sharp look. "I think we've done enough of your work for you," she told him pertly.

TWELVE

Standing in the street outside 21 Dupont, Trent glared at Granville in the dim light cast by the lone streetlamp. "They were rude about Miss Frances. Why'd you let them run on like that?"

"When people are answering questions, you don't stop them to disagree."

"But they were lying."

"About what?"

"About—everything!"

"Which facts did they have wrong? Exactly. Tell me," Granville said.

Trent said nothing, his features set in stubborn lines.

Granville nodded. "That's what I thought. If you're going to be of any use to me, you have to make sure you're working with facts, not suppositions or how you think things should be."

Trent's face changed. He looked up eagerly. "Am I?"

"Are you what?"

"Going to be of any use to you?"

Granville grinned. He'd walked right into that one. "Well, I don't know," he said. "It depends on . . ."

As he spoke, two dark figures reared up behind them. Before Granville or Trent could react, one of them grabbed the boy. The other went for Granville, and would have had him, too, except for the patch of sheer ice in his way. The attacker's feet shot out from under him, and his head met Granville's fist, then rebounded off the ice with a dull clunk. He wouldn't be moving for a while, Granville thought, shaking out his throbbing arm, noting that the stitches seemed to have held.

Trent let out a muffled groan. Granville turned to help him just in time to see Trent's elbow shoot out and catch the other man in the stomach. The second ruffian grunted, but didn't release Trent. Grabbing a broken barrel stave from a pile of rubbish by the steps, Granville swung at him. He missed, but he caused the man to drop Trent and jump back.

Granville went after him, the stave cutting through the frosty air with a whoosh. The fellow ducked, then swung back with fists like clubs. He caught Granville a glancing blow on the chin. As Granville backed away, ears ringing, Trent stuck out a foot, tripping his assailant, who went down like a heart-shot grizzly. Recovering, Granville hit him on the head with the stave. Trent sat on him, then looked at Granville. "So what do we do now?"

Granville examined the men at their feet. "First we find out who these two are, and who sent them. But you might want to stand back. He's down, but he's not likely to stay that way."

"Oh." Trent stood up and backed away. Granville moved to stand in front of his young companion, clutching his makeshift weapon.

"Keep an eye on that one. Let me know if he moves," he said to Trent, who was next to the first attacker and regarding him warily.

"Why don't we just get out of here?"

"This is the third time I've been set upon in three days. I want to know why."

The man he was guarding stirred and groaned. Granville raised his weapon. "Who sent you?"

Hearing no reply, Granville nudged the fellow's ribs with his boot. "Who sent you?"

Still nothing.

Granville raised the barrel stave higher. "Talk, or you'll regret it."

The fallen man's face set in stubborn lines, but his eyes tracked Granville's every move.

"Granville, I think I know this one." Trent was bent over the fallen man, trying to make out his features in the uncertain light.

"From where?"

"At the warehouse, with your friend Blayney. He was one of the men guarding me."

"You're sure?"

"Yeah. I remember the scar on his neck."

Granville leaned a little closer to the second man. He didn't recognize him. He turned back to the first. "If you worked for Blayney, you might as well say so. There's nothing he can do for you now."

There was no response.

"Unless it's Gipson you work for," Granville continued. "I understand he has his own ways of punishing disloyalty." He didn't actually know any such thing, but he knew enough about Gipson that it seemed a safe assumption.

The resentful eyes flickered.

"So it is Gipson. Now, why do you suppose he's so interested in me?" Granville said in a thoughtful voice. The second man once again didn't answer. Granville hadn't really expected an answer. He nudged the man again with his toe. "It is in your interest to answer me."

"Why?" It was a growl.

"Because I can hurt you as much as Gipson can, and I'm here. He isn't."

"This one's stirring," Trent said.

"Better talk fast," Granville told his charge.

"He never tells us why." It was a sullen mutter, but the words were clear.

"What did he tell you?"

"Said he wanted you roughed up. Run out of town."

What kind of threat did he pose to Gipson? Granville wondered as he brought the barrel stave down on the second man's head, sending him back into unconsciousness. Was it because he'd sworn to find Jackson's killer? He hadn't been looking for a connection between Jackson and Gipson, but now Blayney was dead, too—and Blayney had worked with both Gipson and Jackson.

Was Gipson behind the murders of Jackson and Blayney? Or were these attacks on him more personal? What kind of threat could he pose to the man? He knew Gipson was a rotten snake, but so did half of Dawson City. Based on what Flo had said, it wasn't exactly privileged knowledge in Vancouver, either. More significantly, anything he knew about Gipson, Scott would also know. But Scott was already safely locked up and facing death, while he was being run out of town. What sense did it make?

"Come on, Trent," he said, grabbing the boy's elbow. "We've got what we needed."

"Where are we going?" Trent asked as he hurried to keep up.

"I need to have a little chat with my partner."

"Now?"

"Why not?"

"Because you've been beaten up three times in three days," Trent muttered as he hurried to keep up.

"What was that?"

"Nothing."

When the one-armed jailer opened the cell door for them, Scott was lying on the bunk, staring up at the rough bricks that made up the ceiling. Granville was shocked to see how haggard he looked.

"Doesn't look like they're feeding you too well, partner."

Scott turned to face him, and for a moment Granville saw the misery in his eyes. Then it was quickly hidden behind a broad grin. "Naw, I just don't want to put on fat, all this loafing around I'm doing," he said, sitting up and swinging his legs over the edge of the bunk.

He looked over Granville's shoulder. "And who's this?"

"You don't recognize him?"

"Should I? Hand me that lamp. I can't even see you in this light. Not that that's a bad thing." He peered at Trent. "Nope, can't say he looks familiar . . . wait a minute. Didn't you attack us the other night?"

"Correct," Granville said.

"What's he doing here?"

"He's helping me find Jackson's killer," Granville said, at the same time wondering if it were true.

"Where did he come from?" Scott asked.

"Good question. He showed up one night and I haven't been able to get rid of him." He had meant it as a joke, but Trent thought otherwise. "Actually, he's given me some good leads," Granville hastened to say as the boy glowered.

"He has?"

"Sure. Trent worked for both Jackson and Blayney."

"He means I ran errands for them," Trent said before Scott could say anything. "I'm not very important, but I notice things."

"What kind of things?"

"All kinds."

"Like?"

"Like Mr. Blayney didn't like Mr. Jackson very much. And Mr. Jackson had packages delivered to businesses all over the city."

"Did he, now?" Scott said. "That's interesting."

"Is it? Why?" Granville asked.

"I'll tell you later," Scott said, rolling his eyes toward the cell door and their unseen audience.

"No, you'll tell me now, or you might not have a later," Granville said brutally. "Scott, I've had enough of these games. I don't know whom you're protecting, or why, but you have to make some effort to help me."

"Or else?"

"Or else you'll be hanged for Jackson's murder," Granville told him in very precise tones.

Scott said nothing.

Granville watched him closely. Figuring he had nothing further to gain, he changed the subject. "What do you know about Gipson's business in Vancouver?"

Scott was startled. "Gipson? What's he got to do with this?"

"That's what I'd like to know. He's had me attacked three times in the last three days, and I've only asked him a question or two so far."

"He never did like you, you know."

Granville grinned. "I know. I can't say I much care for him, either. But that is not what this is about, and you know it."

"I do?"

114

"Listen to me. I need to know *now*. Have you had any dealings with him since you came to town?"

"He tried to bribe me when I first started guarding the silk shipments. Guess he imagined easy pickings."

"And what did you do?"

"Told him what he could do with his money."

Granville sat down on the bunk opposite Scott. "So what happened then?"

"Nothing much. He sent over one of his enforcers the following week. I packed him off with a thick ear."

"I can see you didn't endear yourself to Gipson. What do you know about his business?"

"Nary a thing," Scott said, but his eyes shifted away from Granville's.

So he did know something. "Rumor has him involved with smuggling and women, and trying to challenge Benton on the gambling."

"Keep your voice down."

"I'm sure it's no surprise to the law. Look, Scott, who are you trying to protect?"

"Protect? Nobody!" But it was bluster, and they both knew it.

"I hear that Jackson was killed by a woman, a tall, dark-haired woman," said Granville, and watched the shock spread across Scott's face.

Scott shook his head, his face set in stubborn lines. "Whatever you heard, you heard wrong. It wasn't a woman that shot Jackson."

"Oh? Were you a witness?"

Scott didn't answer.

"Then how do you know it wasn't a woman who killed him?"

Scott was still silent when Trent spoke up. "You don't have to worry, Mr. Scott. Your sister didn't shoot Mr. Jackson."

Scott leaped to his feet and grabbed Trent. "What do you know about my sister?"

Trent's face went white, but he stood his ground. "We talked to her, and she was doing her show that night. Miss Frances couldn't have shot Mr. Jackson."

The tension in Scott's face relaxed and he sank back onto the bunk. "Of course she didn't shoot Jackson."

As Granville listened, several things were clear to him: Scott knew—or thought he knew—who had murdered Jackson; he was trying to protect her; and whoever she was, she was connected with his sister. The question now was who was it Scott was willing to die to protect? And how could Granville, with time running out, learn the identity of the person his partner was protecting?

THIRTEEN

Monday, December 11, 1899

Walking toward Lord's tea shop, where Frances was waiting for him, Granville straightened the collar of his coat. Such places made him uncomfortable, but she'd chosen it for their meeting, and he'd been too desperate for information to argue. He was starting to realize how little he really knew Scott—the man hadn't even told him about his sister until after Granville had met her.

And what a sister, Granville thought, as he rounded the corner to see Frances in a window seat, her hair gleaming with glints of red in the sun. Julia had hair like that. He pushed the memory to the back of his mind; Julia was part of his past, gone as surely as Edward was gone. Saving Scott's life was what mattered now.

It was a small establishment, crowded with round tables and dainty chairs, with a hum of feminine voices filling the air, accompanied by the soft clatter of fine china. The smell of freshly baked cakes set his mouth watering. Ignoring the interested looks he was attracting from the gathered ladies, Granville strode directly to Frances. Seating himself opposite her, he leaned forward and placed both hands on the table.

"Thank you for meeting me. Let me start by being frank with you. Scott is running out of time and he refuses to tell me what is going on. You have also been refusing to tell me what is going on. It seems that the only person who will talk to me is Benton, and I'm not sure I can trust him."

She smiled. "You show good judgment."

Scott's sister was even more fascinating in her plain green dress than she'd been in last night's feathers and glitter, he thought. It was the contrast between her dramatic features and the demure gown that did it, and for a piercing moment, something in the grace of her movements reminded him of Julia. A feeling of regret stirred inside him, though whether for Julia or for Frances he wasn't sure. Ignoring it, he said, "Perhaps. But it isn't helping me get any closer to finding out who killed Jackson. Or to getting Scott out of jail."

She raised delicately etched brows. "I hear you're a detective. It doesn't sound like you're too good at it."

She was quick, and she'd been talking to Benton, which wasn't surprising given what he'd learned about their relationship. He thrust the unwelcome picture of Frances and Benton out of his mind, concentrating on what he hoped to learn from her. "I have nothing to work with, which is why I'm asking for your help."

"I told you, talk to Sam."

"You haven't even heard my questions yet."

"I don't need to hear them. But I suspect you won't leave me alone until I do, so ask."

"Are you and Sam the only children in your family?"

Was that pain he saw in her eyes? "Just the two of us."

She was lying. She'd brought her eyes up to meet his, but couldn't hold his gaze. Why would she lie? What did she feel the need to hide? Granville reached across the table and took her hand, which twitched in his as though she'd been about to withdraw it and then had changed her mind. "I dearly want to help, Frances," he said. "I owe your brother my life. I want to save his."

She was silent. He watched her face, so smooth and still, with just the quiver of her darkened eyelashes betraying her. "We had a sister," she said eventually, looking up to meet his eyes. "She is—lost to us now." Her voice was firm, her eyes steady, but her hand shook a little as it lay under his.

"Lost? Did she die?"

She shook her head and her eyes glazed with tears. "I can't speak of it. But she is no part of this."

"What was her name?"

Frances hesitated. "Elizabeth. Lizzie. But she can tell you nothing."

Granville noted her use of present tense; so Lizzie was not dead. Lost? What did that mean? He watched as Frances regained her composure, wondering what question he could ask that would give him the answers he so badly needed; Scott had only seven days left. Seven days! It wasn't nearly enough time.

Frances gave him a haughty look. "Back to staring at me, are you? Did your mother never teach you manners?"

Granville grinned at the thought of his elegantly remote mother teaching her children anything. Nanny had taught him his manners, and made a thorough job of it, too. "My apologies," he said, bowing over the hand he still held. "I did not mean to appear rude."

She glared at him. "You don't have to make fun of me."

Granville mentally kicked himself. It wasn't like him to be so clumsy with a woman, especially not one as beautiful as Frances. He was nearly two years out of practice, and it showed. "Frances, I don't mean to insult you. I need your help. Tell me about Lizzie."

Frances looked at him for a long moment, then her expressive eyes filled with tears. She pressed her napkin against her mouth. "I'm sorry, I can't talk about it anymore," she said. Pushing back her chair, she fled.

Granville half stood and watched her go, aware of the curious glances cast at them, the women whispering behind their fans. He felt like a cad. It was a good thing he'd left Trent behind; the kid would never have forgiven him for upsetting Frances. Seating himself again, Granville lifted his teacup and drained it. So Scott and Frances had a sister, and she was still alive, somewhere. He was willing to bet that somewhere was Vancouver. Was that what had brought first Frances and then Scott here?

"Mr. Granville? May I join you?"

The soft voice broke into his thoughts. Before he could respond, a young woman with tilted green eyes slid into the seat Frances had just vacated. "I'm sorry. Do I know you?" Granville asked, sure that he didn't but unwilling to offend.

She flashed a dimple as she smiled. "No. You don't know me, and I am afraid I am intruding, not to mention risking social ostracism by talking to a man I haven't been introduced to. But I saw your companion leave, and I had been wracking my brain trying to think how to talk to you, ever since I spoke to Bertie."

"Please sit down. You must be Miss Emily Turner."

"Why, yes. But how did you know?"

"I have only met one Bertie since I came here."

"How very logical. And you don't mind my interrupting you?"

"Not at all."

"You're not just being polite?"

He grinned at her. "When I am being polite, you'll notice."

"Well, as long as you are sure," she said, blushing slightly.

Her directness was refreshing. Granville was enjoying her company —even her blushes. Much to his surprise.

"Now, about Bertie," she was saying. "He says you have agreed to help him. Have you?"

Granville nodded.

"I want to help, too." Her voice was still soft, but she sounded determined

"Help?"

"Find out what happened to Bertie's cousin, of course."

"How?" he asked, watching her expression.

She glanced around the tea shop. "Would you ask the waiter to bring a fresh cup, please? They only notice women if there are no men with them, which I find quite annoying"

As requested, Granville signaled the water for another cup.

"Thank you." As the waiter departed, Emily lifted the pot. "More tea?" she asked.

"Nothing, thanks."

She put the pot down and looked at him. "Now, you were asking how I planned to help you find out about Bertie's cousin?"

Watching her and wondering about her motives, Granville had nearly forgotten the question. "Yes, that's what I was curious about."

"To be honest, I don't quite know. I will rely on you to tell me where my assistance will be of the most use."

"Bertie and I are going to trade information," Granville said. "We've agreed that he will help me, and then in turn I shall help him.."

"He's to help you in finding Mr. Jackson's killer?" She looked pleased. "But that's wonderful."

"How do you know about the murder?" he asked. She must have been listening while he'd talked to her father. Would she admit it?

"It was in the paper." She glanced over his shoulder. "I think I had better rejoin my friends. They've gone from shocked looks to outright glaring."

She stood, and Granville did as well. "Good-bye, Mr. Granville," she said, extending her gloved hand to him. "I did enjoy meeting you. I'll have Bertie keep me advised on your progress. And when you need my help, you can pass a message through him."

With a rustle of silk skirts she swept past him and toward the rear of the tea shop. Half turning, Granville watched her rejoin a table where two other young women were seated, wearing identical expressions of concern.

Emily's humor and her daring appealed to him. She was nothing like the women he was usually attracted to, nothing like Frances, nothing like his Julia. Julia had bottomless blue eyes, the face of an angel, and a voice that could make a devil weep. But she was Edward's sister, and she could no longer bear the sight of her dead brother's best friend, the man she blamed for his death. "If you hadn't set the example, he would never have lost everything." He could hear her frantic tones ringing in his head. "Edward was no gambler, but he believed you could do no wrong, God alone knows why, and anything you were doing he was determined to do."

Granville had never pointed out that gambling was expected of gentlemen of their class; he felt too guilty about the number of gambling hells Eddie had followed him into. Taking a hasty swallow of tea, Granville wrenched his thoughts back to the present, and Emily Turner's offer of help. What kind of assistance did she think she could give him, anyway? Not that it mattered at the moment; saving Scott was a matter of more urgency than locating Bertie's missing cousin. Draining the last of his tea, Granville signaled the waiter for the bill.

FOURTEEN

"Emily, I can't believe you did that!" Clara leaned across the table to speak, but her piercing whisper could probably be heard on the other side of the tearoom.

"Shush, Clara. He'll hear you," said Susan, indicating with a motion of her head who "he" was.

"No, he won't," said Clara, lowering her voice anyway. "He is nice looking, though, Emily. Such thick, dark hair, and those eyes! It's too bad he doesn't have a mustache. I do think a man with a mustache looks so dashing. Where did you say you met him?"

"He came to call on Papa," Emily said. Privately, she agreed with Clara's assessment of Mr. Granville, except for the mustache; personally, she preferred a man to be clean shaven, especially when his chin was as firm as Mr. Granville's.

"I can't picture your father introducing you to a man who looks like that," Susan said.

"Nor can I," said Clara, with a suspicious look at Emily. "He *did* introduce you, didn't he? Emily?"

"Well . . . ," said Emily, biting her lip.

"Emily Turner! I don't believe it! You just walked up and took tea with a strange man." Susan's face had turned pink even saying the words, and she stared at Emily as if she no longer recognized her.

"He's not all that strange."

"But what are you going to tell your mama?" Clara asked.

"Nothing at all, I hope."

"Oh, I think she'll have a few questions when Mrs. Smithers gets through telling her about today," Susan warned.

Emily turned just in time to see the redoubtable Mrs. Smithers leaving one of the tables near the front of the room. "Oh, dear," she said. "She must have come in after we got here."

"She did," said Susan.

"Why didn't you tell me?"

"You didn't tell us what you were planning to do, so how could I know it would matter if she saw you?"

"I didn't exactly plan it. It just suddenly came to me when I saw him sitting there alone. It was the perfect opportunity."

"The perfect opportunity for scandal," Susan said. "Your mother will never forgive you."

"Well, I think it was brave of you, Emily," said Clara. "But what did you want to talk to him about?"

Head held a little to one side, Emily considered her friends. Clara was a dear, but inclined to be a chatterbox, and Susan was simply too conventional. She'd never understand the need Emily felt to help Bertie, and she'd certainly never want to get involved in solving a mystery like that of Bertie's lost cousin. Emily gave them a half smile, keeping her lips closed and hoping she looked mysterious. "I can't talk about it. It is not my story."

Clara's face lit up. "Oh, a romance! How exciting. Is it one of your sisters?"

Emily nearly groaned aloud. Now Clara would never let this one go. "No. No, it isn't my sisters. But I can speak no further."

"Well, whatever it is, I don't think you should have got yourself involved in it. Not if it means speaking with strange men," Susan said. "And how are you going to explain yourself to your mother once Mrs. Smithers has told her tale?"

Emily didn't know how she was going to explain any of it, but discussing it with Susan certainly wouldn't help.

Her thoughts raced. Maybe they could help if she told them part of what was going on. But which part? "Mr. Granville is a sort of sleuth."

Susan looked horrified.

Clara, however, was intrigued. "A sleuth? Oh, how fascinating. But why were you talking to him? What do you need detected?"

"It isn't for me," Emily said. "One of my father's employees is accused of a murder he didn't commit. Mr. Granville is trying to find the real killer."

Susan patted her napkin against her lips, watching Emily's face. "And what does that have to do with you?" she asked.

"I am going to assist him."

"Emily!" Susan said in a shocked voice.

"Well, I think it's wonderful," said Clara. "But how?"

"I haven't worked that part out yet," Emily told her. "I thought perhaps you two might be able to help me."

"Us?"

"How?"

Susan and Clara spoke at the same time, then looked at each other. Clara gestured to Susan to speak first.

"How did you think we could help?"

She sounded curious, Emily thought. This was turning into a surprising day. She plunged ahead. "Well, between us we know a lot of people, and we hear a great deal of the gossip."

Susan still looked skeptical. "How can a little gossip help? It is a murder he is investigating, is it not? We would never meet any murderers."

Before Emily could answer, Clara said, "I know what we can do. We can visit that medium."

"What medium?" Emily asked.

"The one who always advertises as in the *World*," Clara said. "You know, the one who says she'll give advice on all business matters. Well, this is a business matter, isn't it?"

It was a ludicrous idea, but she didn't have any better ones. And the more Emily thought about it, the more of an adventure it sounded.

It was a typical gentlewoman's parlor. Every surface was draped in fabric and covered with ornaments, and crystal pendants dripped from the chandelier, reflecting the afternoon sun. Little shards of light danced against the wallpaper, while twin lamps on the matching side tables sported velvet shades and more crystal drops. Emily was disappointed to note that the draperies were a rich burgundy velvet, not black. Somehow she'd expected to find more sinister aspects in a medium's house. A real medium's house, that is. Emily hoped this Mrs. Merchant would prove to be genuine, but she didn't really expect it. And she wasn't entirely sure how she'd know what comprised an authentic meeting with departed spirits, anyway.

"Good afternoon. And what may I do for you?"

Emily spun around. She found herself confronting a short, rather dumpy woman with graying hair twisted into a severe bun at the back of her head. "Mrs. Merchant?"

The other nodded. "I am. And you would be?"

"I am Emily James. And these are my cousins, Susan and Clara." Emily was rather proud of herself. By using their own first names, none of them would slip and wrongly address one another, while saying they were cousins meant they only had to remember one surname.

The medium looked at the three of them for a moment. Then she said, "Fine. Which of you would like a reading?"

They looked at each other. It was a question they hadn't anticipated. "Actually, we are here about a business matter that affects all of us," Emily said. "But I will be asking the questions."

Mrs. Merchant waved them toward a lace-bedecked round table in the corner. "Please, seat yourselves."

They arranged themselves around the table in high, straight-backed chairs. Mrs. Merchant looked from face to face, finally focusing on Emily. "What is this business matter you wish information on?"

"A man, a business associate of my uncle's, was killed several days ago. We need to know anything you can tell us about his death."

Mrs. Merchant's thick eyebrows rose. "How was he killed?"

"He was shot."

"I see. And his name?"

"Jackson. Clive Jackson." Emily had memorized the name.

"And the nature of your business with Mr. Jackson?"

Emily darted a quick look at Clara and ran the tip of her tongue over suddenly dry lips, feeling her heart pounding in her chest. What were they getting themselves involved with? "I'm afraid that is private," she said, meeting the medium's assessing gaze with an effort of will.

After a pause that seemed endless, Mrs. Merchant nodded. "Very well," she said, standing up and walking to the window. Reaching up, she drew the heavy curtains, leaving the three of them sitting in the dimness. "We will see if we can reach your Mr. Jackson, or another spirit who might know him," she said, reseating herself.

"But don't you need complete darkness to call the spirits?" Emily was sure she'd read somewhere that was how it was done.

The medium spoke firmly. "Only charlatans require total darkness, so they can fool the gullible. For a true spiritualist, the spirits will come anywhere, but the soft light helps me relax. Now, silence, please." She sat back in her chair, closed her eyes, and took several deep breaths. Her face seemed to smooth out, losing all expression.

Emily watched her carefully. She'd expected to be asked to join hands around the table, not to sit in separate silence.

"We seek the spirit of Mr. Clive Jackson," Mrs. Merchant said in a low voice. "Clive Jackson, are you present?"

There was a long moment of silence, then the medium gave a shudder. The muscles of her face tightened into a scowl and a deep voice spoke. "I am," it said. "Who seeks me?"

Emily jumped. It certainly sounded like a man. Could this be a genuine séance, after all? But, then, she had no idea what Mr. Jackson had sounded like in life. Just as she was about to ask a question, a hand moved in the dimness and clamped itself onto her arm.

She could feel her heart thumping in her chest. Silly, it's only Clara, she chided herself as she patted Clara's hand reassuringly. If there was any possibility this was real, it might be of use to Mr. Granville. This was no time to succumb to nerves. "We have questions for you, Mr. Jackson," she said, keeping her voice steady with an effort.

"Ask, then."

It seemed a very obliging spirit. Emily wondered if that had been Mr. Jackson's nature in life, though she suspected that it had not, given the manner of his death. "How did you die?" she ventured.

"I was shot," the deep voice replied.

Well, that matched what had been in the newspaper article, so it offered no guarantee yet that the speaker was not, in fact, Mrs. Merchant.

"He knows! It is him!" Clara said in an excited whisper.

Emily patted the hand again but ignored the comment. "Why were you there?"

"I liked to stroll along the wharves in the evening."

"Who shot you?"

"It was dark."

"Could you see nothing?"

"A movement in the shadows. Little else."

This could be a fraud. Their hostess, disguising her voice, would have reason to say as little as possible. "Did you also hear nothing?" she asked.

"She said I deserved this and more."

She? "A woman shot you?"

"Yes."

"What else did she say?"

"Welcome to hell."

Emily was shocked. It was a horrible thing to say, but then killing someone *was* horrible. "Did she say anything else?"

"No. Then she shot me."

Clara's hand still clenched Emily's arm, and on her other side Susan sat stiff and straight, staring at the medium. Emily made a mental note to ask Susan what she'd observed during the session. "Did you recognize the voice?" she asked.

"No. She'd changed it, disguised it."

"Could it have been a man, disguising his voice?"

"No. It was a woman." He sounded sure. Or Mrs. Merchant did, if it was indeed still her speaking.

"Was there anything familiar about the voice? Did it remind you of anyone?"

"It was somewhat familiar."

"Do you know who it reminded you of?"

"No. I couldn't recognize her."

Emily paused, her brain racing. The voice was slippery, telling her only what she thought to ask. What hadn't she asked yet? She thought quickly, then recognized the question she'd missed. "If it was so dark that you couldn't see her, how did she see to shoot you?"

There was a pause, then he answered. "There was one streetlamp. I stood beneath it. She stood in the shadow beyond its light. She could see me clearly, I could see nothing."

It made sense, but was it too pat? Why the hesitation? "Did you smell anything?" she asked.

"Saltwater, tar, and rope."

"Nothing else?"

"A fragrance of musk, very faint."

"Musk? Her perfume?"

"Possibly."

"Do you know a woman who wears musk perfume, has access to a gun, and would want to see you in hell?"

It was Mrs. Merchant's lighter tones that now responded. "He has gone. Did you get the answers to your questions?"

Emily regarded the medium with suspicion. She seemed very composed for someone who had just come out of a trance, and the room felt no different with the spirit gone. If it had ever been there at all. "You didn't hear?"

"I never do, my dear. The spirits use my body as a vehicle, which includes use of my eyes and ears."

"I see. Yes, some of my questions were answered. But he left before he could answer the most important question."

"I am sorry to hear it. The spirits are often unpredictable. Do you wish to book another session to ask your question again?"

"No, thank you. We've heard enough." It was Susan's voice.

Emily nodded. She suspected she would want to see the medium again, but she didn't wish to contradict her friend. It was time to go.

FIFTEEN

Granville sat in Dr. Barwill's waiting room, Trent at his side, wishing the coroner were a little more punctual. The room had once been opulent, but now the upholstered side chairs had lost their stuffing and the air smelt unpleasantly of damp. Dr. Barwill's nurse had also not weathered well; her iron-gray hair was drawn back severely from craggy features that had settled into a permanent frown. She looked up every few minutes to give them a disapproving look. They'd been waiting more than a quarter hour, and they were the only ones in the room. Eventually the door at the end of the room opened, and Dr. Barwill's head appeared.

"Who's next, Miss Hinch?"

"These gentlemen have asked to see you," she said, her eyes disapproving. "On business," she added.

So that was her problem; they weren't paying customers. Granville wondered if the practice was doing as poorly as the decor seemed to suggest. It made him wonder at the reason behind its decline.

"Now, what can I do for you gentlemen?" the coroner asked.

"I have a couple of questions about the man who was shot earlier this week. Clive Jackson?"

The white brows drew together. "You'd do better to talk to Chief McKenzie."

"I have." Which was true, as far as it went. "These are questions relating to the inquiry."

"Oh?" Dr. Barwill opened the door fully and crossed the room toward them, accompanied by a strong smell of whiskey. Scotch whiskey, unless Granville missed his guess. Which answered the question of what had happened to the good doctor's practice. "And just what would those questions be?"

"The time of Jackson's death. And the caliber of the bullet you dug out of him."

"And why should I answer your questions?"

Granville played his hunch. "I have a bottle of aged Lagavulin you might appreciate."

The nurse frowned and cleared her throat. Dr. Barwill ignored her. "Lagavulin, eh? Scotch is good for the lungs, you know. This damp climate is hard on my lungs."

He paused, and for a moment Granville thought the doctor's scruples might have gotten the better of his thirst.

"Very well, then," Dr. Barwill said. "Jackson, was it?" he muttered as he turned and went back into his office. Granville and Trent followed.

They found the doctor rifling through an unsteady stack of files, piled on one corner of a battered desk. With a grunt of satisfaction, he pulled one out from halfway down the stack. Granville watched in a kind of horrified amusement as the rest of the stack toppled, spilling its contents across desk and floor.

"Got it, by Jove," Dr. Barwill said, ignoring the chaos now in evidence. "Now, what was it you wanted to know?"

"The time of death."

"Ah, yes." He pulled out a thin file. "It was a cold night, as I recall. Snowing, wasn't it?"

"For part of the night."

"Hmmm. Cold will slow down the onset of rigor, you know. Makes it harder to determine the time of death."

Granville controlled his impatience with difficulty. "What time of death did you decide?"

He looked from Granville to Trent and back. "You sure you want the boy to hear this? Pretty gruesome stuff, you know."

Granville glanced at Trent and nearly laughed at the fascinated expression on his face. "He can handle it."

"Hmmm. Yes, well, the corpse bled a lot, you know. Blood everywhere. Messy."

"I know. I saw him."

"Ah, so you did, so you did. Hmmm, now, let me see."

"The time of death? You were about to say—"

"Very well, very well, I'm getting to it. It looks as if he died somewhere between eight that night and one in the morning."

Beside him, Granville felt Trent stir, and he shot him a look. The boy had agreed to keep quiet; it was the only reason he'd allowed him to come along. "You're sure?" he asked Barwill.

"Of course not. But it'll have to do."

Any skills he'd once possessed had probably been pickled in Scotch years ago. "And the bullet?" At least this question required no competence.

"A thirty-two. Revolver, most likely."

"A thirty-two? I imagine that caliber is pretty easy to buy in Vancouver?"

The doctor shrugged. "You can buy them anywhere in town you've a mind to. Even order them from Eaton's catalog, seventy cents the box. "

"Eaton's?"

"They ship out of Toronto," Trent said. "People subscribe to the catalogs, and you can order anything."

"Including bullets."

Trent nodded. Granville released a frustrated breath and gave up on that line of inquiry. "What was the condition of the body?"

"He was dead. What more do you need?"

Granville kept his thoughts to himself with an effort of will. "Was there any sign of a struggle?"

"Not a thing. Even his hands were unmarked. Is that all?"

It seemed to be. "Thank you for your time," Granville said, too politely, as they stood up to leave.

"You mentioned whiskey, I believe," the doctor reminded him.

Once they reached the street, Trent could contain himself no longer. "He said Mr. Jackson died between eight and one. That clears Miss Frances, doesn't it? She was onstage then."

"Trent, it's important never to let your feelings for people color what the facts tell you."

"Yeah? Well, how do you know Mr. Scott is innocent, then? What facts told you that?" Trent shot back.

It was a good question, one that Granville didn't have an answer to, but he wasn't going to tell Trent that. Bad enough that he himself still had lingering doubts, without sharing them. "We'll go have a chat with the bartender at the Carlton. He should know where

Frances Scott was between eight and one that night," he said in an abrupt voice. They covered the fifteen blocks in complete silence.

The Carlton was busy, men standing two and three deep along the bar. Working his way to the front of the crowd, Granville looked for the bartender. It was the same bear of a fellow who'd been working the other night. He was at the far end pulling a pitcher of ale, his deft movements reflected in the mirror that ran the whole length of the wall behind him. Granville waited until the beer was delivered, then caught the man's eye in the mirror, and held up two fingers.

As the bartender put their drinks on the bar in front of him, Granville laid a bill on top of the coin he'd placed on the bar. "I'm interested in where Frances was last Tuesday night," the Englishman said.

"Last Tuesday? She was here that night." He had to raise his voice to be heard over the hum of voices in the room. "She's always here on Tuesdays."

"All night?"

"Sure. She does two shows."

"Yes, I know," Granville said. "Did she go out between shows?"

"Not that I saw."

"And you would have seen her?"

"Usually." He pulled a grimy cloth from under the bar and wiped at a spill.

"But can you swear that Frances was here all night?"

"No. It was too busy."

Granville sensed that another bill might have affected his memory, but he needed the truth, not convenient lies. He tapped the money already lying on the bar. "Is there anyone else who might know for certain if she was here all evening?"

"Well, Nan might know. They're pretty friendly. Annette is her stage name."

Granville remembered the dancer who'd been molting her feathers the first night he'd been here. "Is she here? I'd like to talk to her."

"'Fraid you're out of luck on that one. Nan's ma is ailing, and she left town last night, probably won't be back for a week or more."

Granville felt his heart sink. Scott didn't have a week. "Where did she go?"

"Frisco."

It was too far, even by steamboat. "I see. Is there anyone else who might know of Frances's movements that night?"

"Nope. No one comes to mind."

Granville pushed the money across the bar. "Well, thanks for your time. I'll be stopping back, so if you think of anything, let me know."

But the bartender had already turned away. As they exited, a blast of cold air hit them. It was starting to snow again, small pellets that stung when they hit. Trent looked at Granville, but said nothing.

"No matter what he said," Granville told him, "Miss Frances is still a suspect."

"But she didn't shoot anyone!"

"Perhaps she did, perhaps she didn't. And if she did? Are you ready to see Scott hang because you don't want to admit the truth?"

Trent's face went white. "I don't want anyone to hang."

"Well, someone will."

"But that person can't be Miss Frances."

"Give me one fact that says she can't have done it."

"Well, you heard the bartender. She was here when the coroner says Mr. Jackson was killed."

"She was onstage for her acts. How do we know she didn't leave after the first show, throw on a cloak, meet and kill Jackson, then get back here in time for the second show? What proof do we have that didn't happen?" He didn't remind Trent that Wong Ah Sun had said

Jackson was shot by a dark-haired woman. That wasn't a fact, either, but it made him very interested in any holes in Frances's alibi.

Trent looked shocked. "I guess she could have," he said slowly. "But she didn't. She wouldn't. Not Miss Frances."

Granville looked at him and didn't say anything.

Trent dropped his eyes, and took a deep breath. "Right," he said after a long moment. "I see what you mean about facts. So what do we do now?"

"We stop standing in the rain and we go to talk to Benton."

SIXTEEN

Sitting quietly in the back parlor, her forgotten embroidery hoop in her lap, Emily kept thinking about the deep voice saying he'd smelled the scent of musk. Musk was such a particular and unusual scent and none of the ladies she knew wore it. She didn't quite believe she'd been talking to a spirit, yet hoax or not, she'd been given some very detailed information. Whether or not it was genuine, it seemed to mean something and she knew it was important to tell Mr. Granville what she'd heard.

The problem, of course, was how was she to do so? She had no idea if he had an office, and it was unlikely that she'd just run into him again as she'd done that afternoon. She tugged on one earlobe as she thought.

"Emily," her mother suddenly snapped at her. "How many times have I told you not to pull on your ear? It is most unmannerly, and will probably end up disfiguring you for life. It's quite enough that I have to hear that you were out walking without your maid. Again! I have nearly given up expecting you to behave like a well-raised young lady. But I do not expect to have to watch you pluck at parts of your body."

"Yes, Mama," Emily murmured. If she looked abashed enough, sometimes Mama would let it go.

"And don't try to fool me with that meek look. You have never been meek a day in your life, and I don't expect you to start now. Sit up straight, girl. Show some of that backbone."

Emily raised her head to meet her mother's glare. The twinkle she saw instead caught her by surprise. "You are who you are, Emily, and don't ever try to pretend otherwise. But there are certain rules you must follow if you are to survive in society. To tell you the truth, I don't much like Mrs. Smithers myself, but no matter how annoying she is, please do try not to be rude to her."

Emily could feel herself flushing. Mama had not yet heard about her behavior in the tea shop. "I'm never deliberately rude, Mama."

"No, I know, child. But the appearance of rudeness is equally bad. You can do better."

Her sisters, who'd been silently embroidering during their mother's lecture, resumed their discussion of what they'd wear to the New Year's ball, and Emily went back to thinking about musk perfume, which interested her far more. She didn't think she'd ever met anyone who wore musk; rose, yes, and lily, lavender, and violet, even orange blossom, but not musk.

"Have you ever known anyone who wore musk perfume?" she asked.

Her sisters stopped their chatter and looked at her. "Musk perfume?" repeated Miriam. "Why are you asking about that?"

"I overheard someone today talking about it and thought it sounded different. I would love to try some, but I don't know where to buy it," Emily said, thinking quickly.

"I don't think I've ever known anyone to wear musk," Jane said.

"It is not a scent that a well-bred woman would wear," their mother said firmly. "Musk is one of the exotic scents, appropriate only for actresses and opera dancers. I forbid you to even think about trying it, Emily."

"Yes, mother," said Emily, returning to her embroidery, her mind racing with this information. What now? Perhaps Bertie would know how to get in touch with Mr. Granville, and then she could impart the full extent of her researches.

Granville was waiting to see Robert Benton. Beside him, Trent was kicking one foot against the heavy oak chair he was sitting in. Granville glanced at the tall clock standing in the corner; they'd been there nearly half an hour and it seemed much longer. The place was nearly deserted, the ticking of the clock echoing in the silence. Benton kept late hours. It was a good thing they'd had dinner first; at least his stomach no longer felt hollow, though he'd give anything for a shot of whiskey.

Granville's mind slid to his conversation that morning with Frances and the revelation of her and Scott's sister, Lizzie. What could have happened to Lizzie that Frances spoke of her as if she were dead? Scott was no help, either. Before he could form the next thought, the opening of the door at the far end of the room signaled Benton's presence. Granville stood up to face him. Trent followed his lead.

"Granville," Robert Benton said. "Here's a pleasant surprise. How's your partner?"

"Still in jail."

"I do know that. In good spirits, though?"

"Considering he's being held for murder, yes, I would say he is holding his own."

"You still haven't figured a way around that one-armed jailer?"

"I prefer to look for a solution that will allow Scott to stay in town."

"Too bad. You're just making things harder for yourself. Who's your friend?"

"This is Trent. My assistant." From the corner of his eye, Granville could see the proud smile that spread across the kid's face.

"But what can I do for you?" Benton asked.

"Well, Benton, I have learned two things about you. The first is that you know a great deal about Jackson. The second is that you don't want Frances involved in this case in any way."

Benton rocked forward so that his weight was balanced on his toes, like a prizefighter facing a worthy opponent. "So?"

"So Trent and I would both like to keep her name out of this. Right, Trent?"

Trent nodded vehemently. "Right. Miss Frances isn't involved in this. She can't be."

Benton shot him a look, then returned his attention to Granville. "I'm not saying Frances is involved, but what is it you want in return?"

"All I need is information that will spring Scott."

Benton looked at them both for a long moment, then turned and walked back through the door. "Come into my office," he said over his shoulder.

They followed him, Trent even more curious than Granville.

Benton, already seated behind his desk, waved them to two leather club chairs. "Whiskey? Cigars?"

Granville shook his head to both offers. He didn't trust Benton enough to accept his hospitality.

"Too bad." Benton lit a fat cigar and inhaled deeply. "These are the good ones." He exhaled a cloud of smoke and inhaled again, watching them as he did so. "What d'you want to know?"

"What do you know about any dealings between Scott and Gipson?"

"Between Scott and Gipson? Not much. Just that the latter is much less trustworthy than the former."

"Why is that?"

"He's crooked."

"Isn't that a bit meaningless, coming from you?"

Benton met Granville's eyes. "You're not afraid of me, are you?"

"No."

"Most men are," Benton said, drawing again on his cigar. "Of what I represent, and the men I can call on, if not of me personally." He paused. "But not you."

"No."

"Hmmm." Benton nodded. "I operate outside the law, but Gipson is crooked. There's a difference. None of his dealings are straight. His word is worth nothing."

"Unlike yours." It was not a question.

Benton blew out a cloud of smoke and considered Granville through it. "I like you," he said slowly. "Even if you are threatening my Frances."

"Not threatening her. Keeping her name out of this."

"Ah. I see."

A silence fell between them. Trent shifted in his chair, but said nothing. Finally Benton broke it. "Gipson and Scott clearly knew each other, and there was no love lost between them. They mostly avoided each other, though Gipson hired Scott for a brief period, mostly to humiliate him, I'd guess."

Benton was an astute observer, Granville thought. "Why would you consider a partnership with Gipson if you think so poorly of him?"

"A partnership? I'd never consider it. Gipson is greedy and has no principles. That makes him a danger to everyone around him."

"Now, I had heard Gipson wanted a share of some of the businesses you run."

Benton laughed. "He might've wanted a share. He wasn't going to get one."

Granville nodded. "Yet according to Trent here, Jackson and Blayney did a fair bit of business together, and Blayney was Gipson's man."

A vein began to throb in Benton's forehead. "What business?" he demanded, glaring at Trent.

To Trent's credit, he met that gaze straight on. "He had me run errands for Mr. Blayney," he said. "I delivered packages for him, mostly."

"What kind of packages?"

Trent shrugged; he'd been through this before. "I don't know. Small ones, mostly, letters and things."

"Where did you deliver these packages?"

"To the warehouse. Taverns, houses, other places."

"Who paid you for this work?"

Granville was impressed by Benton's acumen. He didn't waste any time asking exactly whom Trent had been working for, but went straight to the question that would give him the clearest answer.

"Mr. Jackson did. Sir."

"All the times you made those deliveries?"

"Yes, sir."

"It's a good thing Jackson's dead," Benton muttered to himself. "Saves me the trouble of killing him, though I'd like to know what he was up to."

"Blayney's dead, too," Granville pointed out.

Benton shot him a considering look. "So he is," he said slowly. "I wonder what the two of them knew about Gipson."

"You think Gipson wanted the two of them dead?"

"Someone did."

"True enough. And you think Gipson could have pulled off the two deaths?"

"I think he's capable of it. Don't you?"

"More than capable," Granville said. "Except that he has been trying to get rid of me for the last three days, and has not yet succeeded."

Benton slowly raised an eyebrow. "Maybe you're just harder to kill," he said.

Granville grinned. "That is possible. Or perhaps Gipson just can't find good help."

"Also a possibility."

Trent was sitting on the edge of his chair, looking from one to the other, his expression confused. Granville extended the grin to include him, and Trent sat back, looking marginally more comfortable. He'd have to explain the dynamics of negotiating information to Trent later, Granville thought. "One thing: I heard a rumor that the person who shot Jackson was a woman, a dark-haired woman."

"And you believe it?"

"No, I don't believe it, but I don't disbelieve it, either. I am operating from the premise that anything is possible except that Scott killed Jackson. The question in my mind is do you believe it?"

Benton's pleasant expression vanished. He remained silent, watching Granville carefully.

"Now, we don't want to think that might have been Frances," Granville said.

"Of course not."

"If, on the other hand, Gipson had a hand in Jackson's death, then I need knowledge of him and his dealings," Granville said. "Oh, and I have already talked to the ladies at Twenty-one Dupont."

"I see."

Granville grinned. "I try."

"And if it were a woman who shot Jackson, do you have any idea who this woman might be?"

"Other than Frances?" Granville said, baiting the hook.

Benton gave him a dry little smile. "Other than Frances, of course."

"Of course." Granville paused, then gave his most open smile. "I have no idea," he said, and sat back, crossing his arms. Let Benton make of that what he would; he didn't have to know it was the truth.

SEVENTEEN

Tuesday, December 12, 1899

Emily sat in the parlor, half hidden by a small forest of palms in brightly polished brass pots. She was fuming. She'd come here to wait for Bertie to return from whatever errand Cook had sent him on, but her father's untimely entrance had ruined her plans. He'd been so furious to find her reading his newspaper that he'd snatched it from her hands, telling her to sit there until he decided what her punishment would be. Not ten minutes later, Bertie had gone by the window, a brimming basket in hand, and ten minutes after that, he'd gone by in the other direction, carrying an empty basket. Cook had obviously sent him on another errand, and it would be hours before she got a chance to talk to him, assuming that she was ever released from the parlor, that is. She'd briefly considered rapping on the window and motioning for Bertie to come and speak to her, but she hadn't quite dared.

There had to be another way to find out how Mr. Granville was progressing in solving his two mysteries, there had to be. Emily bit the tip of one fingernail, then realized what she was doing and folded her hands in her lap. Her mother would sigh and give her one of those looks if she saw her biting her nails, the look that said, "How can any daughter of mine behave in so unladylike a fashion?" Emily glared at the window. There were just too many restrictions if you happened to be a girl. Why couldn't she just walk out that door, find Mr. Granville, then sit down and discuss Bertie's case with him? If she were a man, no one would pay any attention, but because she was a girl, it would cause a scandal she'd never live down. For a long, satisfying moment, Emily contemplated doing it anyway. She could almost taste the freedom that would ensue.

The door opened, and Emily started, feeling as guilty as if she'd actually done what she'd been thinking about, and she was sure her face must reflect that guilt. Ninny, she berated herself, trying to will her expression blank, knowing she'd fail.

"I see you've had time to reflect on your behavior and regret what you've done, hmmm?" her father said.

It took Emily a moment to realize that he thought she was feeling guilty about reading the paper. She had to bite the inside of her cheek to keep her laughter from bursting out. If only he knew what she'd really been thinking. "Yes, Papa," she said.

"And you won't make that mistake again, will you, daughter?"

I won't get caught again. "No, Papa."

He nodded, a satisfied look on his face. Poor Papa. What had he done to be given a daughter like her? Emily wondered. She didn't fit into the neat boxes he'd laid out for each of them, and one day she would probably do something that would send him into an apoplexy. But his old-fashioned ideas were so restrictive, she felt as if she were strangling.

"There's a good girl," her father continued, oblivious. "And what are you planning today?"

"I've plans to meet Clara," she said, suddenly thinking of a way to contact Mr. Granville. "We're going shopping."

"Good," he said, patting her head and nodding. "That's good. Can't get into much trouble shopping, now, can you?"

Oh, Papa, if you only knew, Emily thought, giving him a kiss on his whiskered cheek. "I'll see you tonight, Papa," she said and fled the room before he could change his mind.

"So you see, Clara, I must get in touch with Mr. Granville." Emily gripped the telephone more tightly. Using it was still a novelty to her, and anyway, few of her friend's homes had telephones yet. Clara was the exception.

"Yes, I see, but why not send him a letter? And why must we meet him at the Stroh's? No one goes there."

"Exactly. There will be no one to ask unnecessary questions. Or to carry tales."

"But do you think he knows where it is?"

"I'll put directions in my note, or Bertie can tell him. I'm sure he can find it."

"But why there?" Clara persisted. "Why not arrange to meet him in a bookstore or something?"

"Stroh's makes excellent pastries, probably the best in town," Emily said, knowing her friend's fondness for cream puffs and éclairs.

"Oh, all right." Clara paused, and her voice went softer. "Emily, I think meeting Mr. Granville is frightfully thrilling, but what if you are found out?"

Emily sighed. Clara was usually very loyal, which was why she'd not hesitated to involve her in the afternoon's plan, aside from the fact they were best friends, of course. Susan would never have agreed to meet Mr. Granville. "There will be nothing to find out. This isn't a romance. Rather, I am assisting him in his endeavors, and it's perfectly respectable as long as you are with me. You will do this, won't you?"

"I suppose so. If you are absolutely sure."

"Wonderful. I'll see you then." If Clara had been there, Emily would have reached over and given her friend a hug. That was the problem with using a telephone; the person you were talking to was so far away, she thought as she replaced the handset.

"Miss Turner? I got your note. What is so urgent?"

Emily looked up at Mr. Granville, pleased at the success of her scheme. He appeared tired, she thought, but despite the fatigue in his eyes, he exuded an air of strength and determination. He seemed far too masculine for Stroh's.

"Please, Mr. Granville, join us. Clara, this is Mr. Granville. And this is my friend, Miss Clara Miles. Sit down, and I'll tell you everything." Emily couldn't help beaming.

He nodded at Clara, then seated himself.

"Well?"

Emily started. Mr. Granville's tone was abrupt and he looked impatient. "The person you are looking for? The one who killed Mr. Jackson? I have it on good authority that the killer is a woman." Beside her, Clara gave a little squeak, and Emily glared at her.

He looked a little surprised, she thought. "What authority?"

"I'm afraid I can't tell you."

"We went to see a medium," Clara blurted.

Mr. Granville looked as if he wished he'd never met either of them. "A medium," he said slowly, as if searching for something inoffensive to say.

Emily took a deep breath. There was no point in hiding anything now. "That's right. And she appeared to channel the spirit of Mr. Jackson, who said he had been shot by a woman."

"You say she *appeared* to channel Jackson's spirit. You didn't believe her?"

Emily considered the question and said slowly, "Well, there was no proof. It could have been genuine, but it might have been a sham. Something about it, however, contained a ring of truth. I'm not being gullible, I assure you."

"What exactly did this medium tell you?" he asked.

"The spirit was precise," Emily said. "He said he had been shot late at night. And that he had been shot by a woman, but that it was too dark to see her."

"Well, Jackson was certainly killed at night. Anything else? Did he recognize anything about the woman?"

"He said he wasn't sure, but he thought she was wearing the scent of musk."

"Musk?"

Emily nodded. "Yes. According to my mother, it is a scent no respectable woman would wear."

"Don't tell me you've been discussing a murderer with your mother. Or mediums, for that matter."

Emily smiled at the idea. "No, of course not. I just mentioned that I had heard of a new scent and was thinking of trying some."

"Ah," said Granville.

He must have sisters, Emily thought. She smiled at him. "There was one other thing."

Before he could respond, the waiter bore down on them with their order. Emily picked up the teapot. "Tea?"

Granville lifted his cup, and he met her eyes over the rim. "You were saying there was one other thing?"

"Yes, of course. The spirit said that after she shot him, the woman said, 'Welcome to hell.'"

"Welcome to hell?"

"Yes." Emily was proud she'd managed to repeat the words without blushing. Beside her, Clara had turned beet red. It was a good thing no one was close enough to overhear what they were saying.

"What was this medium's name?"

"Then you do believe me?" Emily was amazed.

He smiled. "Let's just say that this is the second time I have heard that Jackson's killer was a woman."

"Then it's possible Jackson's killer really was a woman? If you've heard it from another source, I mean."

"I'm beginning to think so, yes."

"Then what would her words mean?"

"Perhaps she found her own circumstances desperate, and blamed Jackson for them."

"Will this information help you find her, then? The real killer?" Emily waited for his answer.

Mr. Granville lifted his own teacup in a silent toast. "The information you have given me will help a great deal. It gives me a place to begin asking questions. I am indebted to you."

"Oh." To her own embarrassment, Emily now flushed deeply. "It was nothing. I am just glad I could help. I don't know why we decided to visit a medium, but once I'd determined to help you, this idea presented itself. Neither I nor my friends had ever consulted one before."

He laughed, a rich sound that Emily stored for remembering later. "Miss Turner, I need the name and address of that medium. I would like to talk to her myself now."

"I've written it down," Emily said, passing a piece of paper across the table to him. "I would very much like to know how your discussion with her goes. Perhaps you would inform Bertie when you see him next, and he can tell me." Emily looked down at her lap for a moment, then took her courage in both hands. "Or if you happen to be in the area, Clara and I will be taking tea here at two tomorrow afternoon."

"We will? . . ." Clara began, but Emily silenced her with a stern look.

"And we would be pleased if you joined us." Emily listened with the same pleasure as before when Granville began to laugh again.

EIGHTEEN

"No, it wasn't a waste of time," Granville told Trent. "It just wasn't a meeting for you to tag along to."

"Well, she's just a girl. How much help could she be?"

"More than you've been," Granville teased, then relented when he saw the look on Trent's face. "You're my Watson." But that only brought on another hurt expression, and Granville had to explain about Arthur Conan Doyle and his consulting detective.

Trent *had* been useful, Granville thought. But what Emily had told him, even given its unexpected and quite peculiar source, was a potential key to the maze he faced. Either he had to consider the possibility that Jackson's killer really had been a woman, or find out why Bertie's uncle and a medium were both sending misinformation his way.

Emily had surprised him on their second meeting; she had not only had the imagination to set up a meeting with a medium but also had made intelligent observations about what she had heard.

Granville smiled at the thought of the starchy Mr. Turner trying to cope with a daughter like Emily.

"What's so funny?"

Trent sounded annoyed. Granville's smile widened. Obviously he didn't like feeling left out. Granville couldn't blame him. "Nothing. Nothing at all."

"It's not nothing to me, your grinning like that."

"So are you ready to help me with our next interview?" Granville asked to distract him.

The ploy worked. Trent's face lit up. "I sure am. Who are we talking to next?"

"First a Mrs. Merchant. Then I'll need you to find Bertie for me. Think you can do it?"

"Try me."

Two hours later, Granville was standing on the wooden sidewalk outside a neat little brick house in the West End, swearing inventively. Trent looked impressed by his creativity, which didn't decrease Granville's frustration one iota. The visit they'd paid to Mrs. Merchant had been short, and less than helpful. She had simply and categorically denied knowing anything about the conversation between the spirit of Clive Jackson and Miss Emily James.

"I remember nothing from my sessions," she'd said, her expression sanctimonious. "But you are welcome to stay for your own session, if you wish."

He had then sat through an interminable hour in stifling silence, long legs cramped under a tiny table. At the end of it, she'd met his gaze and told him she was sorry but the spirits weren't cooperating that day.

"They are sometimes cautious," she explained as she pocketed his money. "I'm sure they'll talk to you if you return another day."

She had to be a fraud, but a cautious one. Granville was curious what it was about him that had made her wary. She must know something about Jackson's death—but what, and from whom? Clearly he wasn't going to find out by asking her, but perhaps if Emily were to visit her again? Mulling that idea over, he turned to Trent. "Where do we find your pal Bertie?"

"This time of day? Maybe the Chinese laundry over on Richards."

"Can we go there?"

Trent nodded. "Follow me," he said.

The laundry was tiny, barely ten feet wide. It was also hot, crowded, and loud with abrupt conversations that were shocking to Granville's unaccustomed ears. He scanned the crowd. Bertie was not among the customers, nor was his one of the dark heads bent over steaming tubs of water or hanging dripping clothes on the lines that ran along the walls.

"He'll be here," Trent promised. "What time is it?"

Granville pulled out his pocket watch and glanced at it. "Nearly two."

"He'll be here soon," Trent said with confidence.

Nearly an hour later, Trent's confidence had wilted. The heat and the noise had driven them outside, despite gray clouds that threatened more snow and a wind that kept reaching icy fingers down the back of Granville's neck. He drew his collar closer and looked over at Trent. "We've waited long enough. Come on."

"Where?"

"Turner's place."

Trent looked horrified. "We can't go there."

"Why ever not?"

"If you go there and ask for Bertie, you'll get him fired, probably me, too. And it's not easy to get a job, you know."

Yes, Granville thought, watching Trent's expression, that was something he'd been learning in the last few months. All those years as a fourth son, when he'd felt there was no place in the world he truly fit, he'd still never worried about his next meal. Even those lean years in the Yukon, he'd still had the last of the settlement his father sent with him to fall back upon. After that, he had mostly gone hungry till Scott had offered him the job with the CPR. He clapped a hand on Trent's shoulder. "You're right. We'll find another way to talk to him."

Trent let out a sigh of relief, then hurried to catch up with Granville's long strides. "If we're not going to talk to Bertie, then where are we going?"

"We're going to have another chat with Benton. If a woman shot Jackson, there are a couple of things that don't add up."

"There are?" Trent asked, trying to catch his breath.

"There are," Granville said. He'd been doing some thinking. If it wasn't Frances Scott was protecting, could it be their other sister, Lizzie? When Frances had spoken of her, she had been overcome by emotion. Had that been an act, designed to keep him from asking more questions? If so, it had been effective.

Granville considered the possibilities. Lizzie as the dark-haired woman who had shot Jackson, the person Scott was protecting? It made a certain kind of sense. But if he was right, why had Lizzie done it, and where was she now?

Benton looked surprised to see them, but recovering his aplomb, he invited them into his office after a short delay.

"Why are you back?" Benton's approach was direct.

"There was one question I forgot to ask you the last time."

"Oh?"

"You told me the first time we spoke that you would take care of Jackson's murderer. Have you done that?"

A muscle tightened beside Benton's mouth, but his voice was level. "No. The situation has changed."

Of course it has, now that you know he was killed by a woman, Granville thought, his suspicions confirmed. "Changed how?"

Benton gave a sharp nod. "I now believe it to have been a personal matter, only affecting Jackson and his killer, nothing to do with me or my businesses, so I'm satisfied."

Granville didn't believe him for a minute: a man in Benton's line of work could not afford to give up vengeance so easily. "Your second in command is murdered, and it has nothing to do with you?"

Benton drew on his cigar. "Jackson's death had nothing to do with anything except who Jackson was."

Granville nodded, watching his expression closely. "I see. Well, with Scott still in jail, I am not satisfied." He paused. "Your change of heart wouldn't be because his killer was a woman, would it?"

Benton avoided the question. "It was an entirely personal matter."

"Then who killed Jackson?"

"I don't know who killed him, but I do know Jackson brought it on himself."

There was a note of truth in Benton's voice; he believed what he was saying.

"How?" Granville thought he knew the answer, but he wanted to hear Benton's version.

"Jackson was a man of many appetites. He knew people from all levels of society, and used most of them. He got what was coming to him."

Benton was definitely protecting someone. He might not be sure who had killed Jackson, but he clearly had his suspicions. "From whom?" he persisted.

"That's all I can tell you."

"And you won't tell me who you think might have killed Jackson?"

"No." Benton paused, drew deeply on his cigar, and eyed Granville through the smoke. "Why? Who do you think killed him?"

Granville decided to take a risk. "I think it will turn out to be Sam and Frances's sister, Lizzie."

Benton, who was in the process of relighting his cigar, paused and watched Granville through the smoke. "Do you, now? And why would you think that?"

"I have my reasons."

"And what do you propose to do about it?"

"Find Lizzie."

"So why are you here?"

"Because I think you know where she is."

Benton puffed out a cloud of cigar smoke. "You're wrong," he said.

"Are you saying that Lizzie is not the killer? Or that you don't know where to find her?"

"I'm saying you're wrong about all of it."

"Oh? Then Frances is the killer?" Beside Granville, Trent shifted restlessly, but he didn't say anything.

"You know she's not."

Granville felt the muscles in his jaw knot. "I only *know* that a man is dead and that Sam Scott is in jail for a murder he didn't commit." He kept his voice very level. "Beyond that I have conjectures, rumor, and supposition, but no facts. Which is why I am talking to you. I hear that in this town you are the man with the answers, and right now I am running short of them." And even shorter of time, Granville thought, but he wasn't willing to show Benton the desperation he was beginning to feel. He recognized in him a man to whom it would be dangerous to reveal anything the other might see as a weakness.

NINETEEN

Emily was restless. Being dragged from shop to shop by Clara was utterly boring. She looked over at her friend, who was deep in contemplation of the merits of one waist over another, and sighed. On a day like today, with the wind blowing straight off the snow-covered mountains that rose behind the city, it was a wonder that exercise-averse Clara was even willing to walk from store to store. Only her love of shopping could overcome her dislike of the cold. Emily shook her head ruefully; another half hour of such tedious activity and she'd go crazy. She absently fingered a swath of blue velvet lying on the counter, enjoying the soft feel of the fabric, when inspiration struck. "Clara," she said. Then again, "Clara!"

"Emily, which do you think?" Clara asked, turning to face her. "The cerise or the mauve?"

Emily looked quickly from one to the other. Both had a white front, with crossbars of black velvet ribbon; the only difference was the color. She looked from the waists to Clara's creamy complexion and blue eyes and back again. "The cerise," she said. "It will best become you. But never mind that for now. I want to go to visit Papa's office. Will you come?"

"You want to visit your father?" Clara was stunned.

"Yes. The railway offices are actually quite interesting. Will you accompany me?" she repeated.

"Well, I suppose so. Just let me purchase this first."

"Good afternoon, Papa," Emily said, opening the heavy office door and poking her head around it. The room beyond was paneled in aromatic cedar, with a massive oak desk, glass-fronted bookcases, and a beautiful Aubusson carpet. The effect was one of restrained luxury; it seemed more like a home than an office, and Emily took a deep, appreciative breath. She'd always loved the way it smelled: spicy cedar and lemon furniture polish, mixed with the tang of cigar smoke and the richness of leather.

"Emily? And Clara, too," he exclaimed as Emily opened the door wider. "This is a surprise. Is something wrong?"

"No, Papa. I wanted to show Clara your office."

"You're right, Emily, it is beautiful," Clara said.

You couldn't even tell she'd been coached in what to say, Emily thought in relief. "And I love to see you at work," she finished. Her father was too busy showing Clara around to question her last statement, though her mother would not have believed it for an instant, Emily knew.

"From this window you get a good view of the rail yards," her father was saying. "And there, beyond it you can see one of our *Empress* liners. She's set to sail right after the New Year. A beauty, isn't she?"

Emily joined the two of them at the window, gazing at the sleek white steam liner with the swept-back bows. She couldn't believe her luck. "Where is she sailing, Papa?" she asked, attempting to sound casual.

"To the Orient, my dear."

"Oh, is that one of the ships that carries tea and silk?"

"It is indeed," he said, pride evident in his voice. "That beauty is the *Empress of India*. The *Empress of Japan* is due in next month, and the *Empress of China* the month after that."

Clara's imagination was caught by silk, not ships. "Is it very valuable? The silk, I mean?"

"Very. One carload of raw silk is worth more than a hundred thousand dollars, and this last shipment took seven carloads. Biggest we've ever had."

That was over seven hundred thousand dollars. Emily was stunned. It was more money than she could imagine. Why, even her bicycle, the deluxe model that Papa had bought for her the Christmas before last, had only cost thirty-five dollars, and that was the most expensive thing she had ever owned. No wonder they hired men to guard the silk. "Aren't you afraid the silk will be stolen?"

He nodded, looking pleased at her interest. "Yes, that is why the CPR started the silk trains. Add our fastest engines and those trains break records right across the continent. They stop only to take on coal and water."

"So are they going too fast to rob?"

"It does make it more difficult, though mostly the faster we can get the silk to New York, the better our prices. No, we have armed guards on every car of the silk trains, plus we put guards on the empty cars before the silk ever arrives in Vancouver, to make sure there's no trouble in the cargo transfer from the *Empresses*."

"And that's what Mr. Scott does, the man who is in jail? He guards the empty silk train?"

Mr. Turner looked a little concerned. "Yes, that's right," he said. "Though I don't know how you knew that," he added, half to himself.

"Had the *Empress of India* arrived when that man was shot?"

He looked thoughtful. "They found him the morning of the day she docked."

"What happens when an *Empress* docks?"

"There's a great commotion, but the silk is the first thing unloaded after the passengers and their baggage. The bales are transferred directly from the ship to the waiting boxcars. The company pays a bonus if the silk is unloaded quickly."

"Are the bales heavy?"

"Nearly a hundred and twenty-five pounds apiece."

Emily tried to picture it: the ship at the dock, the bales of silk being lifted across, the sense of urgency. "How long does the silk train stay in the station once it's loaded?"

"A silk train leaves the very second that loading is complete."

"And there was no attempt to rob this shipment?"

"No, thank goodness. It arrived safely in New York a little less than eighty-four hours after it left here. A new record," he said, beaming.

Emily had never heard her father talk so openly about his work. He must indeed be proud of his silk trains. She hastened to ask further questions before he changed his mind and stopped answering. "So do you think there is a connection between the silk and the man who was shot?"

Her father's face grew red and he scowled. "No, I don't think there is any connection. How could there be? And why are you asking me this?"

"Well, I just thought that if you trusted Mr. Scott to guard the silk cars, he must not be the kind of man who would commit murder." Emily considered blinking her lashes at him, the way she'd seen her sister Jane do to great effect, but she was afraid she'd look foolish. So she gave him a small smile instead.

"Of course Scott seemed trustworthy. But that doesn't mean he didn't kill Jackson." He looked thoroughly bad-tempered now, the look he always got when faced with contradictory ideas.

"It doesn't?"

"Of course it doesn't," he said testily. "Emily, you know nothing of such men. Which is as it should be."

"But why would Mr. Scott have done such a thing?"

"Jackson deserved to die."

Emily was stunned. She'd never heard her father talk like that, never heard such venom in his voice. "Why, Papa? What did he do?"

Her father looked shocked, as though he'd forgotten to whom he was speaking. "Never mind, young lady. This isn't something you need to know about."

Emily wasn't giving up that easily. "But, Papa, what about Mr. Scott?"

"Run along, Emily. I'll see you tonight," her father said firmly as he herded them toward the door. "It was nice of you both to visit."

The door closed firmly behind him, and Emily and Clara looked at each other.

"I wonder what Mr. Jackson did to your father?" Clara said.

TWENTY

"So you are looking for answers." Benton had lit another cigar and breathed out a cloud of pungent smoke.

"I am looking to get Scott out of jail," Granville said, resisting the urge to stand up and pace the spacious room.

"Yet you weren't at the hearing today."

"What hearing?"

"The one where your friend was bound over for trial, on a charge of murder."

Granville could barely contain his shock. "When was this?"

"This morning. Scott declined to testify, which did him no good in the judge's eyes."

Which explained why Scott hadn't told him. "And when is the trial?"

"Next Tuesday. The nineteenth."

At least it was the date he'd been working toward. Granville forced his mind to focus on why he was here. "The problem is, I seem to be the *only* person interested in clearing Scott's name."

"Frances wants her brother freed."

"Does she? She has a bloody odd way of going about it, if she does. Or is it just that she doesn't trust me?"

That earned a half smile from Benton. "She doesn't know you, does she? Though I think she believes that you want the best for Scott. The problem is that she trusts me."

Granville slowly sat back in his chair, watching Benton carefully, trying to read the expression in his eyes. "You are trying to get Scott out of jail?"

"Let's say Frances wants me to get Scott out of jail."

"And I'm in the way?" Granville kept his face expressionless as he asked the question. Beside him, he could feel Trent tensing.

Benton blew another cloud of smoke. "That's one way of putting it." He slowly tapped the ashes of his cigar into a cut-glass ashtray, then met Granville's eyes. "But I do think I see a solution to my problem with Frances."

"Oh?" Granville said, watching him warily. This man was far more dangerous than Gipson could ever be. Did he know about his meetings with Frances, and the near flirtation that had sprung up between them?

Benton nodded. "For various reasons, I can't deal with the matter of Jackson's killer myself. But for the sake of—shall we say harmony?—I'd like to see your partner released from jail. I think you may be my answer."

"Go on."

"I'd like to hire you to get Scott out of jail." Benton smiled, and the smile reached his eyes, lightening their darkness. "After all, you are a detective, aren't you? That is what I keep hearing."

Granville sat back with a silent groan. He might have known that particular lie would come back to haunt him.

Benton was looking at him with something very like amusement. "You're not worried about taking money from me, are you? It spends the same as anyone's."

"No, I am not worried about the money." There were always the poker tables, Granville thought. "The problem is that I already have a client."

"Scott, I presume?"

"That's right." Even if Scott seemed determined to refuse his help.

"I don't imagine he's paying you much."

"Money is not the issue."

"Hmmm." Benton's eyes drifted over Granville, assessing as they went.

Granville was glad of the quality of his new outfit; outwardly, at least, he had nothing to be ashamed of. Inwardly it might be a different matter, but then every man was entitled to his secrets.

"If I hire you, you'll have access to any information and resources I have."

"Then give me access and save yourself the fee. I will free Scott anyway." Whatever Benton's game was, Granville didn't want to be indebted to him.

Benton's eyes gleamed. "If I hire you, it will appease Frances. If you fail, it's you she will blame, not me. If I don't hire you, Frances will expect me to save Scott." He drew on his cigar, watching Granville. "So if I don't hire you, there's no reason for me to tell you anything."

Granville started to laugh. Against his better judgment, he liked this man, and for some reason he trusted him, at least in this. "How can I resist such a magnificent offer?"

Benton watched Granville for a moment, a hint of something that might have been surprise on his face, then he put down his cigar and reached across the desk to shake Granville's hand. "Good. Consider yourself hired."

"Aren't you going to ask my terms?"

Benton's eyes glinted. "As you just told me, money is not the issue. I'll pay your terms, whatever they are. I am sure they'll be reasonable."

It was a warning, but it was also a joke, and Granville smiled, amused by the irony of it all. "Well, perhaps on the far edge of reasonable."

Trent tugged at Granville's sleeve. "What about me?" he asked, in a hoarse whisper that carried far better than he had meant it to.

Granville grinned. "Of course, those terms will include my assistant."

Benton chuckled. "Of course," he agreed. "How could I not hire such a fervent champion of my Frances?"

"Oh, you noticed that?"

"It's hard to miss."

They both turned and looked at Trent, who flushed under their combined regard.

They turned off Water Street and onto Carrall, striding past the magnificent brick-and-glass facade of the Alhambra Hotel, past ships chandleries and warehouses, stepping aside from the sprays of mud and water thrown up by the horses pulling the delivery vans. "I can't believe you agreed to work for Mr. Benton," Trent said.

"Why not? We are now making good money to chase rumors all over town, and we know that Benton suspects Frances's sister, Lizzie, and so does Frances."

Trent looked at Granville for a moment. "We do?"

"Think about it."

Trent's forehead wrinkled for a moment, then cleared. "You mean because he didn't argue when you said it was Lizzie?"

"And because he was no longer interested in pursuing the matter himself. It would be somewhat awkward for him if the killer is his lover's sister. The complication for Frances is that she wants to see neither her brother hanged nor her sister apprehended for the murder of a man who deserved killing."

"So what do we do now?"

"Now? We get out of this blasted wind and find ourselves somewhere warm. I could use a whiskey."

"Now? But what about our case?"

Granville grinned at the proprietary sound of that "our." He probably shouldn't tease Trent. Still, it was difficult not to. "I have a particular taste for the whiskey at the Carlton."

Trent looked confused for a second, then began to grin. "Oh, I get it. We're going to talk to Miss Frances again, right?"

"Right."

Frances was not pleased to see them. They'd found her seated at the vanity in her cluttered dressing room. She was assessing her reflected image as she held a long diamond earring up to one earlobe, the gems glittering against her hair. The opening of the door had caught her attention and she'd glared at their images in her mirror. Meeting those angry eyes, Granville felt a stab of lust. She was stunning in her fury.

"Why are you back?"

"I just have a couple of questions for you, if you don't mind." He should have waited until she'd had a chance to talk to Benton, Granville thought ruefully as her eyes sparked at him.

"I told you everything I know."

She was a good liar, he'd give her that. "Not quite," he said, watching her closely. Her eyes darted to her dressing table, and it didn't take a genius to realize she was looking for something to throw at him. He had to admire her spirit. "Benton just hired me," he said hastily as she curled one hand around a glass jar full of powder.

"He what?" It was almost a shriek.

"Hired me."

"Why?" Her voice was an interesting combination of threat and fear.

"To clear Scott. Which means I have to find Jackson's killer." He paused, letting silence fill the room, and watched her face. "Benton says you think it might be your sister, Lizzie."

She gasped, the sound loud in the quiet room, and her face went white. Trent started to move toward her, but Granville's outstretched hand warned him back. He needed answers, and to get them, he had to crack through her protective shell. "I want to save Scott's life," Granville said, his voice gentle. "Benton trusts me." Enough to hire him, anyway. "Don't you think you can trust me?"

"Damn you," she said, turning to face him. "Damn you for this."

It shook him, hearing a woman curse. "For making you choose?" He watched her for a moment, looking for the words that would persuade her. "Scott has already chosen. He'll die rather than mention Lizzie." One hand twitched in her lap, then was still. "Is that what you want, to see Scott dead for something he didn't do?"

She blinked, her eyes filling with tears. "No, I don't want Sam to die." Her voice softened but the words were clear and firm. "I asked Benton to save him, but I don't want it to be at the cost of my sister."

"It may not come to that."

"You can't know that."

No, she wouldn't accept false comfort, he thought, and respected her for it. "Just tell me what you know. I will save Scott, and if there's any way I can save your sister, too, you have my word I'll do it."

She gave him a piercing look, as if assessing what his word was worth. Granville said nothing, just met her gaze steadily, and waited. Would she trust him? It seemed forever that he stood, breathing in the mingled aromas of paint, powder, and scent, watching her bent head. When she finally spoke, he had to bend his own to hear her.

"All right," she said, then straightened and gave him a fierce look. "What did you want to ask?"

"Where is Lizzie now?"

"Somewhere in Vancouver."

"You don't know where?"

She shook her head, then sighed. "She'll be in a house somewhere. She's a prostitute."

"Is that why you said she was lost to you?"

"Do I look like a hypocrite to you?" she challenged him. "My life is not exactly what you'd call proper."

"No, but it isn't boring." That earned him a flicker of a smile. "Why did you call her lost?"

She closed her eyes for a moment. When she spoke, her voice was low. "Lizzie has been smitten with the poppy."

It took him a moment to grasp her meaning. "Your sister's an opium eater?" It wasn't as bad as he'd been expecting. Laudanum was prescribed for everything from toothache to nervous conditions; he'd known at least one countess, to say nothing of a poet or two, who'd been addicted to the stuff. There were cures available.

Frances shook her head, her expression fierce. "I wish it *were* laudanum she took. She's addicted to the opium pipe."

TWENTY-ONE

What had Mr. Jackson done to her father? Emily wondered as she and Clara stepped back into the icy wind. It must have been something awful; she'd never heard Papa wish anyone dead before, and his eyes had been filled with anger. She shivered a little and drew her collar more closely around her neck.

"Clara, it worries me that Papa was so very upset about Mr. Jackson. I hope it isn't connected to why he was murdered."

"Slow down," Clara said, her voice breathless. "You are walking too quickly." She paused for an instant then hurried to Emily's side. "I still don't understand why you are involving yourself with that awful murder."

"Because it is the only bit of life in my own!" Emily burst out, then stopped and looked at her friend. "Oh, Clara, I feel so trapped. Papa forbids almost everything, and Mama tries so hard to turn me into a lady, I feel as if I'm choking. It's almost the new century, everything is changing, but it seems I'm going to be locked in the old ways forever."

"I know, Emily. But why a murder? It's so ugly."

"Because this is what I've been given the opportunity to do. Because no one else seems to care that an innocent man will hang."

"If he is innocent, then they will find that out at his trial. And besides, he has that Mr. Granville trying to get him free."

"And what if he doesn't succeed? What if something I could have done or found out could have made a difference but I didn't bother? How will I feel if they hang him and I never even tried to help?"

"If they hang him, maybe it is because he's guilty. It's not up to you to save this man."

"Perhaps not. But I've been given the chance to try. How can I ignore it? How can I say someone else should help him if I'm not willing to do it?"

"But, Emily, it could be dangerous."

Emily shook her head. "We dutifully go to church every Sunday, Clara, and listen to sermons about helping our fellow man. Is that all it is? Words? Is it enough to put money in the collection box to help the heathens overseas?" She met Clara's eyes, and her own twinkled. "And besides, I am *so* dreadfully bored."

Clara gave a soft laugh, her breath hanging frozen on the air. "Now that sounds like you. Oh, Emily, why must you care so much about things?"

"I don't know, Clara. I suppose it is just the way I am. And I have always hated puzzles I couldn't solve." Her forehead wrinkled. "The first thing I'd like to know is how Papa knew Mr. Jackson."

"There must be a way you could find out."

"I don't see how."

"Does your Papa ever bring work home?"

"Clara, you are brilliant. Yes, he has an office at home, and he won't be there for hours yet."

"Well, promise you'll tell me what you find."

"I promise," said Emily. "I'll tell you tomorrow."

"Tomorrow?"

"Yes, when we go to Stroh's."

"So you can meet *him* again. I don't think it's such a good idea, Emily. Really. You don't even know the man."

"It isn't like that, Clara."

Clara didn't look convinced. "He is still a man, Emily, and attractive. And you don't know anything about him."

"I don't need to know anything about him. This is business." And she did know something about him, Emily thought. She knew he was loyal to his partner, and that he had treated Bertie better than most men would have. For now, it was enough.

Angus Turner's study was small, dominated by a massive rolltop oak desk with two pedestals and a pair of tall filing cabinets. Heavy curtains bracketed the windows, and the thin gray light that seeped between them scarcely penetrated the semi-gloom. Closing the door carefully behind her, Emily shivered. It was a room that always felt lifeless to her. She took a deep breath, then crossed to switch on the standing lamp, surveying her father's neat desktop with something approaching dismay.

She daren't spend long here in case someone came in, but she didn't know where to start. With a sigh, she sat down in her father's leather chair and opened the first drawer on the right. A quick glance told her the contents: a fountain pen, some ink, and a pen wipe. The second drawer held a collection of engraved cards. The third and fourth drawers held a loose collection of papers and a few files. Emily thumbed through them, then spread them out on the desk blotter, nearer to the lamp.

It would help if I knew what I was looking for, she thought, turning over one paper after another. Her father's writing was cramped and difficult to read, which slowed her progress. She found no references to Mr. Jackson or to Mr. Granville's partner.

Replacing the papers carefully in the drawer, Emily went through the drawers on the left, with similar results. A hurried search through the pigeonholes and document boxes in the rolltop yielded nothing. She stood up and opened the first drawer of the first file cabinet; a row of files, each carefully labeled, met her eyes. She scanned them, moving several forward so she could read the ones behind. Copies of schedules, contracts, bills of lading. Nothing that meant anything to her. The next drawer was the same, and the third, while the bottom drawer held only a stack of dusty ledgers.

Coughing, Emily closed the drawer and eyed the second file cabinet with trepidation. The first and second drawers were as boring as the previous four. The third drawer, however, caught her interest; it held bills of lading and passenger manifests, filed in date order, for the three *Empresses: Japan, China,* and *India.* Her father had said that the day Mr. Jackson was killed, the *India* had finally arrived. Emily remembered it clearly because her father had been so relieved when the ship docked. She stared at the files, thinking hard. Could there be a connection between Mr. Jackson and that particular sailing?

Sorting through the files, Emily found the manifests for that sailing; the *Empress of India* had left Japan on December 3rd, carrying 1,915 bales of silk, 600 pounds of tea, and 276 passengers. She'd been delayed by a storm, arriving in Vancouver on the 6th. As Emily scanned the list of passengers, she realized with shock that this was the voyage on which Bertie's cousin had vanished; surely the two weren't connected? She scanned the list again, but his was the only name she recognized. Emily wished Mr. Granville were here— he might recognize other names.

Making a sudden decision, Emily removed those pages, folded them tightly, and hid them in her sleeve. Heart pounding, she replaced the files, then hurriedly checked the last drawer, finding nothing of interest. Reaching to turn off the desk lamp, something about the way the blotter was laying caught her eye, and she raised the edge, finding underneath it several half-size sheets of paper with notes in her father's handwriting.

Emily pounced on them, then froze at the sound of footsteps approaching the study. Was someone coming in? Her heart beating an uneven rhythm in her chest, she ducked under the desk, crawled into the kneehole, and held her breath, waiting. She heard voices, then what sounded like two people walking away from the door.

She drew a deep breath and had to choke back a sneeze. It seemed Sally never dusted under the desk. Crawling out, Emily smoothed out the now rather crumpled pages she had been clutching and examined them under the light. It looked as if her father had been doing his thinking on paper, jotting things down.

Jackson's name was there, with several sums listed against it; the smallest number was one thousand dollars, the largest five thousand. Emily drew in a breath at the latter. Five thousand dollars! There were four other names, also with figures listed against them, but none were familiar. Here was the link to Jackson she'd been looking for, but what did it mean? Her father had said he didn't know Mr. Jackson, so what was his name doing here as if he were some kind of business connection? Had Papa lied to her? But why would he do that?

Confused, she turned to the next page, which seemed to be a

rough sequence of events when unloading the silk shipments. The third page listed how long it took the silk from the day it left Japan to arrival in New York; four hours to load, ten days aboard ship, five hours to unload, 120 hours on the train. Why would her father be jotting down such information? Emily looked from one page to the next; it looked like information you'd need if you were thinking of hijacking a shipment of silk. Surely her father couldn't be involved in something illegal, could he?

Emily suddenly felt very cold. This information might help Mr. Granville free his partner, but what would it do to her father? What if he really had done something illegal and she betrayed him? But how could she doubt Papa like this? Surely he could have done nothing wrong. With an abrupt motion, Emily shoved the papers back under the blotter out of sight, then flicked off the light and whirled toward the door. Just as she was pulling it open, her father stepped in.

"Emily? What are you doing here?"

Emily felt her face heat up and tried by force of will to make the blood recede, to keep her expression smooth and innocent. "Hello, Papa. You're home early. I was just checking on Sally's work. She hasn't been dusting anything except the surfaces."

Her father gave her an odd look. Emily, interested in house-keeping? "Then that would explain the dust mice on your skirt," he said drily.

Emily looked down, batting at the offending evidence. "Yes," she said, trying to sound convincing. "Mama always tells us we must be thorough in our inspections if we expect the work to be done correctly."

She could tell from the look he gave her that he didn't know whether to believe her or not. Emily swallowed hard. She'd never felt so guilty or so confused, and she was far too aware of the papers stuck up her sleeve. She worried that an edge might be poking out. Thank heavens she'd put the other papers back. The ones she was hiding hadn't seemed to actually be incriminating, like those others. There had to be an explanation for it all.

Emily felt so guilty she was startled when her father patted her gently on the head and told her that she was a good girl and to run along. Usually she hated it when he treated her as if she was still twelve years old. This time she felt relieved, but more confused than ever. And she didn't know what she was going to tell Mr. Granville the following day.

TWENTY-TWO

"Hell," Granville muttered, bending to pick up the delicate chair Frances had overturned in her rush to leave them. Now what? He felt he should go and comfort her, but he sensed it wouldn't help. The best thing he could do was focus on what she had told him and how it might help free Scott.

Their sister was an opium smoker. It was the last thing he'd expected to hear, and he'd been too blunt in asking how she had become addicted. It was the second time in three days Frances had fled from him in tears. Granville considered the problems Lizzie posed. She was most likely Jackson's killer, but how was he going to find her, and what would he do when he did?

Having Lizzie in jail instead of Scott was not going to make either Frances or Scott very happy, but if Lizzie had killed Jackson, what other solution was there? Granville grimaced. He needed some way to vent the rage and frustration building inside him. He was getting nowhere, and Scott's time was dwindling rapidly. Granville looked over at Trent, who looked worried now. "Let's get out of here," he said.

"But what about Miss Frances? She's upset."

"There's nothing anyone could say that would help her right now. The only thing we can do for her is to get her brother out of jail. Now, are you coming, or aren't you?"

"I'm coming," Trent said, hurrying to catch up to Granville's long strides. "But where are we going?"

"First things first."

At the Turners' house, they crossed the back porch and entered through the servant's entrance, off the kitchen. Granville noted with interest the thick leather-covered door that separated the kitchen from the rest of the house, muffling the sounds and muting the odors of food preparation and cleanup.

When they had found Bertie and told him what they wanted, he looked thoughtful for a moment. "Not many women smoke opium, few are white. I do not know where to look, but I know who to ask."

"Your uncle?"

He nodded. "Yes. I am most sorry I do not go with you tonight, but I am not finished washing up from dinner."

Trent broke in. "What if we helped you?"

"Then, yes, perhaps I can take you."

Bemused, Granville found himself holding a linen towel and wiping crystal glasses. William would have a fit if he could see me now, he thought with a gleam of unholy amusement. Still, Granville thought, he'd had to do far worse just to stay alive; at least for this he was dry and warm, and he did need Bertie's guidance in finding the opium dens. With Bertie's help, they might have some hope of finding Lizzie in time to save Scott.

*   *   *

Wong Ah Sun did not look surprised to see them; he sat at ease in his carved chair, holding a long pipe and filling the air with the fumes of good tobacco. He said something in Chinese to his nephew, then inclined his head toward Granville and Trent. "What may I do for you tonight?" he asked. His eyes gleamed at them through the smoke.

Granville stepped forward and inclined his head at the exact angle of Wong Ah Sun's bow. "It is my request," he began, using the formal speech patterns he had heard Wong Ah Sun use on their previous visit. "I seek the woman you told me of, the one with dark hair who shot Jackson. I have learned that her name is Lizzie, and that she smokes opium. Bertie has said that you may know where I might find such a woman."

Wong Ah Sun nodded and puffed silently on his pipe for several moments. Granville waited, aware this was another test. Minutes passed. Finally their host nodded again, then raised one hand. "Before I tell you anything, I must know that the information I give you shall not go further."

Now Granville felt more out of his depth than ever. "Why? Making, selling, or using opium is not against the law, as long as you have the right licenses. Why should it matter?"

"Opium use is accepted for us," Wong Ah Sun said, his face expressionless. "If it were known that a white woman had become an opium smoker, then public opinion would be even more against us. And life here is difficult as it is."

Granville nodded. Even in the short time he'd been in Vancouver, he understood what the man was talking about. His caution came out of hard experience. "You have my word. I will reveal nothing of what you tell me and nothing of what I may find, except where it is necessary to free my partner."

A smile flitted across Wong Ah Sun's face, turning the fine skin across his cheeks into a myriad of tiny creases. "It is well. You have agreed to more than I asked for and revealed you understand the spirit of what I asked. I will give you what you need."

He turned to Bertie, deliberately choosing to speak to him in English. "Please guide this man, nephew, for it is beyond my ability tonight. There are two places to visit. The first is on the third level beneath Number Twelve Dupont, beside the Wing Sang Company. The other is next to Hip Tuck Lung, at Number Five, but on the fourth level. You know where I mean?"

Bertie bowed. "I know, uncle."

Aware that he shouldn't interrupt, but needing to learn the answer, Granville said, "Is there more than one white woman who smokes opium?"

Wong Ah Sun's face was still as he considered Granville. "Yes," he said, his voice dry and thin. "There are three that I know of, but only two places that will allow them entry. He will take you." He turned back to his nephew and handed him a folded slip of paper, with an instruction in Chinese.

Bertie responded in the same language, then bowed and backed out of the room.

Impressed by the sense of power that suddenly crackled around the old man, Granville also bowed, a little deeper than before. "You have my thanks, and my assurance that I have not forgotten about your son. I will look into his disappearance as soon as I am free to do so."

Wong Ah Sun dipped his head in acknowledgment. "I never doubted that you would do so. You are a man of honor," he said.

Now what had given him that idea? Granville wondered as he bowed again. As he turned to leave, he was pleased to see Trent bowing, as well.

* * *

Less than ten minutes later, Granville found himself standing on Dupont Street in blowing snow, seeking the address they'd been given. He couldn't read the black characters that ran vertically beside the door, but unless he missed his guess, this was an opium factory. It was closed and darkened now, but Bertie rattled the door handle anyway. He didn't seem surprised to find it locked, just nodded to himself and made his way farther down Dupont to Columbia.

Bertie turned right, then right again when they reached the alley running behind Dupont Street. The alley was as poorly lit as the last time Granville had seen it, and the snow made visibility worse. As they drew closer, he realized he was seeing light from several small windows in a low building that was built directly behind the building in front of it.

Invisible from the street, this second building could only be accessed from the alley. Granville could hear sound coming from the building, muffled by the snow. As they drew closer, he could hear drums, and a stringed instrument wailing, then a woman who sounded as if she were in pain. He stopped dead. "Bertie, what is that? What is wrong with that woman?"

"This is a theater, and you hear an actor. They play a great traditional opera, very old."

"Opera?" It didn't sound like any opera he'd ever heard. Again he felt as though he'd left the world he knew far behind.

Bertie nodded, then led them through a narrow doorway into a kind of antechamber. The room was empty, but close and hot, the heat overpowering after the chill outside. A red cotton curtain hung between this room and the next, which blazed with lantern light. Now the music was overwhelming; drums thundered, flutes wailed, and a male voice was raised in anguished response. Trent grimaced, but Granville was intrigued.

The music was unlike anything he'd ever heard, but there was something about it that stirred him. Bertie didn't even pause to listen, but went straight to the far corner and a well-concealed door. He opened the door onto a dark stairwell, producing a candle from inside his coat. Lighting it, he turned to them. "Stay close, stay quiet," he said, then turned back and began to descend, Granville and Trent on his heels.

The stairs were steep and there was no handrail, so they went slowly. "Here, I think," he said.

Granville could see only one sliver of light along the corridor as they moved still deeper into the building. There was an odd smell in the air, not strong enough for him to identify. The cold and damp were bone-chilling and there was no sound, not even the skittering of rats. A shiver ran across his back; the feeling of being trapped swept over him, stronger than when he'd been caught by a cave-in along the banks of the Ouzel when he was twelve. Somehow it felt worse knowing there was a building above him.

Gritting his teeth Granville fought off the fear as Bertie opened yet another door. A thin yellow light shone out, then a thick cloud of heavy smoke that smelled like roasting peanuts swept over them. Trent coughed, and Granville waved the smoke out of his face.

Bertie disappeared through the doorway. Granville followed and stepped into hell.

They were in a small, low-ceilinged room, and his first thought was that it was full of corpses. Smoke filled the room, hanging in heavy layers that seemed to rise and fall like the tide. The smell was overwhelming, so thick it seemed to first smother and then caress him, inviting him to stay. A score of small lamps lit the dimness. On either side of the room was a row of board bunks, erected about two feet from the floor and covered with matting. At the head of each bunk was a wooden headrest, and every bed was filled.

Granville's eyes swept the room. Each smoker reclined on his side, head cradled on the headrest, as though lacking the energy to sit upright. Most held a long pipe with a bowl on one end over a spirit lamp, seemingly inhaling the fumes. Some held a long needle with a small brown blob on the end that Granville assumed was opium, and they were cooking it over the lamps.

As he watched, one man's ball of opium caught fire. It was quickly blown out, then the man caught the opium on the edge of the pipe and stretched it into long, gooey strings, holding those over the flame. Another smoker, having cooked the drug to his satisfaction, was using the needle to poke the opium into the bowl of his pipe. He then lay back with a grunt of satisfaction and began to draw smoke into his lungs.

Granville coughed, then coughed again, as the opium smoke seemed to crawl into his lungs and crouch there. He surveyed the room again, eyes moving quickly from one side to the other. Bertie was in one corner, talking to a short, thin man who was wringing his hands together, and Trent was beside him, eyes huge, but safe enough. Nearly all of the occupants of the bunks were Chinese and all were men, with one exception. She lay on a bunk at the far end of the room, wearing a bright yellow gown that seemed to vibrate in the dim light and holding an opium pipe to her lips.

Granville shot a look at the owner of the den, but he was still focused on Bertie. Hoping Trent would stay where he was, Granville crossed the uneven floor toward where the woman lay. As he got closer, he could see that she had dark hair. Was this Lizzie? Closer yet, and he could make out the languid expression on her face. His gaze was drawn in horror to the bunk beside hers, where the corpse of a thin, haggard Chinese man lay sprawled. She seemed entirely unaware of her neighbor's plight.

Only as Granville moved close enough to touch the pair could he see the slow, shallow breathing of the man he'd taken for dead. Turning his attention to the woman, he received another shock; he recognized her. Despite the slackness of her features, this was unmistakably Gracie, whom he'd last seen at 21 Dupont Street. "Gracie, is that you?"

Heavy eyelids lifted, and Gracie surveyed him through weary brown eyes. "I know you," she said. "You're that fancy man was asking after Jackson."

"That's me," Granville said wryly, amused despite his surroundings at her description. "Gracie, what are you doing here?"

She smiled a slow smile, but the distance in her eyes didn't change. "I find the pipe eases me after a long day. I don't smoke more than twenty pills, though. I'm no hophead." The effort of speaking seemed to exhaust her and her eyes started to drift shut.

"Gracie, do you know a woman named Lizzie?" Granville asked, his tone urgent enough to break through the opium fog. "I believe she smokes opium, too."

Her brow crinkled slightly. "Lizzie? No, no Lizzie." Her eyelids grew heavy again. "Guess I've taken too much this time. I'll sleep it off now."

Granville stood helpless as drug-induced sleep claimed her as deeply as the corpse-man on the next bed. Even in the dim light, he could see how thin Gracie's face was, the sharp angles of her cheekbones. From the little he knew about opium, its devotees cared more about smoke than about food, and often grew lean and haggard. Sometimes they even died, their bodies completely shut down.

"She is only woman here. Is it she you search for?"

The voice at his back made Granville start. He turned to face their guide. "No, this is not the woman I seek. Let's get out of here."

Bertie nodded and led the way to the door.

TWENTY-THREE

Wednesday, December 13, 1899

"I don't know why you insisted on coming here, Emily."

"They do make the best hot chocolate in town," Emily said. It didn't work. Clara was still scowling into her cup. Emily sipped her own tea and thought quickly. Clara was a dear, but when she was out of temper she could be trying. With Mr. Granville due to arrive at Stroh's any moment, she didn't have time to coax her friend out of the sulks. "Clara, I have a problem and I need your help."

Clara, who was clearly still uncertain that they should be keeping this rendezvous, looked at Emily curiously. "Why?"

"When I was searching Papa's study, I came across something I don't understand."

"What did you find?" Clara's curiosity had been piqued.

Emily had intended only to distract Clara, but suddenly she found herself wanting to tell her everything. The question of what to do about her father's secrets had been eating at her since the previous day, and she was still no closer to an answer. Perhaps in talking about it, she could make some sense of what she'd found. She looked across the table and drew in a deep breath. "I found several sheets of paper under his blotter. Mr. Jackson's name was written on one sheet, against several sums of money. Large sums of money."

"Oh, my goodness, Emily. Do you think your father put it there?"

"It was his handwriting."

"You don't think your father had anything to do with Mr. Jackson's death!" Clara sounded horrified.

"No, not that." Emily couldn't quite bring herself to admit that fear, it made it too real. "But it is suspicious, don't you think?"

"Perhaps they did business together."

"No, Papa said he didn't know him."

"Then why did your father say Mr. Jackson deserved to die?"

It kept coming back to this. Emily shook her head. "I don't know."

"Perhaps Mr. Jackson was shipping goods by rail and your Papa was keeping track of what he owed?"

"But then why deny knowing him?"

"Maybe Mr. Jackson dealt with a clerk rather than with your father, making a number of small shipments, but your father was keeping track of it all." Then Clara's eyes narrowed, and she gave Emily a suspicious look. "When did your Papa say he didn't know Mr. Jackson? It was not while I was in the room."

Caught, Emily looked sheepishly at her friend. "When he was talking to Mr. Granville at home."

"And you listened outside the door, didn't you? Oh, Emily!"

Emily defended herself. "It's the only way I find out anything that is going on, and you know it, Clara, so don't take that tone with me. Besides, you would do the same if you weren't afraid of what your mother would do if she caught you."

"I would not. It is not how a young lady behaves."

Emily emitted a sound very like a snort, and Clara looked at her in horror, then began to giggle. It was contagious, and soon both girls were giggling uncontrollably, holding gloved hands in front of their mouths to try to stifle the sounds.

Finally Clara stopped giggling long enough to say, "It's a good thing this is an unfashionable place for tea, or we would be tossed out," which implausible thought set them both giggling again.

"Good day, Miss Turner. Miss Miles."

The deep voice from behind her cut off Emily's giggles immediately. It was Mr. Granville's voice, and she was horrified that he'd seen her behaving so childishly. Turning in her chair, she summoned all the dignity she could muster. "Good afternoon, Mr. Granville. Won't you join us?"

Watching him, Emily realized she wished he'd not been so prompt. The trouble was she still didn't know what to think about her father's interest in Mr. Jackson, nor what to tell Mr. Granville about her discoveries. Emily's mind leaped from one thought to another. Was Papa innocent? If he was not, and she told what she'd learned, would she be betraying Papa? If she said nothing, and they hanged Mr. Granville's partner, wouldn't she feel intolerably guilty? If she told Mr. Granville, what would he do with the information? Could she trust him? What was the right thing to do?

"Have you learned anything that might be useful?"

Emily looked across the table and met his eyes. He looked tired, she thought, noting the shadows under his eyes. Well, there was one thing she could give him with a clear conscience. Reaching into her leather handbag, Emily pulled out the pages she'd taken from her father's files and handed them to him. "These are the manifests and passenger lists from the last voyage of the *Empress of India*."

"The one Bertie's cousin disappeared on?" He accepted the papers, looking intrigued. He moved his side plate out of the way and spread the pages on the table in front of him.

"Yes. I don't know if they'll be of any use to you, but Mr. Jackson's body was found the morning the *India* docked."

He stopped reading and looked up. "So it was. I'd never considered that particular timing. I assumed Jackson went to the docks to meet his killer. Now I wonder." His eyes met hers. "You are a pretty good detective, Miss Turner, as well as a very charming one."

Emily's instincts said she could trust him, and she was going to. It wasn't just his praise—which had made her blush—but the innate decency she sensed in him. Clara was watching her nervously, but suddenly Emily didn't care. "There is one other thing."

He was a gentleman, she was certain of it. "I would ask you to keep this in strictest confidence, to use it only if you must to save your partner."

"Emily, be careful," Clara warned.

Granville looked from one to the other, then focused on Emily. "You have my word."

She took a deep breath. "Under the blotter in his study, my father—" Her voice broke, and she stopped to take a deep breath, then continued. "He had a list of names, with dollars against them. It was a handwritten list, and Jackson's name was on it." She stopped, took another deep breath, then with an effort, finished. "And my father said, in front of Clara and me, that Mr. Jackson deserved to die."

"Many people thought the fellow deserved to die, but they didn't have anything to do with his death," Granville said. "I thank you for telling me." He waited for a moment, watching Emily's bent head, then, when she looked up again, he said, "Do you happen to remember exactly what was on the list?"

"Yes, there were five names: Jackson, Carver, Smythe, Ahrens, and Gipson. And eight amounts—three against Jackson, then one against each of the other names: against Jackson; five thousand, one thousand, and two thousand, then against the others; five hundred, fifteen hundred, one thousand, one thousand, and two thousand."

"I'm impressed you remembered it so clearly. Was there anything else?"

Emily shook her head. She couldn't bring herself to tell him about the other sheets of paper; it felt too much of a betrayal. She'd look into them herself. "Did you recognize any of the names besides those of Jackson and Gipson?"

"No, just those two. But how did you know I recognized Gipson's name?"

"I saw your reaction. How do you know him?"

"You are very quick. Gipson was a business associate of Jackson's. He is a speculator and a banker."

"So the figures my father had written could have been amounts invested."

"Yes, or amounts loaned. I'll look into the other three names and any possible connection with Jackson. I may indeed learn something."

"And what of you?" she asked. "Have you learnt anything since I saw you last?"

His eyes grew cold and distant, and for a moment Emily thought he wasn't going to answer. This caused her to feel both anger and alarm. Surely he wasn't going to shut her out now, not when she'd just trusted him with such upsetting and—even worse—illicitly obtained information.

"I spoke with your medium," he said, his face still grim.

"And what did the spirits say?"

"Not much. It seems I have a dark aura, and they are wary of me."

"How odd."

"I think so, too. And it makes me very curious why she told you what she did, and where she's getting her information from."

Emily nodded. "Perhaps I should pay her another visit. She seemed to like my aura."

"Or the color of your coin."

She smiled at his dry tone. "True. But then your coin is the same as mine, and no spirits spoke to you."

"But Emily, I don't want to go there again!" Clara protested.

"I think Emily would appreciate it if you would go with her, Clara. It would help me immensely if the two of you could find out a little more about Mrs. Merchant."

"Is there anything in particular you'd like us to ask her?" Emily asked him.

"I would like to know her connection with Jackson, but please don't ask anything that will endanger either of you."

"We'll be careful," Emily assured him.

"If your medium is involved in something illegal, she may overreact to any perceived threat. I'd never forgive myself if you came to harm."

"You think we might be in danger?"

"I have every faith in you, Miss Turner," he said gravely.

Feeling she now had a right to pursue her curiosity further, Emily leaned forward and asked, "What else have you learned?"

"That my partner has a second sister in town—whom he's undoubtedly protecting and who might have worked for Jackson. I'm searching for her now." He offered this news as if she'd earned it.

Emily watched his expression carefully. There was something he wasn't telling her.

"You think she might be the dark-haired woman, don't you? The one who shot Mr. Jackson."

She was quick, this little Emily, thought Granville as he debated just what to tell her. But she still seemed far too innocent to be involved in this case. He wasn't about to turn down her offer of help, though, not when it came to saving Scott. "Yes, I do think my partner's sister may be the one who shot Jackson. And he believes so, as well, though he won't admit it."

Emily's lips pressed together and she looked down for a moment. "Poor man. But what are you going to do?"

"I am going to find Jackson's killer and get Sam Scott released from jail."

TWENTY-FOUR

Granville eyed the whiskey set out on the bar in front of him. It was early for drinking, even for him. He threw the shot back, feeling the welcome burning down the back of his throat. Signaling the bartender for another, he glanced around him. The Mermaid was like most of the other bars on Alexander Street: narrow, dingy, and smoky. The main thing was it served tolerable whiskey and also, at the moment, was quiet.

Pulling out the pages Emily had given him, Granville frowned at first one list, then the next. He didn't see anything pertinent, but who knew what he might be missing? He kept thinking about the connection that he had missed and that Emily had seen so easily—Jackson had been killed the night before the *India* docked. He hadn't even been looking for a link between the silk they had been guarding and the man Scott was accused of killing. Hell, he'd been on the docks that night himself, talked to Scott about the *India* coming in the next day, but still he somehow failed to see the clue that was right in front of him.

He'd been looking at things in far too narrow a focus, chasing disconnected bits of information, Granville thought.

Now that he had a potential link between Jackson and the *India*, where would it take him? There were no names he recognized in the passenger ledgers. He'd jotted down the list of names Emily had given him. Jackson. Gipson. Carver. Smythe. Ahrens. What did they have in common with each other, and with Jackson?

He could ask Benton about the three he didn't recognize, but it might be more entertaining to have a chat with Gipson. He hadn't yet confronted Gipson with trying to run him out of town, either. Time to collect Trent and do just that.

"Gipson's office is the one down at the end." Granville said.

Trent's eyes were wide, but his tone was skeptical. "And you expect him to see you?"

"He'll see me."

"Is that why you're carrying a gun? You know that's illegal, right?"

"Not if I'm concerned for my safety, it isn't." Opening the door into the narrow antechamber, Granville was greeted by the sight of two bruisers seated with a deck of cards on a low table between them. "Trent, I believe these gentlemen are acquaintances of ours," he said, walking into the room.

At this, both men leaped to their feet, hands rising into fists.

"I'm here to see your employer, not to settle scores. We have some questions to ask him."

Uncertain what to do, Gipson's men hesitated, obviously unused to thinking for themselves.

"Just tell him Granville wants a few minutes of his time. We'll wait right here. Peacefully."

Less than ten minutes later, Granville opened the heavy door and strolled into Gipson's office. Dusk had fallen, casting shadows in the corners of the paneled room. Cigar smoke filled the air and wreathed thickly above the banker's lamp set on the edge of the heavy desk. At their entrance, Gipson dropped a cigar ash on a ledger he was checking. He brushed it off, closed the ledger, and looked up. "Gentlemen," he said. "And what can I do for you?"

"Just this. You and Jackson were doing pretty well before someone shot him, weren't you?"

"I don't know what you mean."

"Oh, I think you do. But weren't you concerned that Benton would find out and do something about it? He's not someone who tolerates claim jumpers like you."

Gipson's eyes narrowed. "I have no idea what you're talking about."

"No? You and Jackson weren't partners? You really have no idea what he was doing down on the docks the night he was killed?"

"None." A muscle twitched beside Gipson's right eye.

"None at all?" Granville let a smile crease his face. This was starting to be fun. "It's sad when they lie so badly, isn't it?" he said in an aside to Trent, never taking his eyes off Gipson. "So you don't know anything about your partnership with Jackson. How about Carver? Smythe? Or perhaps Ahrens? Any of those names ring your bells?"

Gipson's thin lips tightened. He was silent.

Granville laughed again. "Now, now. Try to be civilized. That is what you're pretending to be, isn't it? You may fool little old ladies and those imbecile enough to invest money with you, but you can't fool me. I know the kind of underhanded game you run as well as any man alive." He showed him the gun he'd just pulled.

Gipson's hands clenched. "You force your way into my office, pull a gun on me, and accuse me of being uncivilized? I expected better, even from you, Granville. You were at least raised a gentleman, were you not?"

"You're the one who has been trying to have me killed, Gipson, and as a gentleman, I call it highly uncivilized."

Gipson attempted a sneer. "If it weren't for your gun, we wouldn't be conversing at all."

With a grin, Granville raised the revolver so it was pointing right between Gipson's eyes. "Thank you for reminding me. Now, what is the nature of your dealings with Carver, Smythe, and Ahrens?"

"They are investors." Gipson still maintained his sneer.

"I see. What kind of investors, Gipson?"

"They invest in mines, among other things."

"And those other things, did they involve Jackson?"

"Some of them may have."

"And what kinds of things would those have been?" When no answer was forthcoming, Granville pulled back the hammer, the sound loud in the quiet room. "What kinds of things, Gipson?"

A bead of sweat appeared on the man's forehead. "You wouldn't shoot me. You haven't the nerve."

"No?"

Gipson met Granville's eyes, staring long and hard. "Importing," he said at last. "We formed a syndicate to import goods."

"Now, that wasn't so difficult, was it?" Granville said, assessing the information. "Benton didn't know about this syndicate of yours, did he?"

"No. It's a private matter."

"And Benton would not have been pleased." Gipson was silent. "Which is why you were so reluctant to talk to me about it." Gipson's hands clenched even tighter, but he still said nothing. "And what did this syndicate import?"

"Various goods. It depended on the markets, on what was in demand."

Granville's voice went silky smooth and his hand gripped the gun more tightly. "You are lying to me again, Gipson. That isn't smart." He sighted down the blued barrel. "And don't think of shouting for your apes out there."

Granville was watching Gipson's expression carefully as he spoke. "It's my hunch you've been bringing in contraband in the *Empresses*. Now, what could be expensive enough to be worth the risk? Opium, perhaps?"

Gipson stared back at him, face impassive. "I don't know what you are talking about."

"No? You don't know anything about smuggling opium?" It was a guess, but it fit the facts.

"Opium is legal," Gipson said, his voice cold.

"Not if you are smuggling it to the States to avoid the duty, it isn't. San Francisco, perhaps, or New York? How were you and Jackson shipping the opium across the border?"

The muscle beside Gipson's eye began to twitch in time with his heartbeat.

"Yes, that's it, isn't it?" Granville sighted his revolver between Gipson's eyes again. "Why did you have Jackson killed? Was he trying to collect what you owed him or something equally unacceptable?"

"I didn't kill Jackson."

"I didn't say you did. I think you arranged to have him killed. What do you say to that?"

"You're wrong."

"Am I?" Granville watched Gipson's tense expression for a moment. "We'll see. Why did you try to have me killed?"

Gipson glanced at the gun, then met Granville's eyes. His eyes were calm again, his voice smooth. "I simply wanted you to leave town."

I'm sure you did, Granville thought, preferably feetfirst. "Why?"

"You know too much about my . . . past," Gipson said, one eye on the revolver. "I have built a certain reputation here, and I intend to protect that reputation."

Trent started to say something. But at a look from Granville, he subsided.

Granville nodded slowly. "For now, we need to reach an agreement. I won't betray your past." I won't have to, once I pin conspiracy to murder Jackson on you, he thought. "And in return, you stop trying to kill me."

"Trying to run you out of town," Gipson corrected him.

"You call off your men. Do you agree?"

"You have a deal." But it was one he didn't look happy about making.

Granville stood, keeping his revolver in his hand. He didn't trust Gipson's word, but their deal just might buy enough time to point the police his way. "Come on, Trent. We have work to do."

TWENTY-FIVE

Thursday, December 14, 1899

Breakfast found the Turners seated around the big mahogany table in the dining room. "Don't pick at your food, Emily. And sit up straight." This from her mother.

With a sigh, Emily put down her fork and straightened her spine a fraction.

"That's better." Her mother looked more closely. "You look pale, dear, and you aren't eating. Is something wrong?"

"No, Mama, I am fine," Emily said. In truth, she had not been able to stop worrying over why her father had those notes on the shipping of silk. "I probably just need some fresh air."

"Perhaps it will warm up by midday, and you can go out then," her mother said.

Emily glanced toward the window. The light looked thin and gray, as if it was about to snow again. She looked at the head of the table, where Papa sat engrossed in his newspaper.

"Papa?" she said.

He looked up, frowning. "Yes?"

"I've been thinking about the silk trains you were telling Clara and me about."

"You have?" The frown disappeared, replaced by a smile. "I had no idea you were interested, Emily."

"I thought it was fascinating, the silk coming all the way from Japan, the race to get it to New York. Tell me, who is responsible for making sure the silk arrives on time?"

He'd put down his paper and leaned forward. "Well, I am, in a way. I advise the head office in Toronto of any problems with the routes of the trains. The train before last was delayed in the Fraser Canyon because of a washout. Now I've recommended that we have a crew on standby when a silk train is scheduled. I just got word yesterday that this suggestion has been approved and will be implemented as soon as possible." He nodded, pleased with himself.

"And what happens if your silk trains are too slow?"

"Well, then our customers lose business to their competition, which then means we lose their business. But our *Empresses* are the fastest ships on the Oriental route; as long as our trains get through, no one can beat us." He resumed scrutiny of his newspaper.

That could explain his notes on the shipping times, on the loading and unloading of silk, Emily thought. And he didn't sound like a man who was betraying his employer; he took far too much personal pride in their successes for that. So probably those notes were innocent, she thought with relief, reaching for a slice of cold toast and slathering it with Cook's homemade preserve. That still left the list with Jackson's name on it, but there could be a dozen good explanations for that, and she had every faith that Mr. Granville would find the right one.

Two hours later, Emily stood shivering as she waited for Clara. Just as she was about to give up, Clara arrived, out of breath and full of excuses.

"Clara, you're always late. It doesn't matter when it's warm out, but I'm freezing. Come on, I don't want to waste anymore time. We need to be off to Mrs. Merchant's."

"Emily, I don't trust her."

Emily laughed. "I don't, either, but that doesn't matter. I just need to ask her a few more questions."

Mrs. Merchant showed no surprise at seeing them. "Welcome, young ladies, welcome," she said. "Only two of you today? But where is your other cousin?"

"She was unwell," said Emily without even thinking. For some reason, she wanted this woman to know as little as possible about herself and her friends. Clara looked slightly startled at such a blatant untruth.

"I'm sorry to hear that," the medium responded. "Perhaps the spirits will have some advice for her on regaining her health. Please, be seated."

"I need to speak with the spirit of Clive Jackson again," Emily said.

"He seems very popular, the late Mr. Jackson."

"Oh?" said Emily. "Have others wanted to speak with him also?"

The medium's eyes glittered. "I cannot speak of my clients to each other, my dear," she said. "Now, close your eyes and I will see what I can do."

Emily closed her eyes, which only made her more aware of the fusty smell of the room. It seemed to be getting worse, almost as if it emanated from somewhere near them. Peeking out from under nearly closed eyelids, she looked around her, but nothing looked any different than it had on her previous visit. Drawing in a deeper breath, she nearly gagged when the odor seemed to intensify. What was it?

The medium's voice distracted Emily. "Spirits, we seek your guidance," she intoned. "Is Clive Jackson present?"

Emily could feel herself growing tense, waiting for a response, and when Clara's cold hand crept into hers, she started. Just as she thought the session was going to be a failure, a deep voice filled the room.

"What do you wish of me?" it said.

"Is that Mr. Jackson?"

"It is." The deep voice seemed to have no point of origin.

Emily was watching the medium carefully from under lowered eyelids. Neither the woman's lips nor the muscles of her throat moved; if it was a hoax, she must have an accomplice. Yet no one knew that she and Clara had come here today. Emily cleared her throat nervously. "May I ask you several questions?"

"You may."

"Why did you go to the wharves the night you were killed?"

There was a pause, then an answer came: "I often liked to stroll along the wharves at night and smoke a quiet cigar, especially when there were ships in port."

In December? Emily thought. "So you didn't go to meet anyone?"

"No."

The terse syllable was not encouraging. Whether it was really the spirit of Mr. Jackson or an accomplice of the medium, he didn't seem to like her question. "Did you see anyone while you were walking?"

"No one. The docks were deserted."

"Except for your killer, you mean."

"Yes, except for my murderess."

Whoever he was, he was lying, but it seemed prudent to stop now.

Drawing in a deep breath and hoping her voice didn't sound as wavery as she felt, she said, "Thank you for coming, Mr. Jackson. I have no more questions."

There was a long silence, then the medium shook herself and said in a bewildered voice, "Oh, are we done? Has he left already?"

"Yes, just a moment ago."

"And did you get the answers you came for, dear?"

"Yes, thank you. I am satisfied." She just wanted to get herself and Clara out of the stifling parlor as quickly as possible. She'd think about the significance of what had been said later.

"Well, that's good, my dear. So many of my clients leave with questions still troubling them."

"No, all mine were answered," said Emily, rising. She put a coin on the table. "I thank you. Come, Clara."

The *Daily World*, one of Vancouver's two local dailies, reported arrivals and departures of prominent locals and visitors, which was a handy feature, Granville mused, when you were looking for someone. This morning's paper, for instance, had told him that both Carver and Ahrens had left town, departing by train to Toronto the previous day. He found it interesting that two of Jackson's former partners had left town. It was especially worth noting, because according to the local gossip he'd uncovered, their departures had been sudden rather than planned. Something to do with Jackson's death, perhaps?

Aloysius Smythe, the third partner, was still in town, however. Granville and Trent were currently kicking their heels in his lavish outer office. Every so often the clerk who was sitting at the cluttered desk to one side of the door would pause in the act of dipping his pen into the inkwell and survey them over the top of his glasses, as if to confirm that they were still waiting.

The hush of a door opening on well-oiled hinges focused Granville's attention. Smythe appeared; he was a thin man, somewhat below medium height, and unnaturally pale. In the dove-gray morning jacket and trousers he wore, he looked almost ghostly. He looked from Granville to Trent, then over at his clerk.

"Mr. Smythe, these gentlemen came to see you. I told them you might not have time, but they insisted on waiting."

Smythe's pale eyes returned to Granville and Trent, scanning them without expression.

"You might as well come in," he said, turning and preceding them into the office. "I can give you a few minutes."

"Why did you wish to see me?" Smythe asked when they were seated. "I gather it isn't about wanting to make investments."

"Why do you say that?" Granville's self-assurance caused a flicker of doubt to cross Smythe's face, and the businessman scanned Granville more closely. His gaze flicked to Trent, quickly dismissed him, and moved back to Granville. He gave a satisfied smile and sat back in his chair. Picking up the gold pen on his desk, Smythe ran it through his fingers. "Suffice it to say I have met your kind before. If you have a question, ask it," he said.

My kind, is it? Granville thought, torn between anger and amusement. So he had been summed up as a remittance man, had he? One of those younger sons, sent to the Colonies with an allowance, allowing the family to forget about them. In some ways, Smythe wasn't far wrong; he was the youngest and he had caused his father no end of grief, but he wasn't dependent on the family largess. He'd stand or fall on his own. "Appearances can be so deceptive. Don't you find? Take Clive Jackson, for instance," he said, and had the satisfaction of seeing Smythe flinch. "I understand you were his partner? Not a likely association, on the face of it."

Annoyed, their host dropped the pen he was toying with. "We were hardly partners."

"No?"

"I barely knew the man."

"But you invested money with him."

"With Jackson? Where did you hear that? Certainly not."

"No? Gipson seemed to think the five of you were partners. But perhaps you have another word for it?"

A silence followed, and Granville let it drag on. Before long, Smythe would be saying anything, just to fill the emptiness. Guilt acted on respectable men this way—Smythe may have had shady dealings, but Granville judged him no natural fraudster.

Finally Smythe spoke. "It was an investment syndicate. We put up the money. Jackson had the contacts and took care of the details."

"Details? Oh, you mean he stole the opium, transported it illegally, and smuggled it across the border."

"Buying and selling opium is legal."

Granville had heard this before. "Certainly, if you have licenses and pay the appropriate duties, but that's hardly what your little syndicate was doing, was it?"

"What is it you want? Money?"

Granville shook his head. "No. I want Jackson's killer."

"Jackson's killer? Why?"

"I believe that is my business."

"I can't help you. I don't know who killed Jackson."

"You must have some idea who would want him dead."

Smythe gave him a bitter smile. "You may put my name on top of that list. But I didn't kill him."

"No? Then why wish his demise?"

"That's personal."

"I am after a killer. Nothing is personal."

"Look, Mr. Granville, or whoever you are, you aren't the police. You have no right to burst in here and ask me these questions."

"Perhaps you'd prefer that I alert the police. I'm sure Constable Craddock would be happy to ask you questions." Craddock was the last person Granville would bring in, but his was the only name that came to mind.

A muscle in Smythe's jaw jerked. "There is no need to bring in the law."

"Then tell me why you wanted Jackson dead."

Every vestige of color drained from Smythe's face, making it even paler than before. His fingers laced tightly together on the clear desktop.

"Look, I have no interest in what Jackson had on you. My only concern is to find out who wanted him dead."

"How do I know I can trust you?"

"You don't have much choice."

Smythe closed his eyes for a moment. "Blackmail." The word sounded forced. "The swine was blackmailing me."

"Is that why you invested with him?"

Smythe gave a tiny jerk of his head.

"And the other syndicate members? Was he blackmailing them, too?"

Smythe nodded.

"Even Gipson?"

"I would assume so. Why should Gipson be any different?"

"Do you know what he had on the others?"

Smythe shook his head, thin lips held tight.

Granville sensed Smythe was being honest with him, and that he would tell him nothing about the blackmail itself. "What about Carver and Ahrens? I understand they left town rather suddenly. Did either of them kill Jackson?"

Smythe shook his head. "No. They are as relieved as I am to see him dead, but we're not violent men."

"Just thieves and smugglers."

Smythe gave him a nasty look. "That was Jackson's doing. And he was cheating us, too—skimming money. We were just in the importing business."

"Importing as in smuggling opium to New York and San Francisco?"

"Look, let's end this. You want Jackson's killer, I can't give him to you."

Smythe referred to the killer as a man, Granville noted. "Then what can you give me?"

"Money."

"I don't want your money."

"What, then?"

"More information. I need to get close to Jackson."

"Jackson's dead."

"So I can't very well ask him, can I? I'm asking you. What was Jackson doing down on the docks that night?"

"We had a shipment coming in."

"On the *Empress of India*?"

"That's right."

"Who was Jackson's contact?"

"That I don't know."

"Was he on the ship or on shore?"

"Knowing Jackson, probably both."

"Do you know any of Jackson's contacts? Or how the opium was sent out?"

"That did not concern me, nor did his associates."

"What about Gipson? Did he know?"

Smythe looked surprised. "Gipson? Why would he know? He's just an investor like the rest of us."

Not quite, thought Granville, but he let it go. If Smythe actually believed that, there was little more the man could tell him. He rose and inclined his head. "If I find you've been lying, I'll be back," he said. Then, gesturing for Trent to follow him, he crossed through the outer office and stepped out into the mist, right into a blow that knocked him to the ground.

TWENTY-SIX

Emily stood in the doorway of the cluttered *Daily World* newsroom. There was no one visible except a red-haired young man seated at a desk in the far corner. She headed his way, Clara trailing behind her.

The sleeves of the youthful reporter's shirt were pushed up above his elbows, and his tie hung askew. As though feeling her gaze, he looked up. If he was surprised to see two well-bred society girls standing there, it didn't show. He looked to be someone who took everything in his stride.

"Ladies. How may I help you?"

"We are looking for Mr. Timothy O'Hearn?"

"You found him."

Emily studied his eager expression, wondering whether there was any point in talking to him and how he would react to her interest in a murder. "I am Miss Turner, and this is Miss Miles. I'm here about the murder of Mr. Clive Jackson."

O'Hearn looked astonished, then disappointed. "But I didn't cover that story. You need to talk to Mr. Thompson. That murder is his story."

"But you wrote about the recent arrival of the *Empress of India*, didn't you? And the loss of that poor Chinese man? I'm sure it was you whose name was on that article."

"Emily, that was Bertie's cousin, wasn't it? Didn't you tell me he was lost from that ship?" Clara asked. She still looked uncomfortable about finding herself in such surroundings, but she had been following the discussion carefully.

Emily ignored her.

O'Hearn looked at Emily and frowned. "But I don't understand. What does my article have to do with Jackson's death? Or are you following up on the disappearance of the Oriental? And who is Bertie?" He paused, and his eyes narrowed. "Hold on a minute . . . It was the same day, wasn't it? Jackson was killed the day the *India* docked."

Emily nodded, pleased he'd seen the same connection she had. He might know nothing about Mr. Jackson, but he had seemed to know his way around the wharves, and she needed someone with that knowledge as much as she needed someone who could connect seemingly unrelated facts. "Yes. I wondered what was happening at the docks that night, and why Mr. Jackson was there at all. The article on the murder didn't say, and if Mr. Thompson had known he would have said, wouldn't he?"

"Probably. But why are you interested? I mean, they have the killer in jail, right?"

"The police think so."

"But you don't?"

She shook her head.

"Why not?"

Emily had given considerable thought as to how much to tell this reporter about Mr. Granville, and had decided it was better to keep him in the dark for now. It would probably intrigue him, she decided. "I'd rather not disclose that."

And she was right. "A woman of mystery, eh?" He grinned at Emily. "You've just found yourself a reporter."

She smiled back. "Good. Where will you start?"

"Why not with the missing cousin? And who is Bertie?"

He was tenacious, which was probably a good thing, but she wanted him focused on Mr. Jackson's killer. "No one who can't wait."

Undaunted, O'Hearn pulled out a notebook. Pencil poised, he told her, "I still need the facts."

"Oh, very well," Emily said, recognizing a spirit as inquisitive as her own. "Bertie is our Chinese houseboy. His cousin was to have arrived on the *India* that same day but was apparently lost at sea."

O'Hearn nodded. "Yes, they think he fell overboard."

"Except that Bertie's cousin was afraid of water and would never willingly have gone up on deck, and he had a great deal of raw opium with him, which also appears to have vanished."

O'Hearn let out a long, low whistle. "This could be a great story."

"Except you can't publish anything, not until we know what happened."

He nodded slowly. "If it *was* foul play, we wouldn't want to print anything that might alert the perpetrators."

Emily let out a relieved breath. For a moment, she'd wondered if she'd told him too much. "Exactly," she said.

"Besides, it will make a much better story when the mystery is solved, especially if the disappearance ties into Jackson's death."

"Do you see the two events as related?"

"Probably not, but what if they were? That's a big story, the kind that makes reputations around here."

"How do you see the possible connection?"

At this point Clara, who had been watching them both with fascination, spoke up. "It's what you've been saying—it's about the *India*."

O'Hearn gave her an approving glance. "Right. And the timing is interesting, since the missing man wasn't discovered until the ship had docked, when Jackson was already dead."

"But you don't know that Mr. Jackson had anything to do with the *India*," Emily said.

"He was in the area. Why else would he be there?"

She looked at him smugly. "My point exactly. Why was Mr. Jackson on the docks?"

O'Hearn grinned. "OK, so that's where I'll start. I'll go down to the docks, see what I can uncover."

"We'll come with you," Emily said, then laughed at the expressions of horrified disapproval that both O'Hearn and Clara turned her way.

"It isn't safe," O'Hearn blurted out. "Especially not when it's getting foggy."

"That's just a mist. Besides, it is still daylight, and you are planning to go."

"But I'm a man," O'Hearn said, as if that answered everything.

And perhaps in his eyes it did. It wasn't an argument Emily had time to take on, not with Mr. Scott's life at stake. "Very well," she said, with a delicate sigh that had Clara looking at her askance. "When will you be able to tell me what you've found?"

O'Hearn looked horrified again. Clara only rolled her eyes. Emily made a mental note never to underestimate her friend. Before

O'Hearn could argue, Emily said, "After all, I'm supplying you with important information. Surely I at least deserve to know what you've found."

O'Hearn didn't look convinced. "I suppose so," he said. "Why don't we meet here tomorrow afternoon?"

"I have a better idea," Emily said. "Why don't you tell me to whom you are going to talk. Then I'll know which of Mr. Jackson's former associates I should be talking to."

"But you can't," O'Hearn said. "It isn't safe."

"Surely you don't expect me to sit quietly and wait until you return with news?"

Since this was clearly what he had been expecting, it left him uncertain how to proceed. "It's too dangerous," he tried out. "No one will talk to a woman. Not a chance," he finished more confidently.

Luckily for Emily, it seemed O'Hearn had grown up without sisters. "Very well, then. We'll just accompany you now and let you ask the questions. It will be much safer."

O'Hearn turned slightly green. Emily was enjoying herself too much to stop now, but Clara took pity on him. "Why don't you meet us for tea tomorrow, at Stroh's? Perhaps at two o'clock?" O'Hearn nodded in relief, and Clara looked over at Emily and winked. Emily ignored her, standing to shake hands with O'Hearn.

"It's been a pleasure, Miss Turner. Miss Miles," he said as he walked them to the door.

TWENTY-SEVEN

Granville opened his eyes to utter darkness. His mind felt numb; he couldn't see or hear. What's wrong with me? was his first panicked thought. Then, as his brain started to sort out the information his other senses were processing, "Where am I?" He said it aloud, just to see if he could hear himself. To his great relief, he not only heard the words, but he also heard a faint echo of them. He must at least be alive, he figured.

He was lying on his back in a confined space. It felt as if freezing water had seeped into his clothes and all around him was the odor of damp and mold, underlaid with the stench of sewage and rotting fish. From the smell, he was somewhere near False Creek, probably Chinatown or close to it. He tried to lift his head and instantly regretted it, as a red stab of pain shot through his head.

Falling back onto the damp ground, he took several deep breaths, waiting for the pain to subside, then with one hand he carefully felt the large lump on the back of his head. He then felt for his gun, encountering the empty holster with no sense of surprise. Whoever had hit him would have taken the gun. He searched his foggy brain. He remembered leaving Smythe's office, but what had happened next? Another memory returned, and Granville sat bolt upright, then clutched at his head. Where was Trent?

"Trent?" he called. It came out as a cracked whisper. Running his tongue around dry lips, he tried again. "Trent? Are you here?"

Nothing. Not even a rat scuttled in the thick silence. If Trent was here, he was unconscious or worse. Cautiously Granville stretched his right hand into the darkness, feeling a rough board wall less than six inches from where he lay. It ran up about five feet, where it intersected with more boards above him. His gut tightened. Stretching out his left hand confirmed his suspicions; he was in a cellar, and he was alone. So where was the kid?

Perhaps they'd grabbed him and left Trent, Granville thought. They hadn't bothered to tie him up, which meant they didn't expect him to escape. They might not have worried about the kid if it was Granville they were interested in.

Granville swallowed, trying to bring moisture to his parched mouth and throat. How had his captors gotten him here? It had still been daylight when he'd left Smythe's office, so anyone carrying an unconscious man would have stood out. Who had abducted him like this, and why? Gipson was the obvious choice, but hadn't they sealed a temporary truce?

There had to be a pattern, a connection he was missing. Why wasn't he dead? Why just confine him? It made no sense, unless . . . He did a mental calculation. Scott had five days left before his trial and almost certain hanging. What if whoever had grabbed him didn't need Granville dead, just out of the way until after the trial? Once

Scott was hanged, they'd expect Granville to give up the search for Jackson's killer, but they'd be wrong, he thought. If Scott died, he'd not rest until the killers were also dead. But still, there were only five days left.

The thought galvanized him. Ignoring the hot spear in his brain, he got his feet under him, then slumped back against the wall behind him until his breath returned. Gritting his teeth, he moved forward onto his knees and crawled around the confines of the enclosure, testing the strength of the walls as he went. They held firm, not giving at all until he reached what had to be the door, a two-foot-wide section of planks that ran vertically. He ran his fingers around its edges. The hinges and its fastening were on the outside, beyond his reach. Using his legs to provide momentum, Granville slammed his shoulder into the door.

Nothing; no movement, no give. When the fireworks in his head subsided, he tried again, and again, until finally the lack of any change in the door's structure convinced him he was wasting his time. Granville collapsed on the floor, out of breath and dripping with sweat. When his head had stopped swimming and he had his breath back, he began to yell. He yelled until he was too hoarse to yell any longer, then tried whistling, but his mouth was too dry for more than a couple of halfhearted efforts. There was no response.

Lying exhausted in the thick darkness, Granville began to curse, using every pithy phrase he'd learned in the Klondike. Was this how it would end, with him helplessly imprisoned while Scott died? In his head, he heard the echo of William's voice, at its most condescending, "Whenever things get too difficult, you give up." As his brother's words repeated themselves in his mind, the truth of them a matter for dispute at any moment but now, he stared into the blackness.

It was Edward's agonized face he saw, Edward's hand clutching the pistol. They had grown up together, the two of them. Yet when Edward needed him the most, Granville had failed him. Oh, he'd said all the right things, but at the crucial moment he hadn't defended his oldest friend, and polite society had condemned Edward for cheating at cards. Edward couldn't live with the shame.

Granville had hated himself that day. He still did. He'd failed Edward, failed him when it most mattered, and there were no second chances. That knowledge had driven him to the Yukon, but he hadn't left his guilt behind. He couldn't get Edward's face out of his mind, or the condemnation in Julia's eyes when he'd told her her brother was dead. Edward and Julia were both there, staring at him in the darkness.

Granville swallowed hard. There was nothing he could do for Edward, but Scott was still alive, and he wasn't going to give up on him. He wouldn't let another friend die. Closing his eyes, Granville took a slow breath, then another, closing out the pounding in his head, the aching in his shoulder, the fear he felt for Scott, the hopelessness. He still had five days, 120 hours.

After striving and failing to see something, anything in the darkness, Granville began to examine by touch every inch of his cage. There had to be a weakness here somewhere that he could exploit. He was going over everything for the second time when he found it; the boards to the left of the door did not quite meet the floor, and the ground beneath them seemed softer.

He began to dig, scrabbling in the hard earth with his hands and then with the toe of his shoe, which he'd removed. What seemed like endless hours later, he'd excavated for himself the ability to stretch one bleeding hand beneath the wall, but it wasn't enough; he couldn't reach anything. With an exhausted sigh, Granville slumped back against the wall. If he didn't rest, he couldn't go on—and he had to go on.

Taking a series of slow, deep breaths, Granville resumed digging. His shoulders felt like they were on fire and his hands had gone numb, but it didn't matter. Nothing mattered except getting out. He deepened and widened the hole he'd already made, then tried reaching through it again. Now he could reach the lower door hinge, but he couldn't get any leverage on it. He kept digging.

On the next try, his arm went through up to the elbow, and he could just grip the top part of the pin that ran through the door hinge. Numbed and frozen, he grabbed and twisted, not expecting any response, but the pin moved under his hand. Stunned, he tried again and it gave a little more. He twisted again and pulled, then repeated the motion. The pin came free, the hinge separated. Granville withdrew his arm and leaned back against the wall, breathing heavily; now he had a chance of breaking the door free.

Taking a deep breath and bracing himself, Granville threw himself against the lower part of the door, then again, and again. The door shuddered but held. He hit it again and there was a loud creaking. Ramming his aching shoulder into the door again brought a louder creaking, followed by a loud crack. Granville continued to throw himself against the door until suddenly it gave under his weight, and he found himself sprawled in a shallow puddle in the outer room, slimy water seeping into his clothes. At the far end of this room, Granville could see a sliver of faint daylight. Gathering his feet under him, he gave a heave and was up and running toward the light, his feet splashing through puddles.

The air was cold and clammy and somewhere water was dripping. As he ran, he listened for any sound that would indicate the return of his captors but heard nothing. He ran down a narrow hallway, emerging into an alley. The mist had thickened into a dense fog, obscuring sound, visibility, any hope of recognizing where he was.

Granville hesitated, looking one way and then the other; he couldn't see a thing. He turned left and kept running, watching and listening hard. At best he could see two feet in front of him, and he could only hope the men who had abducted him were nowhere within hearing distance. He burst out into a street, which seemed largely deserted. Instinctively he headed left again, his feet pounding against the board sidewalk. Before he even registered a presence, he ran straight into a damp figure and bounced back a foot.

"Granville?"

"Trent? Is that you?"

Before the boy could say anything, Granville put his hand over Trent's mouth. "All right. You can tell me everything, but we need to get away from here. I don't know if they're likely to come after me."

Trent's eyes widened and he nodded vigorously.

An hour later they were in Granville's room, biting into hearty sandwiches of roast beef and sourdough, bottles of beer on the battered pine table under the window. "I still don't understand why we had to eat in your rooms," Trent complained. "The saloon is much friendlier."

"Because we can have a private conversation here. And because until we determine who is trying to kill me, I am going to keep a low profile."

"Oh."

"Were you able to see who grabbed me?"

"Not really. Just the backs of two of them, and not very clearly because of the mist. Then another one of them hit me and I don't remember anything else. But I wasn't out for very long, so I started looking for you."

It wasn't much help. They were both lucky their heads were so hard, but what was it all in service of? He'd been assuming Scott's

arrest was due to incompetence on the part of the police, but . . .
maybe someone didn't want him to find the real killer. Had Scott
been set up? Granville swallowed his last mouthful of sandwich and
stood up abruptly. "Come on, Trent."

"Where are we going?"

"The jail."

When the one-armed jailer opened the barred door of the cell,
Scott was seated on one narrow bunk, his head in his hands.
Knowing that the clock was ticking just made it worse. Bad as it was
to see Scott trapped like this, being forced to watch him hang was
unimaginable. Edward's face swam through Granville's mind and he
forcibly shoved the memory away.

At the slamming of the door, Scott looked up. He looked surprised and none too pleased to see them, then he took in Granville's
bandaged hands. "Granville? What are you doing here?"

"I had to find out if you were still alive and kicking before I wasted
anymore time trying to save your flea-bitten hide."

"Well, the bedbugs here are trying to eat me alive, and they're
making a good feast of it, but I ain't seen a flea for a while now."

Granville gave a mock shudder. "Rather you than me."

"I can order some sent down from Dawson City if you're missing
them?"

"Instead of that, why not answer some questions for me?"

Scott's eyes narrowed. "Go ahead."

"Could you have been set up? Someone seems to want to keep you
in jail."

"Why do you say that?"

"I was grabbed and tossed into a locked cellar. I think they were
planning to keep me there until after you were hanged."

Scott went white under the pallor he'd gained after nearly a week in jail, but he choked out a laugh and shook his head at Granville. "That explains why you look so bad. I didn't like to ask."

Granville ignored the attempt at levity. "Well, think about it."

"Think about what?

"We both found the body, but you're the one who's in jail. As far as I know, no one else was even questioned, and the police don't appear to be looking for anyone else. Otherwise why arrest you?"

Scott's lips tightened. "You're wrong."

"I don't think so. Whoever killed Jackson seems to have made sure you'd be the one accused of it. As if they knew you would turn noble and refuse to clear yourself." He looked at his friend. "How would they know that, Scott?"

"I don't know what you're talking about."

"You know exactly what I am talking about. Who are you trying to protect? Your sister Lizzie?"

Scott's eyes met Granville's then slid away.

"What if she isn't guilty, Scott, and someone has convinced you she is? I've heard the same rumor, and Frances is certain it's true." He watched Scott's face closely. "Unless it's a story Frances devised, and she's the one you are protecting?"

"Hell, no," Scott said, then fell silent again.

"I can understand your desire to protect your family," said Granville. "But what if Lizzie isn't guilty? What if your death would only be saving the hide of a gutter rat like Gipson? Would you still remain silent?"

"Gipson?" Scott repeated. "How's he tie into this?"

"That's what I'm trying to sort out, but I need your help. Look, Scott, someone has been working very hard to make sure you and all your allies believe Lizzie killed Jackson. Which is beginning to make me think she had nothing to do with it."

"You think she could be innocent?"

"I'm beginning to."

"What if you're wrong? I won't see my sister die."

"They would never hang a woman."

Scott lowered his voice to a harsh whisper. "They wouldn't have to. Being thrown in jail would kill her within six months."

"All right, then, I'll make a deal with you. Tell me about Lizzie and help me find Jackson's killer. If it was *either* of your sisters, I won't say a word. Anyone else, though, will be taking your place in jail."

There was a long silence. "Fair enough," Scott said finally.

"Good man. What was really between you and Jackson?"

"He was Lizzie's pimp," Scott said in a tone of utter loathing.

TWENTY-EIGHT

Striding through the fog toward 21 Dupont, Trent keeping pace beside him, Granville thought about what Scott had told him. It was no wonder that Scott hated Jackson; Lizzie had been barely seventeen, recently orphaned, and on her own in Denver when Jackson had seduced her, then put her to work. Scott suspected he'd beaten her, too. Easy to understand why she'd become an opium addict.

Jackson had deserved to die, and to die slowly, Granville thought. A bullet had been too good for him.

An opium addict. Granville mentally replayed his visit to those hidden-away dives. He could taste the smoke, touch the heaviness of the air, feel his frustration at not finding his quarry. Eventually he'd seen all three of the white women Wong Ah Sun had said would be there, but only one brunette. That brunette had been Gracie.

Replaying that moment, picturing Gracie in his mind, he felt again his shock at recognizing her, his pity at what she had become.

Breaking stride with a silent curse, he replayed the picture in his mind, and finally understood. Gracie was dark-haired, tall, and would have resembled Frances had she not been so very thin. He could have kicked himself for his stupidity.

Walking into the hot, over-scented room, Granville scanned the faces in the uneven light of badly trimmed lamps, ignoring the irritating tinkling of the piano and the come-hither looks sent his way. Gracie wasn't there. Flo, however, seemed pleased to see him back.

"I was hoping to see Gracie. Is she here?" he asked her.

"I'm afraid she's indisposed," she replied. She tucked a curl behind her ear coquettishly.

Granville raised an eyebrow. "Ah. I'm sorry to hear that, but I only need to ask her a question or two. I'll make it well worth her while, and yours."

Flo gave him a hard-to-read look, then nodded. "Follow me. But he'll have to stay here."

Granville looked at Trent and nodded.

Trent's face fell, but he obediently moved to a scarred brown leather armchair set against the wall and sat down. Granville followed the woman up a wide curving staircase to the second floor, where Flo knocked on a door halfway along the hall.

"Gracie?" she called softly. "Gracie, honey, you have a visitor."

"Go away," called a hoarse voice.

"He's willing to pay, dear. Just sit up, we'll be right in."

There was a groan, which Flo ignored, pushing the door inward and sailing into the room, Granville right behind her. The sight of Gracie was enough to make him wince. The ravages of opium were clear; even in the kind light of a brace of candles, her skin was so pale it looked green, and her eyes seemed to have sunken back into her skull. She was propped against a padded headboard that had once been white, wearing something girlishly pink and covered with frills that made her look even more grotesque. Flo poured a glass of water from the glazed pitcher on the dresser beside the door and handed it to Gracie.

"Just talk with him a few minutes, dearie. You'll soon feel better," she said as she left the room, closing the door behind her.

Granville looked at Gracie with compassion. Avoiding his eyes, she swallowed a mouthful of water. Even the process of swallowing seemed painful, he noted with a mixture of pity and repulsion. If this was Lizzie, he knew exactly what and who had brought Scott's sister to this pass, and the knowledge made him so angry he had to fight to keep it out of his voice.

"Lizzie?" he asked, keeping his tone as low and gentle as he could.

She flinched, spilling water on herself and on the sateen comforter. "My name's Gracie."

"Sorry, my mistake." Granville paused, trying to get her to meet his eyes. "Did I ever tell you why I came here, Gracie?"

"You wanted to know about Jackson's death."

"Do you know why?"

"No. Don't care, neither."

Granville looked at her gravely. "The man accused of Jackson's death, the man they will hang for it next week, is my partner. His name is Sam Scott. Does any of that mean anything to you, Gracie?"

"No. Why should it?"

"No? Well, because I've heard rumors it was a woman who really shot Jackson," he said. "A woman with brunette hair." She felt his gaze, but refused to look up, her eyes fixed on the water in the glass she still held. Her dark tresses fell unbound past her thin shoulders. "Scott's sister Frances thinks he is trying to protect their sister, Lizzie, who is an opium smoker." He let the silence thicken between them. "Do you know a Lizzie, Gracie?"

"That's the name you just said, but I'm Gracie."

"You never met her in any of the opium dens you frequent?"

"No."

"That's odd. I'm told of only three white women in the city here who smoke opium, Gracie, and you're the only one with dark hair. Is there nothing you can tell me of Lizzie?"

"No."

"What about Jackson's death?"

Her skin turned gray beneath its pallor and she barely looked well enough to sit upright. "Nothing."

"You're sure?"

She gave a slight nod.

"Sam Scott's life may rest on your answer."

A slight shudder raced through her wasted frame, but her voice was firm. "I can't tell you anything."

Who was she protecting? Granville wondered in frustration. "Are you Scott's sister Lizzie?"

She shook her head, as vehemently as she seemed able.

"I see. Then I'll go. I'll leave your money with Flo," he said. She cringed back against her pillows at the anger in his voice and turned her face toward the wall.

Scarcely more than an hour later, Frances was following Granville down the same hallway. She was soberly attired, her face lightly painted and very pale. It had taken some effort to convince her to come, but once he'd told her why he thought Gracie might indeed be Lizzie, she hadn't hesitated.

She didn't hesitate now, either. Throwing open the door, she marched in and first dragged open the window, then turned to the bed, hands on hips. She stopped as she saw Gracie's face. "My God! What have you done to yourself?"

Since Gracie, blinking against the light, seemed unable to answer, Granville turned to Frances. "Is this Lizzie?"

She seemed unable to tear her eyes away from the living skeleton on the bed. "Yes," she said, her voice catching. "Yes, this is my sister."

Frances sat down on the edge of the bed and took one of Gracie's hands in her own. "Lizzie, how did it get this bad? What can I do to help?"

Gracie looked at her sister and a tear rolled from the corner of her eye. "You can't do nothing. And call me Gracie," she said, snatching her hand away. "Now go, why don't you?"

"Lizzie, I can't leave you like this."

"It's not up to you. So just go."

"Gracie, if you won't help yourself, will you help Sam?" Granville asked.

"Why should I?"

"Because he's your brother," Frances said.

"So?"

"Your brother is prepared to die because he believes you killed Jackson," said Granville. "Do you want that on your conscience? Or perhaps you did kill Jackson—and now you're happy to have your brother die in your place."

Gracie looked down, her fingers plucking at the coverlet, and murmured something.

Granville leaned forward. "What did you say?"

"I didn't kill him."

"Then who did?"

She shrugged.

"Lizzie." Frances's voice held a warning.

Gracie looked up. "What?"

"You owe him. Don't you remember? He's the one who made sure we got enough to eat when we were both too small to fend for ourselves. Is this how you repay him?"

Gracie's voice broke. "He left me there alone when they died. You both did."

Frances swallowed hard. "By the time we got the news our parents had died, we couldn't find you." She moved to put an arm around her sister, but Gracie cringed back against the headboard.

Frances sighed. "At least let me take you out of here."

"I don't want to go. Not with you."

Granville watched them, a sense of pity mingling with surprise. Were all families so tormented as the ones he knew?

"Gracie, I have to know who killed Jackson," he said. "Can you at least tell me whom I should be talking to?"

"Talk to my brother," she said.

TWENTY-NINE

Friday, December 15, 1899

Clara reached for a petit four. "You have cream on your nose."

Emily swiped at her nose. "There. Better?"

Clara nodded and took a bite of her pastry. She didn't look in the least worried, Emily noted, in fact, she'd probably be relieved if neither of the men they were waiting for appeared. Emily knew she was lucky Clara had even agreed to come with her today. Just as she was about to look at the watch in her pocket, she heard her friend say, "Hello, Mr. O'Hearn."

Emily turned her head. "Hello," she said. "What were you able to find out, Mr. O'Hearn?"

"Wait till I sit down and I'll tell you," he said, proceeding to do just that.

"Well?" she prompted him.

Before he could respond, Mr. Granville and Trent appeared, both looking curious at the unexpected extra man.

"I see we have a party," said Mr. Granville.

Emily introduced the three men. "Mr. O'Hearn has been looking for anyone who was working on the docks the night Jackson was killed," she explained.

Granville regarded him with interest. "Did you have any more luck than I did?"

"Don't know. Seems Jackson was in and around the harbor for most of the evening, though."

"He was?"

"Yeah. I found a couple of longshoremen who remembered seeing him."

"What was he doing?"

"Pacing. He seemed to be waiting for something."

"Or someone."

"Possibly."

"When was this?"

"The night he was killed. It was dark, but it wasn't snowing yet, so they saw him pretty clearly."

"Wait a minute. It snowed off and on all day, but I remember that by about half after nine it was snowing heavily. Are you telling me he was on the docks before then?"

"According to my witnesses he was."

"So where did he go? He couldn't have been standing around all night, it was too cold. Even Scott and I had a fire, and we're used to Yukon cold. This damp imitation of winter you have here is pitiful."

"You haven't heard everything. I did find one witness who thought he saw Jackson meeting another man."

"A man! Is your witness sure it wasn't a woman?"

O'Hearn gave him an odd look, then threw another look at Emily.

She could see he was wondering if this was a nugget of information she'd kept in reserve.

"Not unless she was wearing a frock coat and top hat," O'Hearn said.

"A top hat?" Granville was taken aback.

"*Brown's in Town* was playing at the opera house that night," Emily said. She turned to O'Hearn. " Where was Mr. Jackson found?"

"Near the CPR docks."

"It's probably a ten-minute walk from there to the opera house."

"Did you attend that night?" Granville asked Emily.

"Yes, I did."

"When was it over?"

"It started at seven thirty and ended at ten thirty."

"And the intermission?"

"There were two, one at eight thirty and the other at nine thirty."

Granville turned back to O'Hearn. "The timing fits. Do you have a more detailed description of the man Jackson met?"

"Not a very good one, I'm afraid. Jackson was taller than the other man. Both had beards. That's about all."

"It's better than nothing. No one saw anything else?"

"No."

"It doesn't give us much to go on."

"It was the best I could do," O'Hearn said. "And I think it entitles me to hear some of the information I sense you're holding back."

Granville looked at Emily. "Can we trust him?"

Pleased by the sound of that "we," Emily nodded.

"Trust me to do what?" O'Hearn asked.

"Not print anything until we get Scott out of jail."

"Scott. That's the one they're holding for Jackson's murder?"

Granville nodded.

"Then, sure, you can trust me. As long as I get the full story once he's free."

"You have my word on it."

"Then you have mine." The two men shook on it across the table.

"Jackson may have been meeting one of his investors," Granville said. "They were smuggling opium to the States, and I'd wager it was coming in on the *Empresses*. The *India* was already late because of the storms she'd encountered at sea, and Jackson's contacts in the States probably weren't too pleased by the delay."

O'Hearn pulled out his notebook and pencil. "Jackson was smuggling opium to the States?"

Granville nodded. "That's what I've been told."

O'Hearn was scribbling quickly. "But why was he on the dock that night? The *India* didn't arrive till the following day."

"If Jackson had a contact in the CPR, he would have known she'd arrived in Victoria by midday on Wednesday. He probably expected she'd sail to Vancouver that evening. The railroad was as anxious to get their silk on the next leg of its journey to New York as he was to get his opium shipped. The plan may have been that if the *India* came into port, they could get the opium off and shipped out immediately. Unfortunately for all concerned, the weather didn't cooperate, and she overnighted in Victoria."

Trent's face lit up. "I think maybe I know something that'll help," he said.

Granville shot him a skeptical glance. "And you just learned this something?"

Trent grinned and shook his head. "Nope. I just figured out it was important."

"Go on."

"That night you and Scott caught us? Down at the yards?"

"I remember."

Trent flushed. "Yeah. Anyway, we weren't really trying to break into the railcars."

"No?"

"Nope. We'd been hired to create a distraction, draw your attention away from the cars."

"A distraction?"

Trent nodded.

"And it was Jackson who hired you?"

"Well, Mr. Blayney paid us, but Mr. Jackson gave the directions."

Granville smacked his hand against his forehead. "I'm a fool. How could I have not seen it?"

They all looked at him.

"What?" Trent asked.

"I've been paying no attention to who killed Blayney. Once the police decided it wasn't me, of course."

O'Hearn looked from one to the other. "There's another murder involved in this?" he asked, then looked thoughtful. "Blayney. Blayney. I've got it. That was the English gent found dead down on Cordova. They haven't caught anyone for that yet, have they?"

"That's the problem. I don't know," Granville admitted.

Emily was watching Trent. "Why a distraction?" she said. She looked at Granville. "You and your partner were guarding the silk cars, weren't you?"

"Yes."

"So if you were to be distracted, presumably someone wanted access to the cars. But why?"

Granville thought for a moment. "Any number of reasons. To disable or weaken a coupling, to loosen the wheels or a door, anything that might make the silk easier to steal once the train was under way."

"What if they wanted to leave something?" said Emily softly. "If Mr. Jackson was smuggling opium to the States, what better way than hidden in a train that had special status along its route and was guaranteed the fastest delivery time to New York?"

"By Jove, I think she's onto something." O'Hearn was staring at Emily with approval.

"But if Jackson had already put the opium in the railcar, why would he have gone back the following night?" asked Trent. As they all turned to look at him, he added, "It doesn't make sense."

"It depends how much opium Jackson was smuggling," Granville said, tapping one finger against his cup. "If only some of his opium came in on the *India* and the rest from somewhere else, he might ship part of it in the silk cars and ship the stuff that came in on the *India* some other way."

That was why her father had all those papers about the loading of the silk trains, Emily realized with a start of joy. He must have suspected something and was trying to work out what it was, maybe how to stop it. So it was all right, he wasn't being dishonest. Unless he knew about Jackson, she realized with a sinking feeling. And he hadn't been at the theater with his wife and daughters that night; he could have been anywhere.

"That makes sense," O'Hearn was saying. "But it still doesn't tell us who killed him."

"Clara and I went to see the medium again," Emily said, partly to keep from blurting out her fear about her father.

Granville turned to look at her. "And?"

From the corner of her eye, Emily could see O'Hearn's intrigued look, but she concentrated on Granville's reaction. Trying to read his expression, she told them what had happened. "I think she's a fraud," she concluded. "But I can't decide why she'd tell us the story in the first place."

"She tells people what they want to hear," Granville said. "And she probably made the mistake of thinking you were harmless."

"Unless she had some reason for wanting to spread the story that a woman shot Mr. Jackson, and she thought we were gullible and likely to gossip about it," Emily said. "Mr. Granville, you said someone else had told you Jackson was shot by a woman. Who was it?"

"Bertie's uncle."

"Bertie's the one whose cousin disappeared, right? Your Chinese houseboy?" O'Hearn had been following the conversation with great interest, his pencil flying. "Is this uncle the cousin's father?"

"That's right."

"They've never found any trace of the cousin or what happened to him. What does his father think happened?"

"He believes he was murdered for the opium he carried. He's asked me to look into the matter for him."

"And you think the two cases are connected?" O'Hearn asked. "That it was this cousin's opium Jackson was waiting for?"

"And that got him killed?" Emily added, feeling excited. This could mean that her father had played no part in the opium smuggling. "It seems to make sense. Except why would Bertie's uncle tell you about the woman?"

"Who's this woman?" O'Hearn asked.

Emily ignored him. "If he thinks Jackson was responsible for his son's death, he would want Jackson's killer found so the facts could come out, wouldn't he?"

"Not if he hired Jackson's killer himself. He wants me to find his son's killers, and that trail may lead to Jackson, but it also leads to someone else. Jackson was not on that ship."

Emily felt her heart thump. "The passenger lists. The answer could be there."

He nodded. "Yes, thanks to you."

O'Hearn looked from one to the other. "You have the manifest from that sailing?"

Granville looked at the expectant faces; two of them already knew the answer. "Yes, I do," he said.

THIRTY

Ignoring the murmur of voices and clatter of dishes all around them, the five pored over the passenger lists for nearly an hour without recognizing a single name linked to Jackson.

"This is getting us nowhere." O'Hearn flung down the page he was reading, a disgusted look on his face.

"Do you have a better idea?"

Surprisingly, the comment came from Clara, and from the laughter that sparkled in her eyes, she was flirting with O'Hearn.

Well, well, Granville thought, glancing at Emily to see if she'd noticed. She had. She was watching Clara with an odd expression on her face, then her gaze switched to O'Hearn. Was she jealous? Was she interested in O'Hearn herself? Granville found to his surprise the idea unsettled him.

Clara looked at O'Hearn and the young man turned red again. "I'm planning to see what I can learn about the Blayney killing, for one thing," he said.

"That's a good idea," Emily said. "And I want to talk to Bertie about his cousin."

"I think I want to talk to the coroner again. He said Jackson died between eight and one in the morning, but if so, what was he doing from the time he was spotted earlier in the evening until then? Trent can accompany me," Granville told them.

"We'll need to share what we find out," Emily said. "Shall we continue our practice of meeting here?"

"Yes," Granville said. "Same time tomorrow?" Even if they had made little clear progress, he found his mood had lightened.

"When is your friend's trial?" O'Hearn asked.

"Four days from now."

"Then we haven't much time."

So much for Granville's better state of mind.

Dr. Barwill sat alone in his dingy office. "So you're back," he said. "What d'ye want now?"

Without saying anything, Granville put the bottle of malt whiskey on the desk with a thump.

"What can I tell you?" Barwill asked, his tone now indicating a grudging servility.

"I want details on exactly how Jackson was shot and killed."

"Ah. Well, first off, being shot didn't kill him."

What? "It didn't?"

"Nope. The bullet missed everything important. He bled a lot, though."

"So whoever shot him left him to bleed to death? In effect killing him?

"Well, I suppose that's one explanation. But he didn't die of blood loss, either."

"So what did he die of?"

The doctor shrugged. "Probably from the blow he took to the head."

"What blow?"

"The one that dented the side of his skull. Drove a spur of bone right into his brain. Poor bastard," he added. He was eyeing the whiskey covetously.

"And you are certain the shot didn't kill him?"

Barwill seemed to think about it. "Might've, I guess, if it had turned bad. Or if he'd kept bleeding. But no reason for him to stand around doing so."

"So he *could* walk? He could have gone for help?"

"If somebody hadn't cudgeled him first, that's so."

It raised another question. "You told me Jackson died between eight and one. When was he shot?"

"Dunno. He hadn't been patched up, though, and most men don't stand around bleeding from a bullet wound for long."

Granville's mind raced. That meant . . .

"Why didn't you tell me this before?"

"You didn't ask," the doctor replied.

Granville wasn't sure whether he was angrier with the doctor or with himself. Barwill had misled him, but because he'd seen the bullet wound in Jackson's corpse, Granville had immediately assumed Jackson had been shot to death. He hadn't questioned Barwill about anything other than that bullet wound and the time of death. How much time had he wasted? Time a man in a jail cell couldn't afford to lose. "What was Jackson hit with?"

"Some kind of bat, maybe. Left quite a dent in the side of his head."

Granville pictured the heavy baseball bat Scott had been carrying. "What kind of dent?"

Doc shrugged. "A dent. What do you mean, what kind?"

"What shape?"

Doc took another slug of whiskey, then stared at his hands. Forming the right one into a half circle, he held it out. "Like that."

"You've told the police this?"

"I have."

"Then why aren't they looking for the weapon?"

"I believe they think they have the murderer. And how do you know they haven't got the weapon?"

Because I would have seen it at the site, Granville thought, picturing how Jackson's body had lain. "Wait a minute. I saw the body, and there was blood from the shot, but I saw no sign of a blow to the head."

"It was on the side of his head, under his hair."

"He was lying on his face when we found him. And all the blood was on the front."

"The blow to the head didn't bleed much."

"But head wounds always bleed. Unless the victim is already dead." Even Granville knew that much.

"Or he dies instantly. Or the wound bleeds internally."

"So how did this one bleed?"

"Internally."

"And you are certain the blow to the head killed him?"

"Yes."

Granville's mind raced. "Could a woman have delivered a blow like that?"

"A woman? I doubt it."

"Why is that?"

"Jackson was what? Six feet? His assailant had to have been an inch or two taller."

Granville thought about Benton and Gipson, both shorter than

Jackson. He pictured Scott at six foot four, and his heart sank. "What if Jackson wasn't standing?" he asked, afraid he already knew the answer.

"Hmmm. If he was kneeling or bent over? With that angle? In that case, yes, yes, it could have been someone shorter than he was."

Granville's feeling of relief was punctured by the doctor's next words. "It could even have been a woman."

THIRTY-ONE

Trent held his silence until they'd closed the door of Dr. Barwill's office behind them, then he burst out, "How many times was Jackson killed, anyway?"

Despite his own frustration, Granville had to chuckle.

Trent wasn't finished. "I thought he did an autopsy."

"He did. And held a coroner's inquiry."

"I don't understand. Why didn't he tell us before what killed Jackson?"

"Perhaps he wanted to confuse us."

"But why? Oh, you mean someone has paid him off?"

"It's possible, don't you think?"

"But what did he tell the police?"

"Why don't we go and ask them?"

Granville didn't find McKenzie's spartan office any more pleasant when he was the one doing the questioning. "I am very unwilling to let Sam Scott hang for something he didn't do," he told the chief.

"No point jumping to conclusions. Case hasn't come to trial yet."

"No, but my partner's the one sitting in jail. Are you making any attempt to pursue other lines of inquiry?"

"No reason to."

"And are you aware Jackson didn't die from the bullet wound, but from a blow to the head?" Granville asked, watching closely for McKenzie's reaction.

"About the kind of wound a baseball bat might have caused, wasn't it? Like the one your friend was carrying."

It seemed the good doctor had been more forthcoming at the inquiry than he'd been with them, Granville thought. "What about the motive?" he heard himself saying, then immediately realized how it would play into the other's hands.

"Scott's motive? Bad blood between him and the deceased, I hear. Jackson loaned Scott some money and was pushing to get it back. Wasn't there something about a sister, too?"

Had everyone except him known the real story? Granville wondered bitterly. "And what about Blayney's murder? Have you managed to locate any suspects for that one? Or are you planning on laying that one at Scott's door, too?"

"Funny you should ask. Had a young fellow from the *Daily World* in earlier, asking questions about Blayney."

"And what did you tell him?"

Chief McKenzie smiled, but there was no humor in it. "Same thing I'll tell you. We have no one in custody, and until we do, anything else is police business."

"Have you any suspects?"

The chief's eyes narrowed. "I'll not say it again. I suggest you leave now, else you'll find yourself answering some hard questions."

"Fine." At the door, Granville stopped to give the chief a long, appraising stare. "I've not finished yet. I intend to see this through to the end and see the real murderers occupying your cells." Fine words, Granville thought as he let the door slam behind him, but how the hell was he going to fulfill them?

Inside the house at 21 Dupont, Granville spotted Flo on the far side of the room and strode over to her. "I'd like to see Gracie."

"She's indisposed." She looked troubled.

"Still?"

Flo nodded.

"What's wrong?"

"She can't eat, can't keep food down. She has no strength."

"I'd like to ask her a few questions."

"The same arrangement as before?"

He pulled out his money clip but took nothing from it.

"All right," she told him. "Follow me."

He handed her a folded bill. They proceeded to the stairs.

In the doorway to Gracie's room, he paused, taken aback by how wasted she looked, only two days later. He'd seen that pinched look before, and few survived who had it. His nose confirmed what his eyes were telling him, the sweetish smell of the dying nearly over-powering the musk he'd noted the last time. Then Gracie looked at him, and the fierce light in her eyes belied her wasted frame.

"Thank you," he said to Flo and she took the hint, closing the door behind her as she went.

Granville took a deep breath, trying to come to terms with what he was about to do. He wanted to be gentle with Gracie, but he needed answers. Her brother was running out of time, and by the look of it, so was she. Walking to the side table, he poured her a glass of water and took it to her. She reached for it with hands that shook slightly, but her eyes never left his face; she seemed to be bracing herself for his questions. "I know you shot Jackson, Gracie."

She went paler, and pushed herself back against the headboard, as if to put as much distance between them as possible.

"But I don't think you killed him."

In a move that might once have been seductive but now was only pitiful, she ran her tongue over her lips. "I . . . ," she began, then stopped and lifted the water to her lips.

Perhaps if he used her real name, it would speak to something of the girl she'd once been. "Look, Lizzie," he began, then stopped, halted by her expression of revulsion. "Gracie, then?"

She nodded slightly.

"Look, Gracie. I don't care why you were there that night or what you did. My only interest is in saving your brother."

She wouldn't meet his eyes.

"I need anything you know about why Jackson was there that night, and at what time you saw him. Please."

Still she was silent; there had to be a way to persuade her. Except for the killer, she was probably the last person to see Jackson alive, and the information she possessed might be the key he needed to free Scott. But how could he convince her? "If it is money you want, I can pay anything you ask." She gave him a contemptuous look and turned her face away. Now what?

It was Trent who provided an opening: "Are you worried they'll arrest you for shooting Jackson?" he asked.

"You didn't kill him, Gracie. I'll make sure you have the best barrister in town. I can guarantee you'll be set free," Granville said.

At that she laughed, a sound that was entirely mirthless. "I don't think a jail would hold me for more than a few days." A cough shook her frail body.

Granville forced himself to keep his gaze even. He found it painful to see a woman suffer so. "Is there anything I can do to help you?"

"Feeling sorry for me now? Don't bother. And thanks for the offer, but no. There's nothing anyone can do to help me now." She clearly sensed his distress, but it seemed only to harden her resolve.

"Then why won't your help your brother?" Trent burst out. "If you have nothing to lose, then why not save him?"

"I didn't say I had nothing to lose."

Granville shook his head. He had no idea what was going on. Clearly they were asking the wrong questions, with Gracie weakening by the moment. "Look, let me be honest with you; I am bound and determined to save Sam. If you have something or someone you need to protect, I will protect them when you no longer can, but only if you tell me everything you know about the night Jackson died."

She gave a harsh laugh. "How can you protect something if you don't know where it is?"

"I'll find it for you," he pledged recklessly.

"Do you mean that?"

"Every word," Granville said, wondering what he had committed himself to.

She put every ounce of her strength into the stare she gave him. "How do I know I can trust you?"

"You have my word as a gentleman."

"And just what is that worth?" There was a wealth of bitterness in her tone.

"If I were lacking in honor, why would I be fighting so hard to save your brother?"

She was watching him, a fleck of color high on each cheek. Then she gave a quick nod, and a sigh that seemed to shake her entire body. "All right, I'll trust you. But you have to do what I ask."

"Agreed. What do you want me to do?"

"I have a daughter. Somewhere. You have to find her for me."

A child. It was the last thing Granville had expected to hear, and Gracie didn't seem old enough or strong enough to have borne a child. For a moment he hesitated; it could be hopeless. Then he thought of Scott, and the reality of a hanging, and shuddered. He could not lose another friend, not if he could prevent it. "Agreed," he said, before he could change his mind.

She gave him a smile that was half a grimace. "I think you'll regret that promise, but you'll honor it. Ask your questions."

"When did you last see Jackson?"

"That evening, the night he was killed."

"Why?"

"It's personal."

"Scott said he was your pimp?" Granville felt like a brute, but he had to ask.

She shook her head, her breathing shallow. Granville watched her face, and the pieces began to fall into place. "He was your lover."

She nodded.

"And the father of your child?"

Another nod, then a choked sob. "Yes."

"What did Jackson say when you told him she was his child?" Granville asked softly.

"He denied it. Then he said she was the daughter of a whore and deserved to grow up like the filth she was."

"And is Jackson the reason you don't know where she is?"

Gracie choked on a sob, nodded. "We lived in Denver before we came here. He made me leave my baby behind, said we'd bring her later. Then he refused, wouldn't tell me where she was. I don't even know if she's alive."

It was as well that Jackson was dead, Granville thought. "I'll find your baby for you, Gracie. Sam will help me."

There was no answer but another choking sob.

"Is that why you shot Jackson that night?"

"He said I'd never see my baby again."

"What happened then?"

"He . . . he put a hand to his shoulder and swore at me."

"What did you do?"

"I ran."

So she hadn't seen anything. Granville nodded, hoping his expression hid his disappointment. "What time was this?"

"Ten. Maybe a little after."

"Ten? Not earlier? You're sure of that?"

"Maybe it was a little earlier."

The timing concerned him. "Do you know whom Jackson was meeting that night?"

"No, I couldn't recognize him."

"You mean you saw him?"

She nodded.

"Who was it?"

"I just said I didn't recognize him."

"But you saw him. Clearly?"

She gave a faint shrug. "It was snowing."

"What did he look like?"

"He looked short beside Jackson. He was stocky, and wearing some kind of dark jacket and trousers; black, or maybe navy. His hair was white. I couldn't see anything else."

"How short?"

"My height. Maybe a little more."

So five foot four, perhaps five five. Too short to be Gipson, unfortunately. "And he wasn't wearing a top hat?"

"A top hat? No." A puzzled look crossed her face.

"Could he have been carrying one?"

"No."

"You're sure of that?"

"Yes, I'm sure. He had nothing in his other hand when he was hitting Jackson."

"Wait a minute? Do you mean you saw Jackson killed?"

She nodded. "He was sort of bent over. This other person came up behind him and started hitting."

There was no point asking why Gracie hadn't tried to stop it or gone for help. The point was, she'd have killed the villain herself if she'd had the strength. Or better aim. "What did he hit him with?"

"Some kind of short stick."

"A stick? Did you see him pick it up? Did he leave it there?"

"No, no, he brought it with him. And took it with him when he left. Maybe it was a club."

"Not a bat?"

"No, shorter than that."

"And this was when? What time?"

"It had to be nearly ten thirty, because it was eleven when I got back here."

"And the killer. His hair was white?" None of his suspects had white hair; no one he could think of did.

"It was snowing," Trent reminded him.

"You're sure you didn't recognize him?" he asked Gracie again.

She shook her head.

"Could it have been Benton?" He was the only man shorter than Jackson who came to mind.

"Benton? No. Him I'd have recognized."

There was pain in her voice. He wondered what had gone on between them, and if it had anything to do with Frances. There was no time to find out now; Scott was his focus, had to be. "What was Jackson doing there that night?"

"He was looking for information on the ship. I think he was still hoping to unload merchandise through the tunnels."

"Tunnels?"

Wearily she said, "Ask your friends in Chinatown about the tunnels."

"What tunnels? What about the tunnels?" he asked urgently. But her eyes had suddenly closed and she was breathing shallowly. Granville knew the interview was over.

As they stepped out into the icy wind, Trent looked at Granville. "Are we going to Chinatown?"

"We have one stop to make first."

Frances opened her dressing-room door to Granville's knock and scowled at him. "What are you doing here?"

"I have to talk to you."

"Is this about Sam?"

"No."

She started to close the door, but Granville stuck his foot in the way. Pulling the door wide, she glared at him. "What?"

"Please, Miss Frances, you have to listen to us. And you don't want to hear this standing in the hall." Trent's face was earnest and his eyes pleaded with her.

Her expression lightened as she looked at the boy. She turned and walked into her dressing room, leaving them to follow. Seating herself, she looked from one to the other. "I'm listening."

"Frances, did you know Gracie has a child?" Granville asked bluntly.

"Gracie . . . you mean Lizzie? Has a child? Oh, God! No, no, I didn't know. But how do you know?"

"She told me," Granville said.

"She told you? Why? Where is it?"

Assuming Frances meant the child, Granville said, "She's probably in Denver."

"She? A girl? But I don't understand, why is she in Denver?"

"Jackson made Gracie leave her behind. Gracie's asked me to find the child for her."

"Jackson? What does he have to do with this?"

"He fathered your sister's child."

"Jackson did? The swine! If he wasn't already dead, I'd shoot him myself."

"Are you sure you didn't?"

"Didn't what? Kill Jackson?" Frances gave a hard laugh. "Yes, I'm sure. Though I'm rather flattered you think I'm that tough."

She looked back at Granville and her face darkened. "Lizzie was our baby sister. She was adorable. She had the biggest brown eyes and masses of golden curls and a dimple when she smiled. Sam adored her." She stopped speaking for a moment, looking down at her hands lying slim and still in her lap. Finally she looked up. "If her daughter is anything like her, she'll be a little angel. How could Lizzie . . . Gracie leave her behind?"

"Jackson gave her no choice. And when Gracie wanted to send for her, Jackson told her she'd never see her baby again."

Her lip curled. She shook her head. "If Benton had known, he'd have made Jackson acknowledge his child. He'd probably have forced him to marry Gracie as well."

"Benton?"

She nodded. "Yes. His father abandoned him and his mother

when Benton was very young. He considers abandoning a child one of the few things that are unforgivable."

"Could Benton have forced Jackson to find Gracie's child and acknowledge her?"

Frances mouth formed a cruel smile. "Oh, yes."

Granville wondered what it would have been worth to Jackson to make sure Benton never found out about the child. Who else had known about her? "Did Sam know?"

"About Gracie's child?" She shook her head. "No, of course not."

Granville nodded, then he said what he'd come to say. "Your sister is very ill, perhaps dying. I think she might accept your help now."

One of Frances's hands flew to her throat. "Dying? Little Lizzie? No! I won't have it." Standing and tossing off her shawl, she motioned them to the door. "You'll have to excuse me," she said. "I thank you for that information."

Emily and Clara sat by the fire in Emily's bedroom. At Emily's insistence, they'd retreated there to discuss all that they had learned. Clara was humoring her, she knew. But someone must have left the opera house to meet Mr. Jackson, she thought. Who? There was no way of guessing, but surely someone had noticed his absence. He had to have been gone for longer than the twenty-minute intermission, it seemed, but how to find out? She sighed heavily.

"Clara, how am I to track the movement of one man in that crush? Everyone in Vancouver seemed to be there."

"I wasn't," Clara reminded her. "I had a headache that evening. But I do have a idea."

"Tell me," said Emily.

"Why not ask your sisters? After all, they're among the most prodigious gossips in the city."

"Clara, that's brilliant." Mentally apologizing to her friend for every harsh thought she'd had, she leaned forward. "But I need your help. Join us for tea?"

It was Clara's turn to sigh. "Jane and Miriam are so boring." She rolled her eyes. "Oh, very well, for your sake I will endure it."

Sitting in the front parlor, Emily watched her mother pour tea from the silver pot. The room was over-furnished and overdecorated, but no one except herself seemed to mind.

"How have you been, Clara?" Miriam was asking.

"Very well, thank you, Miriam. And you?"

"I'm also well."

"Did you enjoy the play at the opera house the other night?"

Good for you, Clara, Emily thought.

"*Brown's in Town?* Yes, I enjoyed it very much. Yourself?"

"I'm afraid I had to miss it, and Emily is not the most reliable critic."

"No, indeed," said Jane, with a sideways glance at her sister. "Sometimes I wonder if she even attends the same performance we do."

What an old cat, Emily thought. As if her taste was so wonderful.

Clara's face showed nothing of her thoughts. "So you enjoyed it also?"

"Yes, I did," Jane said.

Clara had brought the conversation round quite nicely, Emily thought, sitting forward. They'd not suspect anything now. "It was unevenly performed, you must admit," she said.

"I thought it amusing enough," Jane said.

"Then why did so many people leave at the intermission?"

"No one left. The men just went out for a cigar," Miriam explained. "They all returned."

"Except for the Dunsmuirs' guest," Jane said, turning to face

Miriam. "Don't you remember? Mary told us he came back after the second act started. She was so embarrassed." Jane's eyes gleamed at the tidbit.

Miriam brightened. "Oh, now I remember. How rude."

Clara and Emily's eyes met. "I don't think I've ever heard of such a thing," Clara said. "Who was this guest?"

"A Mr. Smythe," Jane said.

"I've not heard of him. Who is he?" Clara shot Emily a glance.

"I believe he's a business partner of Mr. Dunsmuir's. Rumored to be very well-off. Of course they'd invite him," Miriam said.

"And of course they'd overlook any rudeness," Jane finished.

"More tea, girls?" Mrs. Turner asked.

It was like her mother to change the subject when the gossip grew too personal, Emily thought. "No, thank you, Mama," she said. "Clara has to leave early."

"Thank you for the tea, Mrs. Turner," Clara said, standing on cue.

"Smythe," Emily hissed as soon as she and Clara were in the hall. "Did you hear? He was one of the investors that Mr. Granville talked to. Do you think he's the one who killed Mr. Jackson?"

"We must wait until tomorrow and see what Mr. Granville thinks," Clara said.

THIRTY-TWO

Saturday, December 16, 1899

Catching sight of Emily and Clara sitting at their table, Granville made his way to them. Emily smiled back and her eyes lit up. Once again, he was surprised and amused at how much her welcome pleased him.

"O'Hearn hasn't come yet?" Trent asked as he and Granville sat down.

Clara shook her head. "Not yet."

"I have news!" O'Hearn's excited voice announced his arrival. "You'll never guess what I found out," he said as he pulled out a chair, his red hair standing on end as though he'd run his fingers through it.

"Blayney was killed in the same manner as Jackson," Emily said.

Tim's face was almost comical in its disappointment. "You knew?"

"I guessed, but only when I saw your excitement. Then I knew there had to be a connection."

"Oh."

"I, for one, would never have guessed," Clara said. "How did you find out?"

"I started with what we'd published on the death, which wasn't much. Then I talked to the coroner, Dr. Barwill. Did you know the man's a raving idiot?" O'Hearn grimaced, then went on. "Blayney died from a head wound. He was hit with a heavy rounded implement, and so was Jackson. So I think we're looking for one killer."

Listening to the young reporter, Granville was even more annoyed with himself for missing the true method of Jackson's death for so long. But what use could he make of this new information? Who had hated or feared both Jackson and Blayney enough to kill both of them?

"And I think I know who that killer is," Emily said.

Every head except Clara's turned toward her. Clara calmly spooned sugar into her tea.

"Mr. Smythe," Emily said. "He disappeared during the intermission of *Brown's in Town* and didn't return for nearly an hour, and he was wearing a top hat."

"So it was Smythe Jackson was talking to, was it? I'll have to have another chat with the man," Granville said. Smythe was too skinny to be the killer, but it was good to have that detail resolved, and the man might know more about Jackson's death than he'd admitted to. "Thank you, Emily. That's good work."

"It was Clara's idea."

"We did it together," Clara said.

"I'm glad to have the name. Unfortunately I don't believe he's the murderer. I don't think it's Gipson either, much as I'd love to see the man hang."

"Why not?" Emily asked.

"I have an eyewitness," he said, then held up a hand before they could say anything. "She saw Jackson being hit and she says the killer was a short, stocky man. Which lets out Gipson, who is too tall, and Smythe, who is too thin. Also, whoever it was wasn't wearing a top hat, wasn't even carrying one. And the timing does not fit."

"But isn't your partner a tall man?" Emily said. "Doesn't that exonerate him also?"

"It would, except that my witness would have no credibility in court. She's a prostitute and an opium smoker."

"How did you find her?"

"She's Scott's sister."

"Oh, the poor woman," said Emily. "But isn't Mr. Scott's sister the woman rumored to have shot Mr. Jackson?"

"That's right. And she did shoot him. Only she didn't kill him."

"Oh."

"Exactly."

"So where does that leave us?" O'Hearn asked. "We have two murders, an unreliable witness, and no killer."

"What do the police say about Blayney's murder?" Granville asked him.

"Not much. The case is still open, but they have no leads and they don't seem to be looking hard for a killer."

Odd, Granville thought. "Why, I wonder?"

O'Hearn shook his head. "What's your reasoning?"

"Blayney was Gipson's man," Granville said. "And Gipson is not one to overlook an insult, which is how he'd see the murder of one of his key men. So why is he not raising hell with the police?"

"Maybe he wanted Mr. Blayney dead," Trent said.

"Perhaps he did at that," Granville said.

"But you said Gipson didn't kill Jackson. And Jackson and Blayney were killed the same way. So Gipson couldn't have killed Blayney," O'Hearn said.

"Unless he hired someone to do it for him," Emily suggested.

"True enough. If we assume Gipson wanted Blayney dead, where does that take us?"

"Maybe Mr. Blayney knew too much," Trent said.

Granville nodded. "It's possible. So Gipson hires the same man who killed Jackson. Why?"

"Maybe he paid for Jackson's killing, too?" O'Hearn said.

"Or he found out who killed Mr. Jackson, then blackmailed the killer into killing Mr. Blayney."

This came from Clara, and they all looked at her in surprise.

"Could Smythe have been a witness?" O'Hearn asked. "Was he still at the docks when Jackson was killed? Could he have told Gipson?"

"What time did Smythe return to the opera house?" Granville asked Emily.

"Around nine thirty."

"Then no, Smythe could not have seen the murder. Jackson was killed closer to ten thirty. But Gipson might have other ways of finding out who the killer is."

"So how do we find out?" Trent asked. "There's no other way of getting Mr. Scott out of jail, right?"

"Right, so I need to talk to Smythe again. He didn't see the murder, but he did meet with Jackson. He may have seen something that will help us. Then I think I'll ask Gipson who our killer is."

"Yes, I'm sure he would be happy to tell you," said Emily.

"Oh, he will talk to me," Granville assured her. "I know that, at least." But in fact he knew that the agreement they'd made would be honored only so long as it suited the man.

"The interesting thing is that the killer carried the murder weapon with him," Granville said, voicing the thought that had just occurred to him.

"He did?" Tim stared at Granville. "I wonder why? There's no shortage of handy planks down on the dock."

"Maybe he planned the murder," Trent said.

Granville nodded. "Or perhaps the weapon is something he habitually carries."

"Like a cane?" Emily said.

"Possible, though my informant seemed to think it was shorter than that. She was uncertain on the details, though. But the coroner did tell me a little of the shape of weapon."

No one said anything. And Granville couldn't help recalling that Trent was the only one of them who had any familiarity with cudgels. "After I talk to Gipson, I plan on visiting Chinatown," he told them.

"Chinatown? Why there? Isn't it dangerous?" O'Hearn looked intrigued.

"I have a contact there. Scott's sister said something about Jackson using tunnels from Chinatown to the docks that night. Have you ever heard of such tunnels?" he asked O'Hearn.

"No, never, though it wouldn't surprise me."

"Well, it may be nothing. But I think it's worth looking into."

Skirting puddles of slush that spilled onto the sidewalk on Seymour Street, Granville considered how best to approach Smythe. Beside him, Trent seemed deep in thought. "What if it was Smythe?" Trent suddenly burst out.

"What if what was Smythe?"

"That killed Jackson. He was gone long enough. He's short."

"He's too thin," Granville reminded him.

"He could have been wearing an overcoat. If he was bundled up enough, he could have looked stocky, and besides, it was snowing, remember? Hard to see."

"All good points. You'll just have to trust my instincts on this one. Smythe didn't kill Jackson."

Trent didn't look satisfied. "Then why are we going to see him?"

"To see what he'll say."

"Hmmm. I thought we didn't have time to waste."

THIRTY-THREE

In Smythe's office, Granville ignored the clerk's "Mr. Smythe isn't available," and walked straight into the inner office. A frantic squawking followed him, and Granville's eyes glinted. Seated behind his wide desk, Smythe gave them a disdainful look. "I will have to ask you to leave."

"We know you saw Jackson the night he was murdered, Smythe," Granville said. "You met him on the dock."

Smythe's distant expression cracked. "I . . ."

"Don't bother to deny it. You were seen."

"Please close the door," Smythe said, then waited until Trent had done so.

"Yes, all right, I was there. But I didn't kill him."

"Why not tell us this before?"

"Would *you* have?"

Granville considered the man in front of him. He probably

wouldn't have said anything either, but that wasn't the point. Scott's life was the point. "Why did you meet Jackson, Smythe?"

"I will tell you, but you have to promise not to bring in the police."

"I'm not promising anything. But if I can keep your name out of it, I will."

"Fair enough. It was part of our partnership agreement. And I needed the money."

"Why?"

"I owe Gipson."

Gipson again. "How much?"

"More than I can afford to pay."

"So you borrowed money from Gipson?"

"At his terms? My foolishness was of a different sort, Mr. Granville." He sighed. "My venture with Gipson was intended to make money as a cushion to see me through periods when my primary sources of income were adversely affected."

Granville knew what was coming. "You bought mining stock from him."

"To my shame, yes. And I bought more against what he told me was the greatly increased value of the shares I held."

"Then he told you the stocks were worthless, and you ended up owing him money."

"A great deal of money." Smythe looked at him in surprise. "Have you invested with Gipson also, Mr. Granville?"

"No, but I have had dealings with him in the past. I know his methods."

"I see." Smythe looked at his hands as they lay resting on his desk. "When I owed so much, Gipson suggested I invest with Jackson. He even loaned me the money to do so," he said with a bitter laugh. "And indicated that he would be more lenient with my interest if I could persuade several of my friends to invest also. Lenient. My God, he could foreclose on my business if he chose to, so I betrayed my friends to save my living."

Granville said nothing; Smythe would not want expressions of sympathy, but Gipson deserved to be behind bars, and Granville would be pleased to put him there. Smythe's thoughts had apparently been following a similar line. "When you say you've had experience with Gipson's methods . . . do you imply the failure of the mine could have been a setup?"

"There was probably no mine."

For the first time, a flush brought color to Smythe's face. He said something beneath his breath.

"Have you copies of your share certificates?" Granville asked.

"Yes. But bringing action will take time, and I suspect Gipson will simply leave town if I get too close."

"Not if he is behind bars he won't."

Smythe met Granville's eyes. "What can I do?"

"I need to know everything that happened that night, everything you saw or heard. Everything, right down to the smells."

Smythe nodded. "Jackson insisted I meet him, said I had to help him if I ever wanted to see a penny."

"Help him? How?"

"Jackson sent word when he realized the *India* wouldn't be docking till the following day, in daylight. He wanted me to help a passenger and his luggage get to San Francisco. Jackson said his face was too well known for him to do it personally, and he couldn't afford a delay."

The passenger would be Jackson's insider, the man who killed Bertie's cousin, Granville thought. "What passenger?"

"A Chinaman."

"He was Chinese?"

"Yes. Name of Wong Fung, or something like that."

Bertie's cousin. Alive? "And his luggage?"

"Mostly opium, I think, but I saw him on his way. And don't ask how, for I shan't say."

Wong Yu Fung had betrayed his own father? From the little Granville knew of Chinese culture, that was almost unheard of. What kind of persuasion had been used to cause such a betrayal? It was a piece of news he wasn't looking forward to conveying to the young man's father. "So you did what Jackson asked."

"Yes."

"When did you last see Jackson?"

"It must have been nine fifteen or so. I was back at the opera house by nine thirty."

It galled Granville to realize he and Scott had been less than four blocks away while all this was going on. "Did you see or hear anyone else when you were on the dock?"

"No one."

"Did Jackson say anything about meeting anyone else that night?"

"Not to me."

"Thank you, Smythe. I think we'll pay a call on Gipson now and see what he can tell us."

"Good luck. And be careful."

"Do you really expect to get answers from Gipson?" Trent asked as they left the building.

"No, I just want to rattle him a little."

Granville strode up the stairs and into Gipson's office, slamming open the door. It was late, and this time there were no thugs to stop them. Looking at Gipson's smooth expression, thinking of the resignation he'd seen on Scott's face earlier, Granville was furious. It was time to stop Gipson's little game. He looked at the chunk of fool's gold sitting on Gipson's desk and thought how apt it was—he had made a business out of turning men into fools, chasing after gold in all its forms. It was time someone turned the tables on him. "I've just come from an interesting meeting with Smythe," he said.

"Interesting?" Gipson raised an eyebrow.

"I didn't know he had invested with you."

Gipson looked at him calmly. "Many of the key people in this town have invested with me. My transactions are, of course, private."

"Naturally. But there is just one more thing. I am looking for a short, stocky killer. I wondered if you happened to know such a person?" Granville watched as the expression on the man's face changed.

"I have nothing further to discuss with you."

"I'll take that as a no. Well, my thanks for your time, in any case. Come along, Trent. Oh, and by the way," Granville said, stopping with one hand on the doorknob and turning to face Gipson. "If you plan to send someone to attack us after we leave, I will infer that you do know the killer. I think Chief McKenzie may have a question or two for you after that."

"He really hates you, doesn't he?" Trent asked as they went down the stairs.

"The feeling is mutual, believe me."

"Why?"

"It's a long, and not very edifying story. I'll tell you one day. But right now I'm going to Chinatown and you are going home."

"What? But why?"

"I don't know what I'll be walking into. It may be dangerous."

"All the more reason to take me with you."

Granville looked at Trent's determined face; he wasn't going to give up easily. "Very well, you can be my backup, but if it is dangerous and we both go in, we'll neither of us return. You can come with me, but only as far as the bar at the Carlton. I'll meet you back there in an hour. If I don't show up, you go get Bertie. All right?"

Trent sighed. "All right," he finally agreed. But his expression was mutinous.

THIRTY-FOUR

Emily couldn't sit still; something was wrong. This was more than the impatience she'd been feeling since Clara left, but she didn't quite know how to explain it. What was wrong with her?

She had a sudden vision of Mr. Granville's face. Was something wrong with him? Perhaps Trent would know; Bertie would know how to find him. She left her room and walked to the servants' uncarpeted stairs, not caring, for once, what her mother would say.

"Trent!"

Bertie and Trent were standing just inside the kitchen door, heads close together. The stone sink was half full of the china Bertie had been washing. Trent started, but didn't turn to face her. "Yes, Miss Emily?"

"Trent. Look at me."

He wouldn't meet her gaze; he knew something. And why was he here? "Trent, something is wrong with Mr. Granville, isn't it?"

Trent looked at Bertie then back at her. He nodded slowly.

"Where is he?"

"Chinatown."

"Is he in trouble?"

"I think he might be, Miss Emily."

"So what are you doing about it?" Her eyes went from him to Bertie, and narrowed. "The two of you were going to rescue him, weren't you?" Neither answered her, neither of them met her accusing gaze.

"Take me with you."

Bertie met her gaze, a look of shock in his eyes. "Miss Emily? You cannot go to Chinatown."

"What kind of trouble is Mr. Granville in, Bertie?"

His eyes darted away. "I do not know."

"I think you do. Take me to Chinatown, Bertie. Take me to your uncle."

He turned back to the sink, as if to finish washing the dishes, and Trent leaned back against the kitchen door, tension in every line of his body. "I cannot," Bertie finally said. "Is not safe for you."

"Is it safe for Mr. Granville?"

No answer.

"If I asked you to go, to protect him, could you do that?"

Still no answer.

"Bertie, if you have any respect for me at all, please take me to him."

"I cannot, Miss Emily. Your papa be very angry. Chinatown is not safe."

"If I were with you, I would be safe, wouldn't I, Bertie?" She could see him hesitate. "Please, Bertie. Please."

He looked at her for a long moment. "You know what you ask?"

Trent was watching the both of them, and his uncharacteristic silence said more to Emily than anything else.

"Probably not," she said with a shaky half-laugh. "But I ask it anyway. Please, Bertie."

His expression was grave. "Very well. You need a coat."

She ran to get it.

Emily found Chinatown as unsettling as she'd imagined. She'd entered a world that was foreign to her, and she felt out of place and vulnerable, conscious of eyes watching them, watching her. Every time she looked behind her she saw no one, but they were there, watching, she could feel them.

The streetcar had let them off at Carrall. Though it was already dark, the wide, well-lit streets had felt safe enough. They'd passed by the opulent Alhambra Hotel, where every window was glowing with light, and the sounds of the orchestra and men laughing floated on the chill air. She had even felt a frisson of excitement at the forbidden nature of it all; being out alone, after dark. The fact that Bertie and Trent were with her didn't count. If this little escapade were discovered, she would be worse off for having been with the houseboy and the odd-jobs boy than if she had been totally alone, but it didn't matter. The urgency she had felt, the sense of danger for Granville, eclipsed everything.

Turning onto Dupont, the feeling changed; being here with only Bertie and Trent for company suddenly seemed foolhardy, not brave. I won't change my mind now, she thought. I cannot.

"Miss Emily. This way."

She responded instantly to Bertie's hand on her arm, the urgency in his soft-voiced command. "What is it?" Heart pounding, she drew in a shaky breath, conscious of the cold air freezing in her nostrils and the back of her throat.

"Do not look ahead. We go this way." His hand on her arm tugged her firmly toward a narrow passageway between two rickety buildings. Despite his warning, Emily took a quick look in the direction they had been going; three men were coming toward them, none of them tall or heavily built, but they exuded an air of menace that had the breath stopping in her throat. Emily quickened her step.

Before the three men had gained ground on them, Bertie stopped at a small gate and rapped four times. The gate swung silently inward, as if someone had been standing waiting for them. Emily looked, but saw no one. Bertie bowed as he went through, and Emily tried to copy the motion, though it felt awkward to her.

The room was long and narrow, the near end brightly lit, the other end in shadows. On the sidewall was a fireplace, flanked by dragon statues. Emily drew a deep breath and looked around her; candles flickered in long holders, and the air smelled of some sweetish incense she couldn't name. At first glance the room seemed empty.

She looked over at Bertie, found his eyes were fixed on a dark shape lying along the sidewall. Her eyes took in the bundle, unable to decipher what she was seeing, until a tiny movement showed her the bend of an arm against dark cloth. Her breath caught in her throat. It was a man, lying there draped in some kind of dark cloth, nearly motionless. Granville?

Subduing the urge to rush to Granville's side, if indeed it was him lying there, her eyes sought Bertie. He was bowing toward the farthest, darkest end of the room, then standing, statue still. The look on his face froze Emily where she stood.

Slowly turning her head, she followed his gaze. At first she saw nothing but the shadows cast by the candle flames, but gradually she made out a figure standing there. He was wearing a robe of some dark material with a silvery sheen to it. A white beard fell over the front and his hands were hidden in the sleeves. His eyes gleamed at her, but he made no sound.

Unnerved by the silence, she glanced sideways at Bertie, who didn't seem to have moved. He didn't even seem to be breathing. For the first time since she had proposed coming here, Emily felt truly afraid. Her stomach clenched painfully tight and her legs felt shaky. Seeing Bertie's fear, she realized how little she knew about this world, how little right she'd had to demand to be brought here.

I assumed Angus Turner's daughter would be safe anywhere, Emily thought in sudden terror. I had no idea anyplace in Vancouver could feel so alien. Bertie moved then, bowing his head low, and Emily's heart pounded so loudly she was sure she would faint. I can't faint now. I never faint, she thought. Never.

"Honored Uncle," Bertie said, his head still bowed.

The response, in a voice as dry as spider's silk, was incomprehensible to Emily.

Bertie said something else, but he was no longer speaking English. His tone sounded harsh to her unaccustomed ears. His posture was subservient, though, even nervous.

Bertie's uncle replied sharply. He was angry, Emily thought, watching both of them closely. Very angry. Then there was a long silence and Emily could hear the crackle of flames devouring oxygen. Suddenly breathless, she put a hand to her throat, and those dark eyes watched the movement.

Wong Ah Sun said something else. There was no emotion in his voice, but Emily's heart began hammering again. With an effort, she held her head high. Showing her fear could not help Granville.

There was another exchange. Emily sensed Bertie was talking about her. Whatever he said was not well received. She drew in a quick breath, held it, as Bertie's head turned, ever so slightly, to look toward the corner where Granville lay. Bertie said something. His uncle's reply was long and Bertie seemed to Emily to cringe back, though he didn't actually move.

Emily wanted to leap forward and explain herself and Granville, but held her tongue. The environment was too alien; she was afraid of saying the wrong thing. She would have to trust Bertie to speak for her. But it was harder than anything she'd ever known not to go to the figure on the floor.

Bertie spoke again, his voice a little louder. He was not giving up, or so it seemed to Emily. The old man's response was softer, but it seemed menacing to her. Bertie asked something. The answer was short, the tone ruthless.

Granville was in trouble, she could sense it. Taking a deep breath, Emily stepped forward, mentally rehearsing the name Bertie had so painstakingly taught her. "Mr. Wong Ah Sun? May I say something?"

"Miss Emily, no." Bertie grabbed for her arm, but missed.

The eyes watching her widened slightly, but he made no move. Emily gave a little bow, not knowing if she was doing the right thing. She had no idea what they had been arguing about, but given his anger, she guessed it must have to do with the old man's son. All she could do was give them the information she had, and hope it would help.

"Four hours ago, Mr. Granville believed that Jackson had arranged to have your son killed and the opium stolen. When last I saw Mr. Granville, he was tracking down Jackson's accomplices. If he has told you something different about your son now, he must have found more information. Trent would know." She looked behind her. "Trent?"

Trent stepped forward, his expression determined, but Emily could sense his fear. "Yes?"

"Did you and Mr. Granville talk to anyone before coming here?" Trent nodded. "A gentleman named Smythe."

"What did he tell you?"

"That Jackson had asked him to get a man named Wong Fung and his belongings to San Francisco. And that he did so."

"My son," Wong Ah Sun said softly. His gaze moved from Trent's face back to Emily's. "Perhaps your Mr. Granville told the truth about my son, though it pains me to think it, but there are other matters he spoke of, things he has no business knowing."

"Trent?" she said. "Was there something else Granville learned of that might concern Mr. Wong Ah Sun?"

"We were told of the tunnels," Trent said.

Beside her, Emily could feel Bertie tensing. "Would that be a concern?" she asked the old man.

"Perhaps." There was no emotion in that voice, nothing showing on his face.

"He is only interested in looking for Mr. Jackson's killers." She paused, then decided the gamble was worth the risk. "He is a man of his word. He did not ask again about the woman you told him of, did he?"

Wong Ah Sun's gaze flicked to Bertie, then returned to her. "No."

She nodded again. "No. I thought not. He has already found her. And she did not kill Jackson."

A groan distracted her; it came from where Granville lay. Well, at least she knew he was still alive, Emily thought. Now all she had to do was convince a man more alien to her than any she'd ever met that they meant no harm. All!

She'd have laughed if she dared, but instead drew in a long breath, willing her nerves to steady. She could almost feel the presence of death in the room, hovering. Granville had come too close to things that needed to stay hidden.

Wong Ah Sun watched her. "And who are you to him, that he should tell you these things?"

"I am his fiancée. We are to be married," said Emily recklessly, ignoring the little start Bertie gave beside her. Somehow she had to convince this man to take her seriously, to believe that Granville meant no harm.

"I see." His eyes searched her face, then shifted to the still body on the floor. That piercing gaze snapped back, fixed itself on Bertie's face. "Is this true, nephew?"

He hadn't missed Bertie's reaction, either, Emily realized. "Bertie doesn't know. Neither do my parents. I . . . we kept it a secret."

There was no chance that Trent wouldn't react to her lie, but she felt sure he was intimidated enough by their surroundings to save his comments for later.

Wong Ah Sun's glance now turned to him, but Trent was staring at the floor.

In silence they all stood there. It seemed like forever to Emily. Her heart jumped when Bertie's uncle suddenly spoke. "Nephew, escort Miss Emily and Mr. Granville and their friend wherever they wish to go. Though you may have to assist Mr. Granville. He is feeling rather unwell."

"Yes, Honorable Uncle," Bertie said with a deeper bow.

"Thank you, Mr. Wong Ah Sun," Emily said, copying Bertie's bow. "But if I may, there is just one thing?"

He did not reply, only waited.

"We still need to know if Jackson was here the night he died. Not about the tunnels," she added hastily. "Just if he was here. And when he might have left."

When she'd finished, there was a tense silence. Emily wanted very badly to look away, but she forced herself to meet Wong Ah Sun's eyes.

"You have courage. Yes, Jackson was here, though he did not get what he came for. And no," he said, holding up a hand as Emily began to speak. "Do not ask me what he came for. Jackson took a shortcut to the docks. He would have been there by eight o'clock."

"Thank you," said Emily. But what did it mean? she wondered, then went to help Bertie lift Granville, who came to his feet with a low groan.

With Granville held up by Bertie on one side and Trent on the other, the four of them made slow progress down Dupont Street. Emily had been horrified to see how badly Granville had been beaten. The right side of his face was battered, his lip was cut and swollen, and a bruise darkened his cheekbone. He moved awkwardly. Every step seemed to cause him pain, and she wasn't sure he was entirely conscious, shuffling along in what seemed to be a dazed state. "Mr. Granville, can you walk any faster?" she begged. "We have to get you out of here."

His head had turned slowly toward her. Two gold-flecked hazel eyes laughed at her. "Don't you think you could call me John now? Since we're engaged?"

THIRTY-FIVE

Sunday, December 17, 1899

"What do you have to say for yourself, girl?" Emily's father thundered, his face red. They'd been so intent on getting Granville to the hospital alive, she'd never thought about the possibility of being recognized.

Emily took a shaky breath. She'd never seen her father like this. A glance at her mother was no help. She hung her head and waited for the tempest to blow over. But Papa hadn't finished. "You're confined to your room, and you will stay there until I decide what to do with you. I'm thinking about a convent. It seems the only solution."

"But, Papa, we aren't Catholic."

"I don't care."

Emily took a deep breath. Clearly there was no reasoning with her father now, but she doubted he could get any angrier. Perhaps this was the time to ask him about Mr. Jackson's name on that list. She had to know. "Papa, why were you so interested in Clive Jackson?"

Startled by the abrupt change of subject, he gave her a hard look. "What makes you think I was?"

"I accidentally saw a list when I was tidying your study. His name was on it, and since he is now dead . . ."

"You shouldn't even know of such things, much less be asking questions about them."

"I am sorry, Papa. I was worried about you." It was true.

"Worried? What, that I'd killed him?" When Emily didn't deny it, he glared at her angrily.

"But, Papa . . ."

"Enough. I won't hear another word. Go to your room. Now."

"But . . ."

"Go."

Emily went.

Emily sat in her bedroom, wondering what would happen to her. She'd probably be sent away, somewhere miserable; too many people would know of her adventuring for Papa to let her stay. And she'd never be allowed to see Granville again, or to find out what happened with their investigation. She sighed and walked slowly to the window, peering out into the darkness.

THIRTY-SIX

Monday, December 18, 1899

They'd strapped his ribs too tightly, Granville thought as he entered Stroh's Tea Shop, but at least he could walk without wincing. He was looking forward to seeing Emily, and he wanted to thank her for what she'd done. At the time he'd been too groggy to really recognize how brave she had been, and how much she had risked by helping him.

Granville ignored the other patrons gaping at the sight of his bruised and battered face. His eyes went straight to her table, but she wasn't there. Tim O'Hearn sat alone, looking oddly bereft. No sign of Trent either, though he was supposed to meet him here.

"Where is everyone?"

"I'm not sure."

"Emily's being held prisoner!" Trent said, arriving out of breath to provide part of the answer. His cheeks and nose were red from the cold and from hurrying.

"What?" Granville exclaimed.

"And Clara?" O'Hearn asked at the same time.

"I don't know about Clara," Trent said. He was relishing his role as bearer of such dramatic news. "I've just come from the Turners'. Her father is furious; he's locked her in her room."

"I see."

Trent went on. "Cook says her reputation is ruined and no one will ever marry her."

"I'll marry her myself." Granville had never thought to hear himself speak those words. But he realized he didn't regret having uttered them.

Trent widened his eyes. "But they blame you. I know that much."

Granville wasn't surprised to hear it.

"Cook says her parents accused Emily of consorting with Chinamen and criminals. Like you," Trent said.

Granville ignored this. "She's all right, though?"

"She's just being kept in the house. Cook says nothing like this has ever happened, and that it's for her own good . . ."

Granville nodded. "Then she'll be all right until tomorrow. I'll deal with her father then."

"But that's not all!" Trent said. "She smuggled me a note to bring you!" He handed a folded paper to Granville, who opened it and read:

I'm sorry I can't meet with you this afternoon. Trent will explain why.

I have been doing some thinking about the murder weapon. If it was heavy, shorter than a cane, and something someone always carries, could it have been a nightstick? The kind police carry?

E.

Granville read the note, and read it again. He could almost hear the click as all the pieces fell into place.

"It was Craddock. He's the killer," he said.

O'Hearn and Trent both looked at him.

"Craddock? Who's he?" O'Hearn asked.

"One of the constables who was first on the scene of Jackson's murder. He's short and stocky and he hates Scott." He handed the note to Tim, and waited while the two of them read it.

"A policeman?" Trent said.

"Sure," O'Hearn said, nodding. "We're still waiting to hear the results of the judicial inquiry. Being sworn to uphold the law's only words to some of them."

"But why would he kill Jackson?" Trent asked.

"According to Scott, Craddock lived in Denver before he moved here. So did Jackson."

"So?"

"So Jackson and Gracie had a child together. Jackson has kept the whereabouts of that child from her mother. And I'd be willing to bet Craddock knew about it."

"I don't understand," Trent said. "Why does that matter?"

"Blackmail is one possibility?" O'Hearn said.

"Yes," Granville said. "According to Scott, Craddock has a gambling problem, which probably means he's short of money. I'd be willing to bet he tried to blackmail Jackson. It would explain a few things."

"So what do we do now?" Trent asked.

Granville turned to O'Hearn. "That judicial inquiry. Where does it stand on McKenzie? Is he clean?"

"McKenzie? Not exactly," O'Hearn said. "He says he is, but from what I hear, the evidence is piling up against him. I, for one, will be very surprised if he holds his position into the new year."

"So we can't trust him." The line of Trent's jaw was hard as he said it.

"But McKenzie won't stand for murder," O'Hearn said.

"Are you sure of that?" Granville asked.

"Pretty sure. His problem is in discerning the line between collecting fines for the city and collecting them for himself. Murder's something different."

"You sure enough to risk Scott's life?"

"Not that sure."

"No, I thought not." Granville stopped to think, saying nothing for a few minutes.

"So then what do we do?" Trent asked.

"We dig up everything we can find on Craddock. Then we hire someone smart to defend Scott, and we fight this out in court."

"In court? Are you crazy?" O'Hearn said.

"That depends. Is the judge honest?"

"It's Thompson, right? Yeah, he's honest. Unforgiving, but honest."

"Good. Then the only thing we need is a really good barrister. Somebody who knows how to argue and to convince a jury."

"A barrister!" O'Hearn repeated, shaking his head. "I think I know someone who meets your requirements, but he won't come cheap. And he may not take the case."

"Let me worry about that," Granville said. "We have to convince him to go into court tomorrow morning, and he has to be willing to do as I say."

"Sounds risky."

"It is. But just give me his name."

"Randall. Josiah Randall."

THIRTY-SEVEN

Tuesday, December 19, 1899

The courtroom was narrow and crowded. Granville crossed his arms and shifted in one of the hard chairs they provided for spectators. Sitting in the front row, he could feel the anticipation in the eight rows behind him, hear the excited whispering. The witness stand was in front of him, with the judge's bench to the left and the jury stand to the right. The bewigged lawyers and the defendant sat at two tables set in front of the judge. Granville could see only the back of Scott's head, held at a defiant angle.

Despite the number of people who had squeezed in, the room was cold and the air felt damp. Most of the spectators had kept their coats on, and the few ladies huddled their fringed shawls more closely around themselves. The jurors, seated on hard benches against the wall, looked pinch-faced and miserable. Rain formed a gray stream on the windows, and from somewhere there came an insistent dripping; the courtroom leaked.

For the first time since Scott had been arrested, Granville was certain his friend would be set free.

Watching Josiah Randall cross-examine Constable Myers had been fascinating. Randall's questions were incisive, and he had a slow but insistent manner that seemed to draw out answers the witnesses had never intended to make.

"Constable Myers, you have testified that the defendant came and found you and your partner to report a murder, did you not?"

"That's right."

"And what time would that have been?"

"Six or so."

"I see. And you and Constable Craddock had been on duty all night?"

"Yes."

"Together?"

"Yes."

"So when Mr. Scott came to tell you he had found the victim's body, he found both of you."

"Yes."

"And was there any point during the night in question that you and your partner were not in sight of each other?"

Myers flushed slightly. "Well, of course, there was the occasional . . . necessity."

"I see. But when Mr. Scott came looking for you, you were together?"

"That's right."

"And between, say, ten and eleven the previous night, were you together then?"

The Crown prosecutor hastily stood up. "Objection. This cannot be relevant."

Randall turned to the judge. "Your Honor, I am looking to establish patterns of behavior."

"I'll allow it for now. The witness will answer the question."

"No," said Constable Myers. "We were not together."

"Not during any of that time?"

"No."

"I see. Thank you, Constable. Now, when Mr. Scott reported the murder, did he show any signs of violence?"

"I don't understand."

"Were there any bloodstains on Mr. Scott?"

"No."

"Did he show any signs of bruising?"

"No."

"Was his clothing disheveled?"

"Well, it was damp."

"But not torn, or in disarray."

"No."

"I see." Randall nodded slowly, then fired his next question. "Then why was Mr. Scott arrested?"

"What?"

"If Mr. Scott bore no sign of violence, why was he arrested for this very bloody murder?"

"Well, he . . . Scott carried the weapon."

"Which weapon was that?"

"The baseball bat. The one marked Exhibit A."

"Ah, yes, that baseball bat. And was there blood found on that baseball bat?"

"He'd had time to clean it off."

"I take it that is a 'no.'"

"Yes. I mean, yes, it's a 'no.'"

"I see. Thank you, Constable Myers. You may step down now."

Myers had slunk from the stand, with Craddock glaring at him. Chief McKenzie had not looked too pleased, either. Now Randall was cross-examining Dr. Barwill, and the coroner looked, as usual, as if he'd give anything for a stiff drink.

Granville's glance flicked from Judge Thompson's narrow, expressionless face to the intent expressions of the jury, and he smiled to himself. Josiah Randall was good; he'd liked him immediately on meeting him the previous day, but seeing him at work confirmed everything Granville had hoped. If anyone could put Craddock and Gipson behind bars in exchange for Scott, this man could.

"Now, we all heard Constable Myers testify that the defendant was carrying a baseball bat on the night in question. And you have just testified that the victim had been bludgeoned to death. You did conclude it was the blow to the head that killed Mr. Jackson, and not the gunshot wound, did you not?"

"That is correct," the doctor replied.

"Then let me ask about the nature of the wound itself. For instance, how big would it have been?"

"How big?"

"Yes." Josiah Randall picked up the baseball bat from the table to the right of the witness stand where it had been resting and handed it to the doctor. "Could this have been the weapon, for instance?"

"Of course it could. I already said so earlier, didn't I?"

"That's right, you did. Then the wound was consistent with a blow from the wider part of the baseball bat?"

Dr. Barwill looked at the baseball bat and slowly shook his head. "Well, no, it wasn't that wide."

"Ah, I see. Then it was consistent with a blow from the narrower end." And here Randall held up the bat so the jury could see the grip of the bat, with the larger rounded end.

Dr. Barwill turned even redder. "Well, no, the wound was even in width. That end of the bat has a knob on it."

"Could you clarify that last statement for the jury, please? What do you mean by saying the wound was even in width? Do you mean that both ends of the wound were the same circumference?"

"Yes. I suppose that is what I meant."

"You suppose? Doctor, we need you to be sure. Were the ends the same, or were they not?"

"Yes, that is what I meant."

The jury was murmuring among themselves. Randall had just demolished the largest part of the prosecution's case.

Turning away from the witness stand, Randall looked around the courtroom, his gaze falling on Granville's still-battered face. He walked over to where he sat, accompanied by a low excited buzz rising from the spectators. "Mr. Granville, if I might borrow your cane for a few moments?"

"Certainly," said Granville, handing over the polished black walking cane he had purchased for just this purpose the previous day. His injuries might just turn out to be useful.

"Thank you, sir," Randall said and strode back to the witness stand. "Now, Dr. Barwill, is this object the right size and shape to have left the wound you observed in the victim?"

"I don't know," stated Dr. Barwill, probably seeing a chance to reclaim himself. "I'd have to examine it more closely, wouldn't I?"

Randall handed him the cane.

The coroner rolled the long cane in his hands. "I don't think so. It's heavy enough, but seems too narrow to have caused the wound I saw."

"So you are saying a cane like this one could not have caused the wound that killed the victim?"

"No. It would have to have been a much thicker implement." Barwill looked pleased to be making such a definite statement. He glanced at Chief McKenzie, as if checking for his approval, too.

Randall nodded. "I see. Thank you, doctor." He picked up the cane and returned it to Granville with a nod, then strolled over to stand in front of Constables Craddock and Myers. "Constable Craddock, may I borrow your nightstick for a moment?"

Craddock's expression froze. "My nightstick? Well, I don't know," he said, looking to the chief as if for direction. At McKenzie's nod, he handed it over.

"Thank you, Constable," Randall said and strode back to the witness stand. "Now, Dr. Barwill, is this implement the right size and shape to have left the wound you observed in the victim?"

"Well, I . . . I . . . ," stammered the physician, his eyes darting from the barrister to the prosecutor to Chief McKenzie and back. "I suppose it could be."

"Look carefully now. You need to be certain," Randall said, handing the nightstick to the doctor.

Barwill turned the nightstick over and over in his hands. "It could have been. The dimensions seem correct, and certainly it is heavy enough. But you must understand, there are any number of objects that could have caused such a wound."

"So you are saying that a weapon like this one could have caused the wound that killed the victim?"

"Yes. A weapon something like this one."

Randall nodded and picked up the baseball bat again. "And a weapon like this one could not have caused such a wound?"

"Objection." Arthur Morris, the Crown prosecutor, leaped to his feet. "The witness cannot make such a statement."

"My lord, the Crown brought the doctor in as a witness precisely because he has the expertise to speak to the nature of the wound that killed the victim."

"Overruled," said Judge Thomas. "Please answer the question, doctor."

"Well, no," said Dr. Barwill. "The narrowing proportions of the bat do not match the shape of the wound."

Randal nodded again. "I see. Thank you, doctor. I have no further questions." He returned the bat to the table and the nightstick to Craddock with a nod of thanks.

Granville grinned to himself at the unhappy look on Craddock's face.

Judge Thompson leaned forward and addressed the doctor. "You may step down now, Dr. Barwill." Looking relieved, Barwill scrambled down and headed straight for the door. And the nearest bar, Granville was willing to bet. "Call your next witness, Counselor."

"The Crown calls Chief McKenzie," Morris said.

Once McKenzie had been sworn in, Morris led him through the evidence against Scott. Without the weapon, the case was thin. The defendant had borrowed money from the victim, had had several loud arguments with him, and was known to have hated him. When Morris finished, there was a sheen of sweat on his narrow forehead, and McKenzie's face was pale.

Randall stood up, then paused to read his notes. The courtroom was absolutely silent except for the drip, drip, drip of the leaks. When Randall straightened, he strode over to the witness and gave him a smile. "I have one or two questions for you, Chief McKenzie. Now, you have told the court the reasons my client was arrested for the murder of Clive Jackson. However, there was another murder in the same week, was there not? A Mr. Walter Blayney?"

"Blayney was killed the same week, yes."

Randall nodded. "And how was Mr. Blayney killed?"

"By a blow to the head, just over the right ear."

"The same manner in which Mr. Jackson was killed?"

"Mr. Jackson was shot first, but otherwise, yes, that is my understanding."

"I see. And we have heard from Dr. Barwill that it was the blow to the head that killed Mr. Jackson. Is it your understanding that Mr. Jackson and Mr. Blayney were killed by a similar blow, with a similar weapon?"

The police chief hesitated for several long moments before speaking. "Dr. Barwill has told me that Mr. Jackson and Mr. Blayney were killed by a similar blow. About the weapon, I can't say."

"And your own perception in this matter?"

"The wounds appeared similar."

"Thank you. Now, can you confirm for us where Mr. Scott was on the night Mr. Blayney was killed?"

There was no answer.

"Sir?"

McKenzie's looked decidedly uncomfortable. "Yes. Mr. Scott was in jail that night."

"There is no possibility that he was anywhere else?"

"None."

At Chief McKenzie's reply, the clamor in the courtroom was so loud that Judge Thompson had to call out for silence.

"I see," said Randall when the noise had died down. "And can you tell us where Constable Craddock was that night?"

"Objection." Morris bobbed up out of his chair. "I fail to see the relevance."

"Objection sustained. The jury will disregard the question."

Randall nodded. "Very well. Thank you, Chief McKenzie. You may step down."

There was more noise in the courtroom when Morris stated he had no further witnesses to call. It became almost deafening when Randall stood and called Scott's name. Granville watched his friend walk to the witness stand. As he passed in front of Granville, one eye closed in a wink. Granville nodded back. It was going well.

When Scott had been sworn in, Randall stood back for a moment, as if sizing up his client. The courtroom suddenly grew very still. Granville darted a glance at Craddock, who sat with narrowed eyes and a grim expression. Several of the spectators were leaning forward, as if afraid they'd miss something.

Josiah Randall was not one to waste words. "Mr. Scott, did you kill Clive Jackson?"

"No, I did not," stated Scott clearly. There was a collective gasp at his words.

"I see. You have heard the case against you. Did you borrow money from the victim?"

"No. I'd talked to Jackson about borrowing some money, but we hadn't sealed a bargain yet."

"Mr. Scott, what was your relationship with the victim?"

"I hated him." Scott's voice was clear and hard.

"And why was that?"

"Because he corrupted my youngest sister when she was only seventeen, sold her into prostitution, and took away their child." There was an excited murmuring among the spectators at hearing such shocking revelations. Judge Thompson looked fierce and picked up his gavel, and the sound died away.

"I see," said Randall. "Then why did you try to borrow money from Jackson, if you hated him?"

"It was business. I needed the money, and Jackson was the only one who would lend it to me."

"Why did you need the money?"

Scott hesitated.

"Mr. Scott?" Randall prompted him.

Scott drew in a breath. "Because Constable Craddock said Lizzie's baby had been sold, and that he knew where she was. He said he could get the child back, but it would cost me. If I didn't pay, he would make sure we never saw the child again."

At his words the court went silent.

"So you were going to borrow money from Jackson and pay Craddock."

"Yes."

"But he was killed before you could do so?"

"Yes."

"And you did not kill Clive Jackson?"

"No, I did not kill Jackson." The words were slow and clear, and the hush in the courtroom deepened.

"Thank you. I have no further questions."

"Mr. Morris? Do you wish to cross-examine?"

Morris waved one hand.

"Thank you, Mr. Scott. You may step down. Call your next witness, Mr. Randall." With his sharp, bony profile, Judge Thompson looked like a falcon waiting for prey, Granville thought.

"I call Constable Craddock."

The courtroom broke into a babble of sound. Granville ignored the noise, watching closely as Craddock collected himself. Over the man's shoulder he caught sight of the psychic, Mrs. Merchant, her expression intent and her eyes fixed on Craddock as he swaggered up to the witness stand and took the oath. *Well, well,* Granville thought, shifting his attention between them. Under his bravado, Craddock looked shaken.

"Constable Craddock, on the night of the murder, you were called to the scene by the defendant, were you not?"

"That's right."

"And you found the body down by the CPR docks, as the defendant had told you?"

"Yes."

"Did you recognize the victim?"

"Yes, I knew right away it was Jackson."

"And how do you know Jackson?"

Craddock's expression said he hadn't been expecting the question. "I knew who he was."

"You had no dealings with him? And I would caution you that you are under oath."

There was a movement from the bench, but Judge Thompson made no comment.

"I . . . well, I knew him, of course." Craddock tugged at his collar. "We may have done business together."

"In fact, you did do business with him." The lawyer's words were polite, but his expression was skeptical.

"He may have included me in a couple of his dealings."

"And you lost money on those deals, did you not?"

Craddock scowled. "Yes, I lost money. A lot of money."

"I see. So would you say you were not on the best of terms with the victim?"

"I guess not," Craddock muttered.

"And you knew the victim when you both lived in Denver," Randall said.

"Yeah. So?"

"I believe you knew the defendant before as well, in Chicago?"

"I don't see what that's got to do with it."

"Answer the question, please," the judge cautioned him.

"Yeah, I knew him."

"Well enough to extort money from him?"

Craddock's face slowly turned purple. "I . . . I . . . ," his voice trailed away as his eyes ricocheted from Randall to Scott, to the judge and then to Gipson, seated in the second row. "I didn't extort money from him."

"You didn't receive money from him. But you attempted to extort money from him, did you not?"

Craddock's glanced at Chief McKenzie, seated in the front row, then looked away quickly. He said nothing.

"Constable Craddock, answer the question please," Judge Thompson said.

"But . . . I . . . "

"Just answer the question."

"Well, I might have raised the subject with him. With Scott. And he could have thought it was extortion. Maybe. But, damnit, I wasn't trying to extort money from him."

"Constable Craddock, I'll have no profanity in my courtroom."

Standing in front of the witness station, Randall steepled his fingers together and contemplated Craddock over the top of them. "I see. So you deny trying to extort money from the defendant. And what about the victim? Do you also deny blackmailing him?"

The judge was watching him closely, and the look on Chief McKenzie's face did not bode well.

"I did not blackmail him."

"Are you sure? Remember, you are under oath."

"No. That is, yes, I'm sure."

"I see. Well, then, did you speak to the victim that night?"

"I did not."

"Nor quarrel with him?"

"Objection! Judge, this is harassment." Mr. Morris stood up.

Judge Thompson looked at Randall. "I assume you have a point here?"

"If you will allow me to follow this line of questioning for a little longer, Judge, my point will become clear."

"Very well then. Proceed."

"Thank you." Randall turned back to Craddock. "Could you show us your nightstick again, please?"

Without comment, Craddock unclipped his nightstick from his belt and placed it on the ledge in front of him. A bead of sweat rolled unheeded down his cheek.

"Thank you, Constable." Randall stepped closer and picked up the nightstick. It was black, about a foot long with rounded ends. "It seems to be a very clean weapon. Tell me, do you clean it often?"

Craddock flushed. "Well, no more often than anyone else."

"I see. Constable Craddock, can you tell the court where you were and what you were doing on the night of the twelfth between ten and eleven and on the thirteenth between those same hours?"

"I want a lawyer," Constable Craddock said.

THIRTY-EIGHT

Emily walked into the parlor, her eyes immediately seeking out Granville where he stood by the window, head bent in thought. When Mama had told her he was here, and that Emily should put on her best dress and come down, she hadn't known what to think. It was the first time they had allowed her out of her room in two days.

She paused just inside the doorway, feeling awkward. He must know what had happened, how her parents had behaved, like some mid-Victorian melodrama. The queen might still be on the throne, but a new century was just weeks away, for heaven's sake.

He seemed to sense her presence, turning and grinning at her. His handsome face was still battered, and a purple bruise spread from his right eye nearly to his jaw. All of Emily's awkwardness dissolved.

"Oh, Mr. Granville. Your poor face. And tell me, what happened at the trial?" she asked, advancing into the room with her hands held out.

He took her hands and held them. Realizing what she'd done,

Emily tugged at her hands, but he didn't release them. "I thought I asked you to call me John," he said softly.

Blushing, Emily forced herself to meet his gaze. "I don't think that's a very good idea. Especially not now."

"Why not now?" His eyes twinkled.

"Stop teasing me," she scolded. "And tell me what has happened. The trial was to be today, was it not? Did you free Mr. Scott? Did my note help?"

"Stop," said Granville, laughing. "One question at a time."

Emily just looked at him, curious but cautious. His mood was so different, she hardly knew what to think.

"In fact," he said, "I think it was your insight that solved the case for me. It was indeed a policeman's billy club that killed both Jackson and Blayney."

"It was?"

"Indeed. And a policeman who killed them."

"Who? And why?"

"Constable Craddock. A man of very bad habits, a tendency to gamble being among them, as well as an unseemly willingness to try extortion and blackmail, and a very evil temper when all else failed."

"Jackson undoubtedly deserved his death," she said. "But why Blayney?"

"Craddock still owed money. Gipson needed Blayney dead, and somehow learned that Craddock had killed Jackson."

"The blackmailer was being blackmailed?"

"There is a certain justice to it, you must admit."

"But how did all of this come out?"

"In court, before Judge Thompson. We hired Scott a very flexible barrister who is a demon in cross-examination."

"You mean *you* hired him."

"Well, yes."

"So Craddock admitted killing Jackson?"

Granville grinned. "Oh, yes. He's still claiming self-defense, but it's fairly clear our Mr. Craddock simply got quite angry and hit Jackson. Unluckily for him, it was a killing blow."

"And Mr. Blayney?"

"Ah, that one Craddock is having more trouble explaining. When I left, Craddock was very busily implicating Gipson. By nightfall, I expect to see them both in jail."

"And your friend Mr. Scott?"

"A free man."

"That's good," Emily said, then looked down at her hands. With her questions answered, she suddenly felt embarrassed and at a loss for words. It wasn't a feeling she liked.

She looked up at Granville for a moment, trying and failing to read his expression, summoning her courage. "Granville, what are you doing here?" Realizing what she'd said, she blushed. "I didn't mean . . . I mean, I cannot imagine how you talked Papa into letting you see me, especially with your face looking the way it does now," she added with a smile. "He was very angry with you. And with me."

"Can you not indeed?" He looked amused. "He considers you disgraced, you know."

"Yes, I know. Isn't it the most ridiculous thing you have ever heard of? I mean, this is eighteen ninety-nine, after all. Not eighteen forty-nine." She paused. "I'm planning on running away. I'll get a job."

"A job? What kind of a job?"

At least he wasn't dismissing her plans, like her father had, but this was the hard part. Emily gave him the only plausible idea she'd been able to think of so far. "I plan to train as a typewriter. There is a lot of demand now, you know, and they are hiring women as well as men."

"Yes, I've noticed. But what will you live on while you train?"

"That is the only detail I've not yet worked out. But I will."

"I have no doubt of it. But perhaps I have a solution for you."

"You do?"

He nodded. "I do. I would propose we become engaged, which will save your reputation. We can set a distant date for the wedding. Your father will be appeased, and in the meantime you can take training as a typewriter."

"Papa would never agree to my marrying you." She said this gravely, as if by her tone the offense would lessen.

"Emily, have I ever told you who my father was?"

"No, and I don't see that it could possibly help."

"My father was the fifth Baron Granville." He said it in a tone both reluctant and proud.

"A baron? Then you . . ."

"Alas, I am the fourth son. I have no estate and no title, but I am still of noble birth."

"And your name?"

"The Honorable John Lansdowne Granville."

Emily could feel the blood draining from her face, and for an awful moment she feared she would faint. "I see. That explains why I'm allowed to receive you. But how would you support me?"

He had the answer ready. "Scott and I are opening our own detective and security agency. We will be hiring Trent as our assistant."

Emily looked at him for a moment, then let out a gurgle of laughter. "You're serious. How perfect, but I still don't understand. Why are you offering to marry me?"

"You risked your safety and your reputation to save my life. The least I can do is give you the protection of my name in return."

"But you don't want to be married to me."

"I wonder," he said. His expression was gentle as he regarded her. "We can at least pretend to be engaged. It will give us time to decide what you want to do, and it will keep your father from sending you off somewhere. Who knows," he said, taking her hand. "Perhaps we will come to like the idea of being married to each other."

"Perhaps," she said, trying to ignore the sense of joy she felt.

"Emily Turner, will you agree to being engaged to me?" he asked, his tone formal but with an odd glint in his eyes.

"I accept," Emily said, blushing slightly but meeting his gaze steadily.

"And as your fiancé, if only temporary, do you think I am entitled to a kiss?"

"Oh, yes," Emily said.

Acknowledgment

Special thanks to my editor, Don Weise, for making this dream come true; to my agent, Eric Myers for his patience and hard work; to Michele Slung for an amazing line edit; to everyone at Avalon Publishing/Perseus Books for helping make this book a reality and to Chris Grabenstein for the tips that all first time authors need.

Thanks to my family and friends for being there and for their humor and to my writing buddies for their feedback and enthusiasm.

Thanks also to the staff of the Vancouver Public Library Special Collections for their help in tracking down obscure historical details.

None of the characters in *The Silk Train Murder* are based on people living or dead, with the exception of the one-armed jailor (I couldn't resist.) Although the historical detail in this book is as accurate as extensive research could make it, I did move the December, 1899 arrival of the Empress of India up by a week in the interests of the plot. Please check my website at *www.sharonrowse.com* for historical source materials.